WISHING WILL

A NOVEL

DANIEL HARVELL

WITH

BENJAMIN LUND

This book is a work of fiction. Names, characters, businesses, organizations, places, events, and incidents either are the product of the author's imagination or are used fictitiously. Any resemblance to actual persons, living or dead, events, or locales is entirely coincidental.

www.DanielHarvell.com

Cover by 7Reed Design

DEDICATION

Daniel dedicates this book to David for

helping him to wish again.

Ben wishes to dedicate this book to Olivia, Sydney,

Jill, Jimmy, Haleigh, Mom and Dad.

TABLE OF CONTENTS

DAY 0.1

At 11:03 a.m. Will Cricket dashed into the lunchroom. His stomach gurgled and rattled, but his eyes were glued to his precisely-synched, radio-controlled watch. Time was dwindling, but he needed to refuel. Today was the biggest day of his life. Success depended on his being ready to bounce, which required an energy boost from a delicious helping of ... tuna surprise? Will's upper lip curled involuntarily as he glared at the lunch menu, but he jumped in line anyway. Lunch was, after all, one of the five most important meals of his day.

To his left a group of catty cheerleaders prattled away on their phones; to his right Diego Rouleau, the school bully, poked the tiny and trembling Duncan Sapp. Will tried to avoid them by blending into the crowd, but he wasn't exactly inconspicuous. The only blending he usually did involved milkshakes. Will outweighed almost everyone at Lamone Pledge Middle School by at least 40 pounds—a fact that no one let him forget.

"Someone call Green Peace," said cheerleader Jordan Jesup, as she pointed to Will. "We've got a beached whale they need to push back into the ocean."

"Knock it off," he mumbled, avoiding eye contact. He took a step away from them but nearly tripped over his own feet.

Lucy Logan—another cheerleader—gasped. "That was a close one! A fall from Willy the Whale would've set off an earthquake!" The other girls squealed in delight.

"Yeah, well you're a bunch of ... a bunch of ... pretty girls," Will said, blushing and deflated.

The cheerleaders stopped laughing, then grabbed their throats and gagged.

"Lame!" Cordelia Carson made an "L" with her fingers.

They continued to sling insults, but they were more focused on entertaining one another than on Will. He glanced at his watch—it was already 11:06 a.m. His hands shook nervously. He didn't have time for this!

Will gave his blondish-red buzz-cut a quick scratch as he slowly backed away and accidentally knocked a lunch tray out of the hands of an exchange student. Tuna surprise, green bean casserole, and brownish Jell-O sailed through the air and landed in one giant plop at Diego's feet. He looked up with an expression as mean as a pit bull with diaper rash.

"Willy the Whale," he growled, his twitching eyes staring straight into Will's.

A noise rose from behind him that sounded like a horse with asthma. Diego's best friend and lackey, Jerritt Locke—a tall, lanky boy with thick bottle-cap glasses—laughed.

Will tried to sidestep the two, but Diego's mitt-like hands took him by the collar and yanked him off his feet. "My shoes! You've ruined my shoes, you bozo!"

He looked down at Diego's sneakers, and Jerritt got on his hands and knees to inspect matters up close. Diego's left shoe had a *speck* of tuna on it.

"Surprise?" Will weakly smiled.

"You're gonna clean my shoes with your tongue, Cricket."

Will felt a shiver run through his toes. He ignored Diego and the gawking crowd to look at his watch. 11:09 a.m. Only two minutes to go! He chose his words carefully and flashed over them again and again in his mind. Then he held his breath, gritted his teeth and made a wish.

I've got to get free! Don't let Diego embarrass me in front of everyone! I wish someone would make him stop!

Will knew that an ordinary run-of-the-mill wish didn't stand much chance of coming true. He had to do something to amplify the wish, like wishing on a four-leaf clover or blowing out birthday candles. In the absence of those types of wish-magnifiers, whenever Will needed a wish to come true, he crossed his fingers for luck. Usually crossing two fingers was enough, but this was a dire situation. So Will crossed *everything*. First he crossed his fingers, then his arms and thumbs. He wrapped his legs around one another, which made him look like a human pretzel. He even tried crossing his toes in his shoes.

Diego's fist wound back for the kill. Will was seconds away from needing a full body cast.

I wish it would all stop! Will wished again, now crossing his eyes too.

Suddenly, the cafeteria went silent. All the giggles and gasps ceased. The cheerleaders froze in place; their eyes rolled in disgust. The jocks paused in mid-air like excited apes. The teachers didn't move a muscle. Even the giant apple clock on the wall stopped ticking. Everything, everyone was frozen in time—except Will.

"Wow," he said, prying himself from Diego's grip.

As many wishes as he'd made throughout his life, nothing of this magnitude had ever been granted. Will glanced down at his watch suspiciously. It was 11:11 a.m.

His heart skipped a beat. "The magic minute!"

The date was November 11. A year ago, this day hadn't meant a thing to Will. Then he stumbled upon the magic wishing legend while surfing the Net. One particular website had articles from numerologists who had studied the date and time number-sequence. The theory that Will bought into was the simplest, a long-established rule of wishing: repeating a wish makes it more likely to come true. That's precisely what 11/11 is—the number one repeated over and over again.

There are two brief moments when the wishing magic is even stronger—11:11 a.m. and 11:11 p.m. Wishes made at these times on this particular day were practically guaranteed to come true. But why? Will thought that maybe those times signified when the universe was perfectly in sync and anything was possible. His head pounded just thinking about it.

He sprinted around the cafeteria—his wish had come true!

A spitball aimed at Duncan Sapp hung in midair. Rocky Quick was in the middle of spewing out chewed bits of tuna. Will bumped into Mr. Jorgensen, a seventh grade math teacher, whose statuesque body had froze while trying to jump over a chair on his way toward Diego. Mr. Jorgensen fell to the ground and rolled on his side but didn't flinch.

Will raised an eyebrow, and a smirk came over his face. He ran back to Diego. With all his might, he resituated Diego's fist so that it aimed back at his own face. Next, he moved Jerritt, still on the floor, right behind Diego.

Then he noticed something out of the corner of his eye. On the other side of the room, something moved! Will's knees trembled as he scanned the motionless crowd. He saw a blur of color shoot behind a table. Will backed into the far corner as the shakes in his knees spread to the rest of his body.

A minute passed, and Will thought his mind had just been playing tricks on him. Then, out of the blue, three people popped into sight and stood a few feet away from him. They were the most peculiar individuals he'd ever seen. One was an abnormally tall man with a small body and exceptionally long legs. Another was a kid about Will's age, whose hair changed color with every movement he made—first blonde, then red, then velvet purple! The third wore a jacket that sparkled and glowed. Will was mesmerized, but when he looked up at the person wearing it, the man shook his head disapprovingly.

"Huh—hello there," Will said.

The man with the stunning jacket pointed to the frozen crowd and said, "Time's up, William."

Will turned toward his schoolmates, and the strangers broke away. He looked back, but they had vanished.

All at once, the cafeteria was in full motion again. The spitball hit Duncan in the ear. Babs Bykowski squealed as Rocky's tuna landed on her tray instead of his. Best of all, Diego's fist punched his own face. He gave himself a black eye and fell backwards, stumbling over the strategically placed Jerritt.

"Ow! Watch where you're going!" Jerritt yelled.

The smile on Will's face slowly faded. He thought he'd feel good seeing someone else suffer for a change, but as everyone in the lunchroom began laughing at Diego, Will couldn't take it anymore. He dashed through the cafeteria doors and into the hallway, looking back at the melee.

No one seemed to realize that time had stopped. They were all carrying on as if nothing had happened. Even Mr. Jorgensen, who had wound up on the floor, simply got up and dusted himself off.

But the three strangers who'd appeared when time stood still—who were they? And why had they been immune?

Will was thrilled that he'd discovered the power of the magic wish minute, but furious that Diego had forced him to waste it on a wish to stop time. Will's original wish had been for something he'd wanted his whole life. But he'd get another chance tonight. It was, after all, only the first 11:11 of the day.

★

When Will came out of the bathroom, he was alone in the hallway. He'd barely been able to convince his teacher, Mrs. Griswald, that he needed a restroom break more than he needed to know about the lifecycle of dung beetles. She told him to return quickly, but Will was content to wander back slowly, daydreaming of wishes to come. His fantasies ended abruptly, however, when he heard a familiar stomp coming around the corner. The floor seemed to shake as if a tyrannosaurus rex roamed the halls. This particular carnivore was even worse—Diego!

Will spun around to run and collided with Jerritt. The lanky lackey wrapped his arms around Will and held him tight in a bear-hug. Jerritt did his best to make a scary face, but he looked about as frightening as Kermit the Frog.

"Get off me," Will said, elbowing out of Jerritt's arms.

Diego came up behind him and pushed him against the wall. They were nose-to-nose. Will could smell Diego's breath, worse than rotten eggs. The bully hoisted him up by his shirt and slid him along the wall until Will's collar found one of the hooks used to display the cheerleaders' spirit banners. Diego hung him from the hook by his T-shirt and backed away. Will dangled there, several feet off the floor.

"Sorry, we can't hang out with you, Willy, but we've got appointments lined up all afternoon. I'm terrorizing the chess club in, like, five minutes. See ya, butthead," said Diego. He and Jerritt laughed all the way down the hall.

"Stupid jerks," Will said to himself.

He tried to jump from the wall, his arms outstretched like some superhero, but no luck. He moved from side to side, but he could only run in place. For a moment, he considered wiggling out of his favorite Transformers t-shirt, but the halls would soon flood with students, and the thought of facing his classmates shirtless was not an option. As much as they made fun of his bubble belly with his shirt on, he'd hate to hear what they'd say about him with it off. Will tried bouncing up and down, hoping to pull the hook out of the wall. He put all his might into it, but it was too late. The bell rang, echoing through the halls.

When the doors flung open, and the kids poured out of the classrooms, no one seemed to notice Will at all. They fiddled with lockers, said quick hellos, and rushed to compare notes for upcoming tests. Towering over them as they scurried about their ant-like lives, Will could hear private conversations and see things the other kids thought hidden from view. It was almost as if he were all-knowing, all-seeing, god-like.

So Mason Quattlebaum had an irrational fear of sock puppets, eh?

Connor O'Malley was the one who flung rubber bands at the back of people's heads.

With this sort of power, he could rule the school.

Then someone spotted him.

It started the way it always did, with finger-pointing. Then Mason yelled out, "Will's so fat that when he jumps, the floor moves out of the way!"

"Yeah, watch out below!" yelled Connor.

The roar of laughter was so overwhelming that kids doubled over with stomach pains. The hall was jam-packed. Word of Will's predicament had spread throughout the school.

Will had given up all hope that a higher power—teacher or otherwise—might intervene on his behalf, when a tall, muscular boy pushed his way forward. It was Jensen Macabee, the football quarterback who was two grades higher than Will. Jensen was impossibly good-looking and supremely self-confident—all the guys wanted to be like him, and all the girls wanted to date him.

"Stand aside," he said, gliding effortlessly toward Will.

Jensen stood directly under him. Will could see only the top of his head.

"You're Cricket, right? Kaitlyn Cricket's little brother?" asked Jensen.

Will didn't know what to say. Kaitlyn had warned him ... no, she had threatened him that he was never to mention their familial connection at school, and certainly not to Jensen, her secret crush. She'd never forgive him if he ruined her chances with Jensen—as unlikely as they seemed. But maybe Jensen would help him because he secretly liked her too. Helping Will would be the perfect way to get closer to her. And once the two of them started dating, Will could hang out with them because they'd owe their relationship to his goofball, wall-hanging antics.

"Yeah," Will said softly. "Kaitlyn's my sister. The cute girl in your English class."

"That's what I thought." Jensen ran his hand across his scalp, as if he had hair to straighten. "When you see your sister, give her my regards." Then he snapped his fingers, and the crowd parted. Jensen gave Will's feet a shove before he walked off, leaving him swinging back and forth like a pear-shaped pendulum.

"How could you!" said a shrill voice underneath Will. He knew exactly who it was. Kaitlyn stood there with her hands on her hips, bright red in the face. "What do you think you're doing up there?"

"Kait." Will forced a smile.

"You pulled this stunt just to humiliate me, didn't you? And you talked to Jensen. How could you? What did you say to him?"

"Nothing. Honest. Well, I mean, we did talk about how pretty you are." Will felt his shirt tear a little, and he dropped an inch or so. The hook wouldn't hold him much longer.

"Really?" Kaitlyn chewed nervously on her long, golden brown hair. "He said that I'm pretty?" Some of the other kids snickered, but Kaitlyn was oblivious.

"I guess I'm the one who actually said you were pretty. But he didn't say you weren't. Y'know, maybe if we both wish hard enough, he'd—"

"Just shut up!" Kaitlyn bit down on her lip. "Enough with you and your stupid wishes. I'm so tired of you screwing up my life. You know what I wish? I wish I didn't know you! I wish you were someone else!"

Kaitlyn shoved her way through the crowd, her head bowed low, punching the wall with her tiny fist. Will's shirt ripped a little more, and he dropped another few inches.

The students who watched from below seemed to realize that he might fall at any moment. Those near the front pushed back, fearful they might be crushed. A wave of panic moved through the crowd, and they all began to scatter.

Finally, the hook tore through the last of Will's shirt, and he collided with the floor, landing on his rear—a well-cushioned thing. He was dazed, but he jumped up quickly.

A chill ran down Will's back. He wrapped his arms around his body to feel the damage to his shirt and heard an enormous ripping sound. His shirt, completely torn down the back, slid off his chest and plopped to the floor. If Will had heard laughter at his expense before, it was nothing compared to the enormous cackles and snorts caused by the sight of his bare torso.

"Ew! Put your shirt back on," yelled Mason.

"Go on a diet, fatty!" shouted the Bloom sisters in unison.

Not for the first time, Will found himself wishing sincerely and with all his heart for the same thing his sister had—that he might be someone, anyone other than William Sherman Cricket.

When Will returned home from school, his house on Summerhill Road smelled like wet sheepskin and candied peaches. His father was on dinner duty again.

Kaitlyn barreled past him at the front door on her way to her room. Barely two seconds later, he heard her door slam with more force than her thin frame should have been able to muster.

Will chucked his book bag onto the garish pink sofa in the front room, wishing he could pitch it into the fireplace instead.

"Hey, boy, watch where you're tossing that school junk. You nearly decked me!" said his irritated old grandmother Nonnie.

Nonnie had come to live with his family after Poppa died two years ago on a trip to France. He and Nonnie had been archaeologists, so they spent their lives traveling the world. Now Nonnie sat in the parlor room, gazing out the window and blending into the sofa with her pink hair. Most people thought she was crazy.

"Oh, sorry, Nonnie. Didn't see you there."

"Didn't see me? Must not be eating your Cheetos, eh? Good for your eyes, Will. Good for your eyes." She rocked back and forth as she pulled from a ball of yarn. She wasn't knitting or crocheting. She just unraveled it for no reason at all.

"You're thinking about carrots, Nonnie. But I understand. They're both orange," Will said.

"And both are filled with cheesy goodness," his grandmother said with a smile.

"You bet, Nonnie." Will often humored his grandmother. He didn't like seeing her agitated. She was a kindred spirit. They were two misfits, and they looked out for each other—well, at least Will looked out for her. She typically looked out for striped elephants or talking squirrels.

"So how was school today, my boy? Have fun with all of your little friends?" She tilted her head as if she were looking over the rim of glasses, only she wasn't wearing any.

"Sure, Nonnie, you bet. Loads of fun." He gritted his teeth. "Can't get enough of those guys."

"Why are you wearing a different shirt from the one you had on this morning?"

Will rolled his eyes. For an old lady who didn't know the difference between carrots and Cheetos, Nonnie was pretty sharp when it came to clothes.

"Oh, right, the shirt," he said, stalling. He'd had to change into his smelly gym shirt that had been in his locker for weeks. "We had this thing today ... a game. We played, ah, musical shirts, and I wound up with Rocky's. Guess we forgot to switch back."

"Better than nothing, I guess. Be pretty embarrassing to wander around the school without your duds, eh?" She returned to her yarn. "Not that you'll ever have much to be embarrassed about, so long as you focus on the reason you were put on this earth, your purpose in life."

Purpose in life? I just wish I could go read my Avengers *comic books!*

"Now don't stress your little heart out about finding your life's purpose. It'll find you." She wrapped the white yarn around one ear, looped it under her chin, and over the other ear. "Now go read your comics. I know that's all you want to do anyhow."

He loved his grandmother, but sometimes she gave him the creeps. "Um, I better go check on Dad first. Something doesn't smell right in there."

"You're telling me!" she said.

Will dashed through the dining room and into the kitchen where all manner of dishes and cooking utensils were strewn across the counter tops.

"Dad? Everything okay?"

Will's father had a cookbook in each hand, and his eyes were bouncing back and forth between them. "Hey, Son. Your Pop's got it all under control. I know exactly what I'm doing."

Will picked up a pastry bag that was lying on top of a muffin pan. "So what exactly are you doing?"

Will's father stopped scanning recipes, gazed down at his son, and whispered thoughtfully, "I'm making rice."

Will held up a cheese grater. "You don't know how to make rice, do you, Dad?"

"In the technical sense, no. Personally, I think it's one of those great mysteries in life that has no right or wrong answer."

Will put a pot filled with water on the stove and turned on the burner. "When the water starts to boil, add the rice. Return to a boil, then lower heat to simmer and cover until done."

"Well, sure, kiddo, I knew that. But that's the easy way. Are you sure you wouldn't like to try—"

"Daaaaaaad," Will said firmly, tapping a foot.

"Okay, okay. We'll try it your way."

"Is Mom working late again tonight? I'd like to talk to her too for a change."

His dad took off his spectacles. "Hey, kiddo, I miss her too, but it's not as if this'll be forever. Your mom's a hugely important person at Peach Preserves—you know she was just promoted to

Senior Vice-President of Special Acquisitions after barely two years with the company. This is a busy time of the year for her. The antiquity business always sees a boom during the holidays, and Thanksgiving is only two weeks away."

Will was perfectly aware of the day and time. He glanced at the clock on the microwave. 4:45 p.m. Six and a half more hours 'til he could make that one special wish.

"Yeah, I know. But you have a busy job too, and you're always here when Kaitlyn and I get home from school."

"My job at the *Corinth Chronicle* is a little different. As a freelance reporter, I pretty much make my own hours. I choose the stories, and the paper pays me after I've written them. So don't be so hard on Mom—she helps put food on the table and the shirt on your back."

Will's father gave him a soft punch to the shoulder. He did not, however, notice anything unusual about said shirt on Will's back. If it were any grungier, it would've been solid black.

That was the way things were in the Cricket household, but soon, it would all change. Forever, he hoped.

Will had been in bed since 9 p.m., but he hadn't slept a wink—he'd hardly even blinked for fear of missing his second chance at the ultimate wish. This was the day he'd been waiting for.

Before today, he'd already believed in the magic of the Wishing Day, as strongly as most children believe in the Easter Bunny or the Tooth Fairy. But if he'd ever had doubts, the strange thing that happened at lunch had totally convinced him. There was something exceptional about this day, and in a few minutes, he'd be exceptional too.

The only thing bothering him was the three odd strangers who had appeared unaffected by the time freeze. Who were they? Was it possible he'd imagined them?

Will's Tweety Bird wall clock whistled 11 times. It was 11 p.m. Eleven minutes away from his destiny. Nothing would interrupt his wishing this time. Nothing, maybe, except a tiny knock on his bedroom door.

"Will? Will, pumpkin, are you asleep?" his mother whispered as she opened the door.

She'd missed dinner again for the fourth night in a row. Judging by what she was wearing, she'd only just come home from work.

"I'm still awake," he whispered back, but then winced. He truly wanted to spend a few moments with his mom, but this was lousy timing.

"Oh, Will. I missed you guys tonight. So much happened today."

Will took in a deep breath and forced himself up in bed as his mom sat by his side. "Rough day, huh?"

"Yeah, it was pretty hectic. Feels like I haven't stopped since Mr. Peach gave me that promotion."

She ran two slender fingers across Will's cheek, and he couldn't help but see how petite she was. How had this poor woman given birth to such a large boy? He decided that he owed her as much of these 10 pre-wish minutes as she wanted.

"Maybe I should have a talk with your boss and put him in his place. Want me to rough him up, Mom?" Will balled his fingers into fists and snarled under his breath.

"How gallant!" she giggled. "All the girls at school must love you."

Will never confided in his family about the torture he went through at school. He was too ashamed, but for a moment he considered telling her everything. "Well, Mom ..."

"Pumpkin, look at the time, I can't believe it's this late. Can this wait until tomorrow? I have to be up early."

"Yeah, but ... okay, Mom, we'll talk later," he said.

Will's mom closed the door behind her, and he quickly glanced at the clock. It was 11:09 p.m. It was almost time. He took a deep breath, threw back the covers, and rolled off the bed.

He slipped his feet inside a pair of Spider-Man slippers and shuffled over to the window. The last couple of minutes seemed to take forever. His secret wish ran through his mind over and over again. It was what he wanted more than anything. Just when he thought he couldn't wait one more second, the clock struck the magic number.

11:11 p.m.

The Wishing Minute was here.

Will cleared his throat and stared into the clear night sky. Hundreds of stars seemed to wink at him, encouraging him to make his wish.

"I wish," he said, then cleared his throat. "I wish that I, Will Cricket, was someone else. I wish to be someone completely different. No more Will Cricket. I wish for a brand new life."

At that precise moment, a star shot across the sky. Will gasped in disbelief. Shooting stars were one of the best things in the world to wish on. He was ecstatic, bouncing with adrenaline. He threw open the window to get a better look.

Then a peculiar thing happened. Another shooting star joined the first, and they crisscrossed the sky together until a third star playfully joined them. Everyone knows that shooting stars go *whoosh* across the sky in straight lines, but these stars looked as if they were engaged in a game of tag.

They changed direction and left their playground in the heavens. The stars were coming closer and closer to Earth! The stars were headed straight for him!

Will shielded his eyes and stumbled back from the window. His entire room was illuminated now, so bright that he couldn't see anything. Effectively blind, Will fumbled for the bedroom door, but stumbled over an old jar he'd once used to collect fireflies. He crashed to the floor.

Not only had the room become dazzlingly bright, but it was also getting hotter, which made Will feel nauseous and dizzy. He tried to stand but fell to his knees, whimpering and sobbing. *It's all over*, he thought. He regretted all the things that he'd never had the courage to do like climb a tree or jump the ravine with his bike.

Just when he thought he might pass out, something in the room changed. It was cooling back to normal temperatures, but Will still felt a force all around him. He slowly opened his eyes expecting a swamp monster to be standing over him. The intense light was fading enough for him to see again, but no one was in the luminescent room, save himself.

Will pushed up from the floor. Though his vision wasn't totally back to normal, he was relieved to see everything in order—his comic books, the dirty clothes across the floor, those three black spots on the wall ...

What the? Will thought to himself. *What're those?*

Opposite his bedroom window, three shapeless lumps of black spotted the wall. They sat motionless for a brief second before bubbling like hot tar. The spots of darkness grew and took the forms of human beings, distinctly shaped and somehow familiar to Will.

This situation was way too strange for him, and now that his eyesight was back, Will dashed for the door. He turned the knob and wished with all his might to make it out alive. He had nearly slipped through the narrow opening when a hand grabbed his shoulder, pulling him back inside and shutting the door.

Four dark fingers had come loose from the wall and gripped Will tightly. He started to scream, but another of the shadows slid along the wall in front of him and put a single cold, dark finger up to Will's lips.

He was about to be devoured by soulless shadows that fed on plump boys. There was nothing left but to endure their horrible tortures. Will could already feel the hot stingers of their alien needles in his eyes. Fiends!

The creatures took hold of Will, lifted him up and gently sat him down on his bed—not exactly the rough and tumble treatment he'd expected. One of them reassuringly patted his head and then moved back. For fiends, they were decidedly well-mannered.

Will considered screaming, but the shadows' strange behavior left him more curious than frightened. One of them held up a hand, signaling for Will to wait a moment. All three brushed off themselves, dusting the shadowy blackness from their bodies; it slid off them, disappearing into the carpet.

Will's jaw dropped—there were people underneath the shadows. He saw patches of skin and clothes. When one finally uncovered a mouth, he said, "Sorry, sorry, sorry about that, William. Didn't mean to scare you."

After a few moments more, they were completely uncovered—the three eccentric strangers from school!

The man with the sparkling jacket stepped forward. "Hope we didn't frighten you too much, Will. I'm sure you understand that our line of work often requires a discreet entrance."

"That was discreet?" Will flapped his arms up and down. "I thought it was the end of the world! What are you even talking about? Who are you guys?"

"Come now, calm down, Mr. Cricket," said the second man. He had exceptionally long legs and spoke in a nasally monotone voice, like he was already bored with the conversation. "We're professionals. We rarely dabble in cataclysms."

The sparkling jacket man cleared his throat. "Except the time we accidentally gave that one kid an atom bomb when she'd actually wished for a date with a boy named Adam Baton. Boy, was my face red."

"Wait one second." Will jumped to his feet but stayed on his bed. He was eye-level with the sparkling-jacket man. "Did you say you granted someone's wish? Seriously, who are you people?"

"I tried to tell you he didn't seem very bright," said the long-legged man. "He doesn't even know why we're here. This is going to cost someone their job."

The third figure, a boy, the one with ever-changing hair color, pulled out a notepad and what looked to be a dandelion, using it like a pen to make a series of notes. "Um, Hollywood," he said, addressing the man in the sparkly jacket. "Wasn't your assistant supposed to send Mr. William all of the paperwork?"

"Oh, right, right, right. My assistant, the poor dear." Hollywood turned to Will and produced a dazzling smile that sparkled as much as his jacket. "Here's the thing, Will. Reverie, my executive assistant, she's a narcoleptic."

"Narco-what?" asked Will.

"Narcoleptic. She falls asleep at the drop of a hat. Hardly matters what she's doing. She's a Dreamweaver, you know. But even for her kind, she snoozes a lot. Maybe she was cursed with a sleeping beauty hex at birth. Makes sense—she's definitely got the beauty part covered if you know what I mean."

"Hollywood!" shouted the boy, whose hair went from gold to blaze red. "You're babbling again."

"Oh, yes, right, sorry. Where was I? Ah, Reverie, right, right, right. She's constantly falling asleep on the job. Comes from her being a Dreamweaver. Can't expect her to weave many dreams while she's awake, now can we?"

Will apprehensively chewed on his bottom lip. Strangers always made him nervous, and these were the strangest strangers he'd ever met. But they'd mentioned the magic word: wish. "I have no clue what you're talking about. Are you here because of my wish?"

"Perhaps some introductions are in order, Hollywood," said the tall man.

"Surely the boy already knows me," said the man in the jacket.

"Well, I guess you're Hollywood, right?" Will said.

"See! Obviously he's a fan." He reached into his jacket and pulled out an 8x10 glossy photograph of himself. "I don't normally do signings while on the job, but I think we can make an exception. Should I make it out to 'Will, my number one fan'?"

"Not this again," the tall man sighed.

"Number one fan? Who are ..." Will began to say. He studied Hollywood intently for a moment, hoping it might spark recognition. But once he looked more closely at the man's jacket, he was mesmerized by it, unable to take his eyes away. He soon realized that the coat hadn't been merely sparkling—it was made to look like a scene from outer space with stars and planets. The images of the astral bodies were all in motion, moving across the jacket, giving off actual light—it was like watching the night's sky through a jacket-shaped telescope.

"Like the threads?" Hollywood said. "The girls from the fan club sent it to me for my birthday last year. You're getting a live look at a section of deep space in the Sigma quadrant. Nice place to visit, but you wouldn't want to live there. Overcrowding's an issue, and don't even get me started on fuel prices. It makes a person regret ever becoming a star."

Will stepped to the edge of his bed, still half-gazing into the space scene. "I'm sorry, sir, but I don't quite recognize you. Maybe if you told me what TV show or movie you starred in?"

"Oh, no, Hollywood isn't that kind of star, but don't try to tell him that." The chameleon boy chuckled, and his hair turned from pumpkin orange to magenta. "He's a celestial star. Like the ones you see on his jacket. Like the earth's sun."

Hollywood grinned contently, apparently oblivious that anyone was talking about him.

Will fell back on his bed and smacked his forehead with the palm of his hand. "Wow ... this is ... unbelievable. Are the rest of you stars too?"

The chameleon boy started to speak, but the leggy man put his hand over the boy's entire face and shoved him to the side. "We most certainly are not. Allow me to introduce myself. I'm Peske, Norv Peske. This little ... fellow is our junior associate, Tangible."

"Call me Tang," the boy said, wiping Peske's hand off his face. "As you guessed before, we're here about—"

Peske cut him off, saying, "We're here about your wish, Mr. Cricket. You see, we're in the business of granting wishes, and we'd like to offer you the opportunity to see your wish come true."

"Are you kidding me? Oh man! This is awesome!" Will scooted off his bed, ran to the closet and pulled out a pointed hat and a rounded wooden stick the length of a ruler. He put the hat on his head and said, "So, you're wizards?"

Tang and Hollywood burst into laughter. Peske yawned. Will took off the hat and tossed his toy wand back into the closet. Tang and Hollywood continued to laugh, however, slapping their knees while their eyes watered.

Will crossed his arms and tapped his foot impatiently. If he wanted to be laughed at, he'd go to school. "I don't get it."

Tang, whose hair had blinked through all the colors of the rainbow, settled down and said, "Sorry, Will. We get that all the time. That's good, heh, wizards. Sure, we work our own brand of magic, but we're not wizards."

"Who'd want to be a wizard anyway?" Peske sneered.

"Our people are called Arcanians," Tang said. "Everyone in our race can grant wishes. We practice the art of *wish*craft."

"And we three work for a company that specializes in granting the wishes of human boys and girls," Hollywood added. "It's called the Sky Castle Network and Enterprises, but we call it the SCENE, for short."

"Peske works in the SCENE's legal department," Tang said. "He makes sure that the SCENE's employees and its clients—like you—follow the precise details of the wish contracts. It's the perfect job for him since he represents the aspects of the literal wish."

"Yes," Peske said. "Be very careful what you wish for while I'm around, William—it just might come true."

"And Hollywood is the SCENE's leading wish agent. His status as a Celestial being—"

"Star," Hollywood interrupted, giving Will the thumbs-up.

"His status as a star," Tang said, making finger quotes in the air, "gives him an advantage over most of the other agents at the SCENE. As you know, Will, there's hardly any wish more powerful than one made on a star. No one at the company has a higher wish completion percentage than HW here."

"Or bigger muscles. Right, Tang?" Hollywood bent over slightly, posing and flexing. "I said, 'right, Tang'?"

Tang and Hollywood stared each other down for a long moment.

"Right, *junior* agent Tang?" Hollywood asked again.

A soft growl hummed in Tang's throat, but he finally said, "Sure, Hollywood."

"So," Will said, casually snapping his fingers, trying to break the tension. "You're like a wish agent-in-training, Tang? Does that mean you're a Celestial—I mean, star, like Hollywood?"

"I wish that were the case," Peske said covering his heart with his hand and sighing heavily. "The boy's a Genie."

"Half-Genie!" Tang's hair changed to the color of hot charcoals. Although he still looked like an innocent young man, something about him frightened Will. "I'm a half-Genie, Peske! Get it right!"

"Well, what's wrong with Genies?" Will asked. "I always thought they were cool, y'know, granting three wishes, living in lamps."

Peske crouched and shook a finger in Will's face. "You wouldn't say that if you actually met a Genie. They are by far the worst group of Arcanians alive. They're a nasty bunch, mean-spirited and treacherous. Whereas the rest of us enjoy a life of granting wishes, their only goal is to see humanity destroyed and humiliated. Centuries ago we had several Genies working for the SCENE, but they would always twist wishes into horrible distortions, granting pain and suffering instead of fortune. When we fired the lot of them, nearly every Genie turned against our people. A skirmish ensued, which we ultimately won. We were forced to imprison them in bottles, lamps and the like. I'm sure their tempestuous dispositions have a great deal to do with the cramped living arrangements they were required to endure, but they brought that on themselves. Many of them have since been set free, even though they only served 1,500 of their 3,000-year sentences. Good behavior, indeed! The legal system today just isn't what it used to be. Now they plot revenge against us. Be warned: never trust a Genie, ever!"

Will slowly craned his neck around Peske to look at Tang. His hair was merely smoldering orange now, though smoke still wafted up from it. His bottom lip protruded, and his eyes were puffed up and glassy.

"Um, what Peske meant to say is never trust a Genie, except Tangible," Hollywood said, throwing his arms into the air. "Tang's the goods! Completely reliable chap who was raised by an exceptional set of adoptive parents—Wish Fairies, right, Tang?"

Tang nodded and wiped his nose across the sleeve of his shirt.

"I'm sure your parents are mighty proud of you, Tang— only seven and already a junior wish agent. You know, Will, that's pretty much unheard of in our world."

"Wow," Will said. "You're only seven? I thought you were closer to my age."

"Actually, Tangible's *700* years old," Peske said. "We Arcanians age a bit slower than your people, William. I'm 2,496, myself."

"Ooh-ooh, guess my age, Will, go on." Hollywood rocked backwards on his heels and clapped gleefully. "You'll never guess. No one ever does. I'm cursed with a youthful appearance."

Will thoughtfully tapped a finger against his chin. "Um, geez, I dunno, 1975?"

"Nineteen ..." Hollywood couldn't bring himself to repeat Will's guess. He moved his lips but didn't say a word.

"Oh, brother." Peske rolled his eyes. "He's rather sensitive about his age. Your guess was close—he turned 2001 this year."

"But do I look a day over 1500? I think not! Why, just last week, a nymph asked me if I was a student at Wish University."

"Wasn't that the old water nymph who's mostly blind?" Tang asked.

"No!" Hollywood shrieked. "I'm appalled at you, Tang! That woman has the eyesight of a hawk!"

Will's door suddenly creaked open, and light spilled in from the hallway. "Will? What's going on in here? Do you have the TV on?" Will's father took his time opening the door, but he would be through it any moment.

"Parental alert," Tang whispered as his hair switched to the color of camouflage.

"Don't panic," Peske said. "Initiate Plain Sight Protocol."

Tang gave Will a reassuring wink and then leapt backwards into the air. He tucked his legs between his chest and his arms, tight as a ball. As he spun in mid-air, tiny sparks shot out from his hair. His whole body shifted through a series of colors before settling on sunflower yellow. Tang's skin and clothes melded until he wasn't just tight as a ball, he became one! The Tang ball dropped from the air and onto the floor where it bounced around before settling near a green-flamed skateboard that Will had never once used.

Peske took an enormously deep breath, causing a few of Will's school papers to rustle. His face and limbs became increasingly gaunt, and when he stopped drawing breath, he looked like a cartoon character that had been flattened by a boulder. Peske turned away from Will and the doorway so that they faced his side. He'd made himself so flat that he practically disappeared when viewed from that angle!

Hollywood, far calmer than he'd been moments earlier, reached literally into his jacket, his hand piercing the deep space lining. He extended into the vast area of blackness and stars shown by his jacket and pulled out a handful of something Will couldn't see.

"Stardust," Hollywood whispered to Will. He held his hand to his face, tilted his head back and blew upwards. The stardust twinkled in the air and sprinkled down. A moment later, he vanished.

Will, of course, had no such magical abilities, despite being called "supernatural" by judges after his victory at last year's hot dog eating championship, so he stood still in the middle of his room in clear view.

"Will, what are you doing up?" his father asked, walking into the room.

"I couldn't s-s-sleep," Will stuttered.

"You've got school in the morning, mister." Will's father yawned. He could barely keep his eyes open.

"I know, Dad, I'm sorry." Will crept slowly to his bed, hoping he wouldn't run into Hollywood or Peske, or trip over Tang.

"Wait one second," said Will's father. "I heard voices. It sounded like there were people in your room." He rubbed his eyes and tried to focus.

"Oh, that. Well, ah, you see, that is—" Will began to speak, but a sudden noise grabbed both his and his father's attention.

"You're listening to W-I-S-H, the station where music is magic." It was Hollywood's voice, only throatier. The sound came from Will's clock-radio.

"Whoa! What the—" Will's father jumped several inches in the air. "What's wrong with your radio? I didn't hear it a second ago."

"Yeah, piece of junk. Keeps cutting in and out on me." Will bit the inside of his cheek. He didn't like lying to his father.

Hollywood's "radio broadcast" continued, "Before we get back to those hip happening tunes, let me introduce tonight's special guest Norv Peske. Get over here, Norv, and say hello to the audience."

Will heard a grumble come from the paper-thin Peske. "You've got to be joking," he hissed.

"Ah, Norv, always the shy one. Now don't be nervous—just forget that we're on the radio. Try to pretend that we're in some kid's room with him and his dad and maybe a yellow rubber ball that should take notes because his boss is such the sly master of getting out of sticky situations."

Will's father crinkled his nose. "What kind of weird radio show is this?"

"Um, it's a, well … it's …" Will stammered.

Will's father cradled his head in his hand. "Let's turn this off and get to bed."

"Don't worry about it, Dad. I'll turn it off. It's messed up. The off switch is finicky."

"No, I don't want to hear another word about it. I'll pull the plug, and we can take a closer look at it tomorrow."

As Will's father walked over to the clock radio, Will noticed Peske scoot out of the way though he continued his verbal spar with Hollywood. In fact, Hollywood and Peske were so engrossed in their argument that they didn't stop talking when Will's father yanked the radio's power cord from the wall socket.

"What in the world is going on? I unplugged this thing!" Will's father looked at the radio's plug and back to the outlet.

Will didn't know how to get Hollywood and Peske's attention without further raising his father's suspicions. He spun around and picked up Tang, still in his yellow ball form.

Whispering, Will said, "They're gonna blow it if we don't shut them up. Do you think you can lend a hand ... or whatever it is you've got?"

The ridges of the ball moved and formed a pair of eyes and mouth. Although it vaguely resembled Tang, it reminded Will more of an Internet smiley-face icon.

"Give me a toss and I'll take care of the rest," Tang whispered.

Will cranked his arm back and lifted his leg in preparation for the pitch. He closed his eyes and wished for accurate aim.

As Tang soared through the air, it was obvious to Will that he had the throwing arm of his grandmother. Will had sent Tang heading directly for the back of his father's head. Just as the half-Genie was a split second away from collision, he stopped in midair and made a 90-degree turn. He knocked Peske in his elongated but thin gut and then bounced across to the invisible Hollywood where he crashed into his upper thigh. Tang fell to the ground and rolled back to Will's feet.

Both men were speechless. With his hand, Will made a slashing motion across his neck to indicate his fervent desire for their banter to stop.

Once he believed he had both Arcanians' attention, he said, "I don't know what you did, Dad, but sounds like the radio finally turned off. So now you can go back to bed, and I can get back to business ... that is the business of sleeping, of course."

Will's father scratched the bald spot at the back of his head. "Huh. Well, I'm not quite sure what I did either, but I guess it's fixed for now."

His father shuffled out of the room and shut the door behind him. Will let out a sigh of relief and collapsed onto his bed. "Man! You guys almost blew it," he whispered.

Hollywood became visible again as he shook the stardust from his body. "Good thing I'm so quick on my feet. We undoubtedly would've been in a jam if I hadn't come up with that brilliant radio ruse."

Peske turned back to face everyone. He puffed out his cheeks and a second later, his head popped back to normal size, followed by the rest of his body. "We wouldn't have been in that jam had you not been making so much noise in the first place. Do you have any idea of the legal ramifications had Mr. Cricket discovered us? The SCENE operates under a tight Arcanian license that restricts knowledge of us solely to children, and only children who are our clients, at that. You know this, Hollywood! You could have set the company back years—we'd be facing another Frost Epidemic like the one that nearly wiped us out 200 years ago."

"Come on, guys, stop fighting." Tang's hands and feet reached out from the yellow ball and pushed him up from the ground. As he leaped into the air, the rest of his body stretched out from his ball form. When he landed, he was entirely back to normal. "Let's not get carried away. It was a close call, but the danger's passed. Now let's get down to business."

Peske nodded almost imperceptibly.

"Right-o," Hollywood said. "Here's the deal, Will. We will grant your wish to become a new person—"

Will yelped. "You just said my wish out loud. Doesn't that mean it's not going to come true? That's what I always heard."

Peske rolled his eyes. "Yes, wishes must be nourished in secret; otherwise, they will not come true. It's one of the fundamental rules of wishcraft. So while you shouldn't go around telling just anyone your wish, we are here to *grant* that wish. Of course we're allowed to discuss it openly—that's our job. But no, I wouldn't recommend telling your school chums how you long to be a new boy."

Hollywood nodded. "But the wish doesn't come for free. In order to receive your heart's desire, you must agree to work for the SCENE as a human agent for a period of seven days. Each day *you* must grant the wish of someone you know, child or adult, it doesn't matter."

"But," Peske added, "you can't grant just any wish. It must be a selfless wish. No giving people a million dollars or any such nonsense."

"Wait one second." Will held his hands up as if signaling traffic to stop. "I'm just a kid. How am I supposed to grant wishes? You saw me earlier—I can't even throw a ball!"

"Will, I understand your concern," said Hollywood. "Granting wishes does take extraordinary abilities. That's why we're going to, ah, temporarily give you your very own Mizms. They're superhuman gifts, Will. They can allow you to do almost anything."

Will dashed over to his comic books and plucked one out of the pile. "You mean I'm going to have superpowers like the Incredible Hulk?"

Peske raised one eyebrow, "Allow me to clarify. You will gain the use of a single and different superhuman ability every night for the next seven nights at the stroke of midnight. We can't tell you what power you'll receive each night because even we don't know. That's the way Mizms work. It will be up to you every morning to figure out what power you've been given and how best to use it. But be warned! These Mizms are not to be abused and are never to be used for your own benefit or to harm any person—any such violations will allow us instantly to nullify your contract and any chance to have your own wish granted."

Arms behind his back, Tang stepped forward. "Over the course of the day, you must find a selfless wish to grant, during which time you may use your power to aid in the wish fulfillment. After the wish has been granted, your Mizm for that day will fade away. You must grant a wish each day or your contract will also come to an end."

"Okay, okay," Will said, tapping a finger against his temples. "Seven days, seven Mizms, seven wishes. But how do I figure out what people wish for?"

"Grantable wishes are private, unsaid things, as you well know," Hollywood said. "That's why we're giving you Telewishing—the capability of hearing people's unspoken thoughts. Unlike your other superhuman powers, you'll have this ability continuously over the seven-day period."

Will's jaw dropped, and it took him a long moment to form his words. "Wow. This is unbelievable. I get my ultimate wish granted, and I get to play superhero, and I get to read people's minds."

"Except that your wish hasn't been granted yet," Peske said, "and won't be until your job is done and done well."

"If I were you, I'd forget the notion that you'll be *playing* at anything. Granting wishes is serious work," Hollywood said, gravely.

"About the reading people's minds thing," Tang said. "You'll only hear wishes people make, not their every thought—it's the same way we Arcanians are able to hear humans' wishes. Trust me when I say that there's not a lot of fun involved. On a bad day, it's mind-numbing. On a good day, it can still leave you with a major headache."

Will's shoulders slumped. He plopped down in the middle of his comic books. "This sounds like a lot of work. I never knew wishes were so complicated. I thought you just made your wish and 'bam!' it comes true automatically, just like on *I Dream of*—"

They all stared at Will, as the title of the old television sitcom he'd once thought harmless hovered in midair.

"Ixnay on the eenie-jay," Hollywood said out of the corner of his mouth.

Peske, paying him no mind, said, "The show you're referring to, William, was a public-relations nightmare for us in the sixties. Portraying Genies as attractive subservient blonde women, indeed. If they ever got a look at a real Genie, they'd scream like a child watching a horror movie. Genies are hideous creatures!"

"Ahem." Tang cleared his throat and eyed Peske menacingly.

"Tickle in your throat, Tangible?" Peske asked.

Before Tang could respond, Will said, "Look, guys, before you get into that again, I've gotta tell you I think you picked the wrong guy to help you. I'm not really the active type. I'll take a video game about skateboarding over actual skateboarding any day. I don't think I have it in me to do all this work."

Hollywood clutched his chest, apparently taken aback. "No one's ever refused one of my wish deals before. It's unheard of! What would our CEO say?"

"I think you're forgetting the bigger picture, Hollywood ... again," Peske said. "Will *must* take on this assignment. In your own words, he's the only one capable. You know that. It's why you, of all agents, were given this project."

"Right, right, right. Can't put personal agendas above the greater good, now can we?" Hollywood kneeled down on one knee and grabbed Will's hand as if proposing marriage. "Will, I'll make you a deal. You agree to work for us for your ultimate wish, and I'll have Tang by your side helping you every step of the way."

"What?" Peske and Tang said in unison.

"That is highly unorthodox," Peske proclaimed.

"This is the incredible Wishing Will we're talking about here. He's a special kid. These are special circumstances. Don't forget the bigger picture, Norv. Tang will just serve as a guide. No rules will be broken, I promise."

"Hey, I like Will and everything, but I've got something kinda big already in the works," Tang protested.

"Consider yourself un-busy, Tang," said Hollywood. "Tomorrow morning you'll accompany Will to school as his new classmate. Peske, you'll handle all the paperwork so we can sneak him in without the school knowing he's actually 700 years old."

Hollywood grabbed both Tang and Peske by the arms and pulled them down so all four sat in the mound of comics. "We're an unstoppable team, the four of us. We're going to make this work. What do you say, Will? Ready for a dream come true?"

"Alright, I'll do it," Will said.

"Fine, then let's get the contract signed," Peske said, pulling something from his pants pocket. He handed the item to Will, who knew exactly what it was before it left Peske's grip.

"A wishbone? Like from a turkey?"

"Hmm, I suppose it does look like that, doesn't it?" said Peske. "Tap it against the wall."

Will did as he was instructed. It began to vibrate and hum, as if it were a tuning fork. But when Will gave a closer look, he saw words made of red light scrolling up through the space between the bone's curvatures.

"This is my contract?"

"What else would it be?" Peske said. "Give it a read through. You'll want to understand all of the terms of the agreement, I'm sure."

Will started scanning through the document as best he could, but the legal language mostly confused him. His mother worked with official papers all the time, and he'd heard horror stories about missing a tiny but critical detail in the fine print, but he couldn't imagine these three Arcanians being duplicitous with him. They'd already told him everything he needed to know. This legal mumbo jumbo was just a necessary evil of working for a corporation. *No need to even worry about it*, Will thought to himself.

"Okay," Will said. "I'm ready to sign."

"You've read through it?" Hollywood asked.

"Um, yes."

"And you understand your obligations?" Peske said.

"What's not to understand?"

"Excellent. Then let's make this official. Hollywood, William, each of you take an end of the contract."

They gripped the wishbone on opposite sides, as if preparing to make a wish.

"Now give a pull. If all is in order, you'll come away with the more significant piece, William, and the game will be afoot," Peske said, whipping a hand through the air.

Will had done this dozens of times before, though usually after a Thanksgiving meal. He knew just where to position his fingers to give him an advantage in leverage. Will applied most of the force with his thumb toward the bottom while sliding his fingers across different pressure points for a constant and even pull.

Hollywood, however, was busy with his other hand rearranging a handful of asteroids across his jacket so they'd appear more aesthetically pleasing. He wasn't even paying attention when the wishbone finally snapped.

"Yes!" Will exclaimed in a hushed tone. He'd come away with the larger piece. He was one step closer to his ultimate wish.

"Hmm?" Hollywood said. "Oh, yes, good job, Will. Congrats and all that."

"Way to go, Will." Tang stretched out and gave him a high-five.

"Yes, indeed." Peske collected the pieces of the wishbone and returned them to his pocket. "Now gather your things, boys, so we can let our champion get some needed rest."

They all scrambled back to their feet and made sure there were no traces of stardust on the floor or shadow blotches on the wall. The Arcanians each took turn shaking hands with Will, and Hollywood gave him a particularly zealous shake. Peske reminded him again about following the details of the contract to the letter while Tang stood behind him mimicking his every word.

When they were ready to go, Hollywood plucked three dots of starlight from his jacket. He kept one for himself and passed the other two to Tang and Peske. Hollywood counted to three and then they all popped the starlight into their mouths, chewed them up a bit and then swallowed. A split second later, they glowed like stars. The half-Genie threw open a window and began to leap out, but Peske pushed his way past him. He jetted off into the night's sky, and Tang took off behind him.

Hollywood looked out the window but turned back to Will before leaving. He put a luminous hand on Will's head, which immediately felt tingly and as light as a balloon. "Good luck tomorrow, Will. Nothing to worry about, though. We'll be with you every step of the way. Don't let that stuff in the fine print of the contract worry you at all."

With those words, Hollywood jumped through the open window and flew off into the earth's atmosphere, leaving Will with just one thought.

Stuff in the fine print? What did I just sign?!

DAY 1.1

A squawking sparrow on the sill of Will's open window woke him suddenly. He could barely open his eyes he was so tired. Last night's dream had left him exhausted. His experiences with the three wish creatures had seemed so real, but, of course, that was impossible. Shape-changing Genies, celestial beings come to life and wish-granting lawyers—it was too absurd to be true. He shook his head and focused on reality—a reality that would be much better spent in bed.

Will grabbed for his blanket, but it was nowhere to be found. His fingers grazed something tough and stubbly. He felt around the hard surface, eyes closed from exhaustion until he realized he wasn't lying in bed at all.

"Oh, man, did I fall out of bed?" But it didn't feel like carpet. It was like a wall or ... the ceiling?

"Oh my gosh!" Will bolted up to find himself perched upside-down on the ceiling looking below at his room! His stomach felt queasy, like the time his sister had forced him onto a roller coaster. He felt weightless.

He was floating!

So it must be true. He hadn't dreamed up Hollywood and his crew or the deal he'd made with them. This was his first day to grant a wish, which meant this was also the first day he'd been given a Mizm. This power, he thought, was the coolest Mizm of them all. He could fly! He could fly! He could—

Fall.

The funny feeling in his stomach disappeared, and he dropped into his mattress like a sack of his dad's impossible-to-chew pumpernickel bread. The legs of his bed buckled and snapped under his weight. The frame fell to the ground with a thud, and Will leapt to his feet as quickly as he could.

"Will?" his father called out from the kitchen. "Everything okay in there? Did you break something?"

"Everything's fine, Dad!"

"Alright, well, breakfast is ready and you've got to leave for school shortly or you'll be late. You'd better get flying, buddy."

"No kidding," Will said to himself.

It took Will only a few minutes to get cleaned up and throw on some clothes. As he moved about his bedroom, he tried to figure out how to fly again. He said different phrases like "up, up and away," and "shazam!" and "bada bing!" Nothing worked—until he remembered what he was dealing with.

"I wish," Will said, "that I could figure out how to fly."

With those simple words, Will's feet left the ground. He immediately flew to the ceiling and back down again.

"Cool!" Will said softly. He'd never felt so light in his entire life.

When Will came out for breakfast, his father was clearing the table. "Your sister already left for school, and your mom went into the office an hour ago. Do you need me to give you a ride to school this morning or are you flying solo?"

Unable to suppress a grin, he said, "Flying, Dad, definitely flying." Will grabbed a piece of toast, did a little spin and ran out the door.

He saw movement at the parlor window—Nonnie stared out at him. When Will made eye contact with her, she plucked a shade from one of the lamps, placed it over her head and stood perfectly still. Will shook his head and sighed, "Crazy Nonnie." He wished she'd act a little more normal—not for his sake, but for her own. Will's parents didn't know it, but he'd overheard them talking a lot lately about sending her to a nursing home.

As he passed by a small, deserted park, Will couldn't resist the urge to test his new powers. He took off from the ground slowly at first, holding onto a loblolly pine to steady himself. Once he felt in complete control, he rocketed upward. He stopped just a foot away from a nest of bluebirds. Startled, the birds flapped away but only for a moment. They made a quick U-turn and dive-bombed Will.

He tried to swat them away, but that only made them angrier. They nipped at his fingers as if they thought them to be worms and squawked madly in his ears. His concentration was frazzled, and his stomach felt sick again. He hung in the air for a split second more and then dropped toward the ground. As he fell, Will closed his eyes tightly and tried to concentrate on flying. He thought of planes, hot-air balloons and kites, but he kept falling faster, crashing through the branches of the tree.

"Whoa!" screamed Will. The ground was coming fast. "Please, STOP!"

When Will opened his eyes, blades of nearly dead grass brushed his eyelids and tickled his nose. He hovered just a couple of inches above the ground.

"Ha!" Will said, turning himself right side up and punching a defiant fist in the air. "I did it!"

"Did you now?" said a voice out of nowhere.

Hollywood, Tang and an unfamiliar blue-skinned woman impossibly squeezed themselves out of the tiny knothole of a spruce pine.

"Uh, hi, guys," Will said. "What's up?"

"Well, you, obviously," said Hollywood. "How are you handling things on this fine first wish-granting day, Will?"

"Pretty good, I'd say! I've got this flying thing down pat! It's pretty easy once you get the hang of it. Did you see me brake just inches from the ground? I'm the man!"

"Actually, Will, Hollywood's the man. He was the one who stopped you," said Tang, whose red hair hadn't changed colors since he'd appeared. "We were on our way to meet you when headquarters informed us that you'd experienced a midair power overload. We got here just in time for HW to use a handful of gravity-defying stardust to stop your fall."

"Wait. That was you?" Will said looking at Hollywood. "You saved me?"

"Stardust is the best. I use it in my hair every morning," said the blue-skinned lady. Her silvery hair flowed every which way, even though the air stood still.

"This is Reverie, by the way. She's Hollywood's assistant," said Tang.

"Pleasure to meet you, Will." Reverie took his hand and shook it lightly. "Sorry about that mix-up last evening with me not getting you the contract information ahead of time. I'm sure the boys told you I'm a Dreamweaver. I tend to fall asleep at the worst ..."

In mid-handshake, Reverie's eyes drooped, and her voice trailed off. She stood completely erect and even held tight to Will's hand, but she was sound asleep. She even started snoring.

"Don't take it personally, Will," Hollywood said, pulling a gumball-sized meteorite from the space of his jacket. "Sleep is the natural state for Dreamweavers. When they're around people, like you, with vivid dreams or exciting wishes, they have to fight to keep conscious. A powerful imagination encourages them to delve into a person's dreams and explore. And to do that, they must be asleep, of course!"

"Does that mean things that would bore me to sleep actually keep her awake?" Will asked.

"Precisely." Hollywood placed the tiny meteorite between his index finger and thumb. He brought his hand up to his eye, gave a good look and then flicked the meteorite at Reverie. It knocked her square in the forehead.

Reverie took a step back, releasing Will's hand. She slowly opened one eye and then popped open the other. She took a deep breath and said, "moments."

Will looked at his hand, the one Reverie had held. It was covered with tiny crystals that looked like sugar. They sent tickly vibrations across Will's fingers and up his arm. After a few more seconds, his limb went numb.

"What is this stuff?" Will held his limp arm with his other hand and shook it at the Arcanians.

"Whoops! That's Reverie's sleeping dust," Tang said. "All Dreamweavers carry it. Just don't get any in your eye or you'll be out, sound asleep."

Will used his good hand to wipe the numb one off on his shirt. As soon as he was clean of the dust, he felt a warm tingle run down from his shoulder to the tips of his fingernails. He could move his arm again.

"My apologies, Will." Reverie rubbed her fingers together and watched longingly as sleeping dust sprinkled to the ground. Her eyes drooped again and her head tilted down a bit.

"No, no, no. Not right now! I want you alert while we're out near the masses. You never know when I'll need you to shoo away my throngs of adoring fans."

"Here, read this." Tang produced an enormous book the size of seven encyclopedias and plopped it down in front of Reverie. "It's the 667th edition of *Rules and Regulations for Practicing Wishcraft*. There's hardly any drier reading than that. Should keep you wide awake, Reverie." Where Tang had been hiding a book that size was anyone's guess, though it didn't surprise Will. With these guys, anything was possible.

Reverie sat down with her legs crossed and flipped to the first page, immediately engrossed.

"Wow. You guys have a lot of rules to follow," Will said.

Tang shrugged. "Yeah, but most Arcanians pretty much do whatever they want. The Vanguard—that's the name of our law keepers—they mostly only enforce the laws when it comes to Genies. So even though I'm only a half-Genie, I've got to follow the law to the letter, or else I could be in serious trouble. Even wish-stealing Trolls get more respect than we Genies do."

"Now Tang, that's not true at all," Hollywood said. "Well, the part about the Trolls, that's true, but not the rest. The Vanguard also keeps a close eye on another group of potential lawbreakers: humans who abuse their Mizms."

Everyone glanced at Will, even Reverie.

"Er, right. About the flying thing—" Will looked at the ground. "I understand. I'm sorry. I don't wanna mess this up. I'll try harder, I promise."

Hollywood clapped his hands together. "Good, good, good. With that settled, on to more urgent business. Peske arranged all the paperwork for Tang's admission at your school, Will. Reverie sent all of it over this morning, right, Rev?"

There was no answer from Reverie other than a little snore. Her face was on top of the wishcraft rules book, and a spot of drool collected on the page.

"Reverie!" Hollywood yelled.

She bolted upright and wiped her chin dry, "Yes, of course, I took care of everything just as you asked. I did it during my morning sleepwalk."

"Excellent. So all is ready, I believe. Will's obviously discovered today's Mizm, so that's done. And Tang's got his book-bag filled with all the essentials so he can blend in with Will and his little school buddies."

"You're not worried about him fitting in?" Will hovered about an inch from the ground and circled around Tang, giving him the once-over.

"Best way to go unnoticed is to hide in plain sight," Tang said. "That's what the Genies believe. Even though they were once the Genies' prisons, most of them still live in lamps and bottles, ordinary stuff that's right out there in the open. When it comes to blending in, Genies are the masters."

Hollywood snatched Will by the arm, forcing him back to the ground. "Tang will be using his power as infrequently as possible while assisting you, Will. This is your mission, after all. And it will be an excellent way for Tang to prove himself to the organization."

"So, your hair isn't going to turn Christmas colors or anything when Mrs. Griswald asks you to recite the periodic table of elements?" Will asked Tang.

"I hosed it down with some super-hold, extra-long-lasting hairspray this morning. As long as I don't get my hair wet by snake venom or carburetor oil, we're totally good."

Will sighed. "Yeah, this is going to go well."

★

As soon as Will and Tang arrived at homeroom, Mrs. Griswald immediately dropped everything. Will tried to tell her "good morning," but Mrs. Griswald pushed him out of the way to get a look at the new student.

"What's your name, squirt?" she said.

"Tang, ma'am."

"Tang? Tang what?"

"Tang, ah, Kipperbang."

"What kind of name is that?" Mrs. Griswald scoffed.

"Norwegian?"

Mrs. Griswald's nose flared. "What about your admission papers?" she asked, folding her arms into her rolls of fat.

Tang reached into his book bag and pulled out the documents. He beamed as he handed them over to Mrs. Griswald. His smile quickly vanished, however, when she shook her head.

"No, no, this won't do at all." She shoved the papers in Tang's face and pointed to the bottom of the page. "We need the signature or signatures of your parents or guardians. There are no signatures on this page, Mr. Kipperbang."

Tang was speechless. The documents were supposed to be signed. And since Mrs. Griswald had already seen them, a simple wish was unlikely to fix it.

"I don't have time for any nonsense," said the teacher. "Now I have to go to the office to sort this out, which is the last thing I need right now. You'd better hope I have time for the pop quiz I planned for today!" The class let out a collective groan.

Mrs. Griswald pointed a claw-like finger at Tang. "New boy, you have a seat next to Willy until I get back. All the desks around him are usually empty. All of you, keep your yaps shut."

Mrs. Griswald flung the door open and then slammed it as she left. Tang and Will sank into desks in the back corner.

"How come the papers weren't signed?" asked Will.

"I dunno. Maybe Reverie took a little siesta again," said Tang with a sigh.

"Wait a minute! What's going to happen when Mrs. Griswald calls the number listed on your forms?"

"I have no clue. I don't even know what number they put down."

"We need to get hold of Hollywood right away! Can you give him a ring? What do you guys do, send telepathic messages using brainwaves or something?"

"Even better." Tang pulled a small handheld device from his jacket pocket and hid it close to his chest so the other students wouldn't see. "We text."

The half-Genie punched a few buttons but scowled at the results. "It's not working. Something's interfering with the signal. We'd better come up with a plan and quick. Look, Hollywood should have an open line on you, now that you're his number one client. You're going to have to make a wish and hope that he gets it in time."

Will closed his eyes and concentrated with all his might. *I seriously wish that Hollywood would get down here and save us ... but that he wouldn't embarrass us by offering to pose for photos ... and maybe he could really stick it to Mrs. Griswald while he's here, yeah, that would be cool ... oh, and if Reverie is taking this wish down for Hollywood—Hey, Reverie, lovely meeting you this morning. Hope your day's going well and that you don't fall asleep in your soup or anything like that. Okay, um, thanks. Take care. See ya later ... Bye.*

"Are you done?" Tang asked as he tapped his nose with a pencil.

"Yeah, I think I was rambling. Now that I know someone's actually listening to all of my wishes, it kind of makes me nervous."

"Don't give it a second thought. We're professionals—we don't judge your wishes or how you make them."

"But?" Will asked, knowing there was more.

"But we do have a silliest wish contest every Friday afternoon at the office. You've won like 17 times, Will. I think that's a record."

Flinging his hands into the air, Will said, "Great. You guys must think I'm a total moron. How did I ever get chosen for this job after all of my stupid wishes?"

"There are no stupid wishes. It's just that some are funnier than others. I mean, we get all kinds of wishes, from 'I wish for a complete set of mint condition X-Men comic books'—one of *your* wishes, by the way—to 'I wish for a pink pony that talks and does cartwheels.' See, not only are we dealing with an enormous volume of wishes, but we're also saddled with some pretty hefty ones, like 'I wish my mother would be okay and get out of the hospital soon.' That wish was from a girl in this school. Getting in a little laugh now and then is one way of dealing with the stress of wishes like that. Speaking of, how are you coping, now that you're hearing wishes too?"

Will grabbed at his shirt collar. "Um, you mean I should hear wishes by now? I haven't heard even one. How can I fulfill wishes if I don't know what they are?"

"Great Zorba, that's not good," said Tang. "How'd this happen? Did you activate the Telewish power this morning?"

"Activate? How was I supposed to do that? I thought it was just going to hit me ... like a bolt of lightning or something."

"After our visit last night, we forwarded the activation sequence to your e-mail account. You were supposed to click on the link and follow the prompts for Telewish setup and activation. Don't tell me you didn't get it."

"Okay, I won't tell you I didn't get it."

Tang slapped his forehead. "Didn't you read your contract last night? Your instructions were all there."

Will fidgeted in his seat and looked around the room at everything and everyone but Tang. "It had lots of big words."

"Well, here are three small words for you: breach of contract. That's what's going to happen if we can't get your Telewishing up and running."

"I can't exactly check my e-mail right now. Mrs. Griswald will be back any second. Can't you use your powers to help me out?"

"I'm not supposed to use any extraordinary means to assist you. If only we could get in touch with Hollywood, he could set up the Telewishing manually. Try wishing again. You may have just gotten his voicemail before."

Will closed his eyes again, even tighter this time. *I wish ... I wish ... I—*

"So who's this, Cricket? Your new girlfriend?"

Will's wish interrupted, he opened his eyes to find three of his classmates standing over him and Tang: Benji Zingermann, Mason Quattlebaum and Connor O'Malley. The ringleader, Benji, was an aspiring football jock. He was just about the shortest person Will knew. Mason and Connor didn't take part in football, but they did play a mean game of dodge ball, emphasis on *mean*. Will was their favorite target.

"Or is this another addition to your freak-show family, Cricket?" asked the orange-haired, pink-skinned Connor.

Will's hands shook, and he managed to stammer, "No ... no, this is a new student. His ... his name is Tang."

"Tang?" said Benji. "What kind of name is 'Tang?' Well, nice to meet you. I'm Pepsi, and this is Kool-Aid and Diet Dr. Pepper."

Tang gave them all a nod. "Pleasure to meet you, Kool-Aid, Diet."

The three boys burst into laughter. "He's as big an idiot as Cricket!" Mason said between snorts.

Tang didn't deserve this treatment. Will started to say something, but he caught himself ... literally. He'd forgotten about his Mizm and started to levitate. He grabbed the sides of his desk and pulled himself back down. Lucky for him, no one seemed to have noticed.

Focus, Will, focus, he thought, his eyes closed.

Just as Will settled back into his chair, Mrs. Griswald returned, an angry scowl on her face.

"Willy," she said in a screechy voice. "You and new boy get up here pronto. Turns out just as I made it to the office, new boy's parents miraculously appeared, ready to finish signing the forms."

"My, uh, parents are here?" Tang fidgeted with his hair, probably hoping it wasn't changing colors.

"Yes, and they wanted to stop by and see you and your friend Willy before leaving. I refused, but your father is quite the charmer—almost like some movie star."

"Oh no ... it couldn't be—" Will gasped.

"Hi, Son! Hello, Will!" In walked Hollywood, dressed in a "World's Number One Dad" t-shirt and matching baseball cap. "Hope my little boy is enjoying his first day at this wonderful school. Your mother and I apologized profusely to your lovely teacher ... Miss, ah, Grizzy is it?"

"Griswald, actually, but you can call me Grizzy if you like," the teacher said.

"Uh, right ..." Hollywood puffed out his cheeks. "Anyhow, Tang, your mom and I came to school right away when we realized we forgot to sign the forms."

"Tang's mom is here too?" Will asked.

"Well, of course! We both had to sign, so where else would Mom be? Right, dear?" He looked into the hall where Tang's "mother" stood. "Mom, get in here already and say hello to your son."

"No, that's okay, I'll wait out here," said a squeaky voice.

"Come on, dear, say 'hi' so we can do our thing, and then we'll leave," said Hollywood forcefully.

From out in the hallway, wearing a lemonade pink sundress, apron and bonnet, Norv Peske entered the classroom. "Hi, Tang. Mommy's here."

Peske looked like a cross between a crotchety old woman and a color-blind milkmaid. He wasn't the best looking guy, and he made an even worse-looking lady.

"Mommy?" Tang said, stifling a giggle.

"You better believe it, kid," replied Peske. He stood with his arms crossed and his legs as far apart as possible.

"What are you two doing here?" Will said, keeping one eye on Hollywood and Peske and the other on his strangely silent classmates. Apparently they were too stunned to do anything but stare at Tang's peculiar parents.

"We came to correct that little oversight we made on Tang's paperwork," said Hollywood. "While we were in the neighborhood, we thought we'd drop in, check up on you boys and see if you might need me to jumpstart your ... ah, car ... yeah, right, car."

"Car?" Mrs. Griswald exclaimed. "You let these children drive a car?"

Hollywood kept smiling, as usual. "Um, given your reaction, I'm going to say no, actually. After all, we follow the letter of the law in our household. I'm sorry, boys—no driving until you're 47."

"Sixteen," Will whispered.

"Or 16. Whichever comes first." Hollywood looked out to the class, pointed at a few of the girls and gave them winks. They sighed and giggled in reply.

"Mrs. Griswald, if you'd be so kind, we'd like to have a moment alone with the boys." Hollywood ushered Will and Tang toward the door. With unusual quickness, Mrs. Griswald sped around and flung herself in front of them, blocking their way.

"You listen to me, mister. You may think you can get whatever you want by being all handsome and charming, but you're wrong. If good looks and charisma were so important to me, I'd never have married Mr. Griswald."

"Come now, my dear. Your heart's not truly into making our lives difficult. Focus on the positive, on what truly matters. I bet you're thinking about that trip to Moldova you've planned for the summer, aren't you? Been a lifelong wish of yours, hasn't it?" said Hollywood.

The creases below her eyes softened ever so slightly. "How ... how did you know about my wish?"

"Lucky guess?"

"Fine! You've got five minutes with new boy and Willy, and that's it."

"Lovely woman, your teacher—reminds me of my mother," Peske stated, matter-of-factly as he peered up and down the hallway, finding no one else present.

Hollywood waved a finger at Peske. "You know, with that dress on, you really look like your ole mum."

"Mother always did dress well." Peske smoothed down his outfit and checked his bonnet.

"As much as I'd like to chat about the extreme oddness of dressing up Peske as a woman," said Will, "could we speed things along? I don't want to face the wrath of Mrs. Griswald."

"Right, right, right. Will, I hear you didn't activate your Telewishing this morning. Didn't read the contract all the way through, eh?"

"Well, it's just that my eyes have been really tired lately and—"

"Maybe it's best that he didn't," said Peske.

"What Norv means," Hollywood said, "is that the contract is sooooo boring that you likely would've fallen asleep before even signing the darn thing. What matters now is that we get your Telewishing operational so that you can get underway with today's wish granting."

Hollywood rubbed his hands together, stretched his legs with several squats, pointed to Will and gave him a wink that literally sparkled.

Will tapped his temples and shook his head around a bit. "Is that it? Am I able to Telewish now?"

"Sorry, Will, no." Hollywood's expression became drab for the first time since they'd met. "Unfortunately, you'll know when it's working. Actually, that's why we wanted you to activate it at home, where there weren't so many people around. Now that you're at school, surrounded by children who make wish after wish, this might be somewhat overwhelming. Brace yourself. It's not going to be pleasant. Trust me, though, when I say, this is going to hurt me more than it hurts you."

Hollywood raised his hands to his face and said, "Twinkle, twinkle little star." Suddenly the tips of his fingers glowed. A whirling mass of dark appeared in his palms, like a miniature black hole from deep space. The sparkling skin of his hands began to flake away and fly about the hallway like tiny fairies. They made a sizzling sound, like bacon frying. There was an odd smell about them too, almost as if something was burning, like rubber ... or flesh. Another second passed and Hollywood's hands had vanished entirely, leaving only the stumps of his arms. Hollywood quickly hid them behind his back, even as he dropped to his knees and gasped in pain.

Will choked back a squeal of terror. He moved toward the Wish Agent, but the specks of light buzzed around him like gnats. The swarm grew larger and denser. Will swatted at them, but they stayed in place. He opened his lips to ask for help, and that's when they invaded. The bits flew into his mouth and then his nose and ears.

Will could feel the creatures bouncing around in his head. But there wasn't any pain at all, certainly nothing compared to what Hollywood seemed to be going through. With his mind's eye, Will sensed the creatures of light moving about his brain. They were tweaking and adjusting, as if Will's mind were a computer that needed reprogramming.

After a few seconds had passed, Will sensed something click in his head. He felt a burning cold in his palms. The dark, swirling mass was seated in his own hands now. The sparkling specks suddenly flew out from the mass and shot toward Hollywood. They ran across the agent's body, which glowed for a moment, then moved in unison toward what used to be the wish agent's hands. When the last speck could no longer be seen, Hollywood let out a whimper. He immediately turned away, still holding his arms out of sight.

Tang pulled a small vial from his pants pocket. It seemed to hold a liquid substance, but it was so tiny that it didn't have more than a drop or two.

"It's wishing well water," he said to Will as he uncorked the top of the bottle and emptied its contents onto Hollywood's hands. "We use it for a number of purposes, but it comes in handiest for healing. Don't worry. He'll be fine."

"This is all my fault. If I'd read the contract like you told me to do and followed the Telewish activation procedures this morning, none of this would've happened. I'm really sorry."

Peske walked away from Will without so much as a glance. Will just stood there, shoulders slumped. He was on the verge of tears when something strange happened. Someone whispered something in Will's ear. He turned to see who it was, but no one was there. It wasn't Peske or Tang—they were attending to Hollywood.

Will scanned the halls, checking around the corners, by the water fountain and even on the ceiling. Nothing. Now he heard another voice, deeper than the first. Then a different one—a girl's maybe. The voices got louder and louder. Will clamped his hands over his ears, but the sounds were all the clearer. They weren't coming from the outside at all—he heard them in his head. The Telewishing was working.

I wish Mrs. Griswald would get canned.

I really wish I'd studied for this stupid test.

I wish Mom and Dad would stop fighting.

I just wish Jensen would notice me.

I wish that chubby dork Willy the whale would get transferred to some other school, like one in Malaysia.

After hearing that last wish, Will tried to block out the sounds. While he couldn't make them totally disappear, he found that he could turn down their volume. The voices were like background noise in a busy cafeteria. All it took to quiet them was a little motivation, a little pain, a little anger.

"Will? Will, you okay?" Tang rushed back to him.

"Telewishing is a go, Will?" Hollywood grunted as he and Peske joined the boys.

"Yeah, all those voices just hit me from out of nowhere," Will said. "It's pretty bizarre. I don't know how you guys handle it."

"Lots of practice," Tang said. "And you seem to have adapted in record time, I'd say."

Arms behind his back, Hollywood circled around Will. "Didn't I tell you both that Will was the one? Never bet against me, boys, I know how to pick a winner."

Will couldn't help but notice how Hollywood kept his hands hidden. The agent's trademark smile had returned, but he seemed to be acting. "Look, Hollywood, about what you did just now for me—"

"Ah, ah, ah, Will. I don't want to hear it. A mistake was made, but that's how we learn, right? Besides, all worthy causes require a little suffering. You've certainly gone through your fair share. Let's put it behind us now, okay? We have more significant issues to deal with, namely, you earning your wish. So you two get back in there and be on the lookout for a wish to grant. I think you'll find it smoother sailing from now on."

Hollywood ushered the boys to their classroom. He started to wave goodbye, but opted for a simple nod.

Will faced his classmates for the first time since his transformation and turned up the volume to his Telewishing, listening intently to the wishes that sprung from the minds of those around him. Unexpectedly the wishes of two adult voices broke in. Will caught wind of a private conversation between Peske and Hollywood.

I wish there were another way, Peske.

I wish the same thing, Hollywood, but there's no way around the obstacles ahead for young William.

All we can do is wish for his success … and his safety.

DAY 1.3

Will had yet to find a grantable wish, and it was making him anxious. Despite the crisp autumn temperatures, he was perspiring heavily even before he hit the outdoor track that ran alongside the fenced-in football field. Will had forgotten to bring a new tee for P.E., having worn the other home yesterday after his shirt-splitting incident. He was so distracted, though, that he almost wasn't embarrassed by being the only student in his regular school clothes.

As they waited for their classmates to arrive for phys. ed., Will caught a glimpse of Diego and Jerritt. "Great," Will whispered. "My two biggest fans are over there."

Tang followed Will's hand as he pointed to the monstrously large Diego. The half-Genie's body involuntarily twitched. "Great Zorba! He's bigger than a Troll!"

Will cupped his hand over Tang's mouth. "Shhh! Come on, let's duck behind that group of girls. Diego wouldn't look for me there."

Will dragged Tang behind the bleachers, a few feet away from eight giggling girls. He didn't realize until it was too late that the gigglers were some of the cheerleaders.

Will stopped cold. Tang peered over his shoulder and examined them. "Hey, I recognize that one girl from the file we have on you at the office. The one with the freckles, that's your sister, right?"

Will did a double-take. "Yeah, it's Kaitlyn. Let's just move away from here. I don't want to bother her—"

Kaitlyn spied Will and immediately but slowly stepped away from the others. She approached her brother, her eyes squinted, and her cheeks puffed up. "Get lost, Will. You and your dweeb friend are embarrassing me. Can't you just leave me alone for, like, five minutes?"

"Hi, Kaitlyn, I'm Tang! Nice to make your acquaintance." Tang beamed.

Will's sister grabbed the boys by their ears, twisted them a bit and led them away. *I wish Will would leave me alone forever!*

Will heard her loud and clear. All he could do was sigh.

"Ten-hut!" It was Jensen Macabee, quarterback, and object of Kaitlyn Cricket's desire. He obviously wasn't their teacher, but most of the kids fell in line anyway. "Listen up, kids. Coach Digger is in the office and will be a few minutes late—apparently the principal frowned on him using rabid dogs to get the track team to run faster. So he sent me out to make sure you guys had an authority figure to ..."

Jensen's voice trailed off as a shadow appeared over his shoulder and blocked out his sunlight. Only one person was massive enough to do that: Diego.

"It's that Troll again," Tang yelped, scrambling behind Will.

"Quick. Under here." Will grabbed Tang by his sleeve and rushed under the bleachers.

"Well, well. If it isn't Lamone Pledge's favorite quarterback, Jensen Macaboob," said Diego. "I've got some things to work out with you, jock."

Jensen backed away and flung up his arms in protest. "Whoa, I thought we were cool. Remember last week I left those primo concert tickets in your locker, just like you wanted."

"I didn't want tickets to that stupid rock concert! I wanted ..." he paused and leaned in to whisper, not realizing that Will and Tang were within earshot. "I wanted tickets to the ballet."

"Yeah, but what?" said Jensen. "Ballet? You're into ballet?"

"Keep it down, punk. So what if I like ballet? So what if I keep taking lessons and the only part I get is a stage prop? You think that makes me bitter?"

"Um, no?"

Diego snorted, snarled and even foamed a little at the mouth. "Well, you're wrong. It ticks me off big time! Makes me wanna pummel something in the ground. And I think you just volunteered."

"Look, Diego," Jensen said as he took a few steps to the side. "It wouldn't be smart for you to beat me up. I'm idolized by everyone in this school. I don't get bullied. So buzz off, chump. Go climb a tree."

"No, I think *you* need to climb a tree." Diego shoved Jensen to the ground and pointed to an enormous old white oak, which still held its leaves despite the crisp November weather. "In fact, I think you should climb that one, all the way to the top."

"You're crazy. I could fall and mess up my throwing arm. No way, dude."

"If you don't, I'm gonna mess up your face. Think the girls will still love you then? Now get up there, all the way to the top, and make it fast. I wanna be entertained."

"Yeah, make like a tree and scram," Jerritt said, waving him off.

Jensen stood in place for a moment, glancing beyond Diego to his fellow football players, all of whom looked away when he signaled for help. He was on his own. Defying Diego, as everyone knew, meant certain pain, even for someone as popular as Jensen.

Reluctantly, the quarterback turned to face the white oak. He scanned it from top to bottom. It was at least 10 stories high. Jensen wiped his brow and placed his foot on a knot toward the bottom of the tree. He looked pale and clammy, and his hands trembled as he reached for a low-lying branch.

I wish Diego would drop off the face of the earth, thought Jensen.

"Did you hear that?" Will asked Tang. "Now that's a wish I could get into. I could fly Diego up to the edge of the atmosphere and toss him into space."

Tang shook his head. "Come on, Will. You know that would violate the terms of your wish contract. Remember the part about not hurting anyone?"

"Yeah, I know, but the school day's almost over, and practically the only wishes I've heard have been about clearing up acne, canceling school and Mrs. Griswald getting fired. When is a decent flying-related wish going to—?"

I wish someone would help Jensen—I don't think he's going to make it down.

"I had to open my big mouth," Will said.

"It's what you wanted," Tang said.

"No, what I wanted was for someone to wish for help getting a book off the top shelf in the library. This is insane."

"This is about your wish too, though. How far are you willing to go to succeed?"

"Pretty far, I guess, but there's one more kicker. I'm not sure that the person who made the wish would actually want me to grant it. It was Kaitlyn."

"But she's such a sweetheart." Tang took in a deep breath and sighed. "She must be the best older sister ever. Why would you be worried?"

"Man, what kind of twisted sister do you have to think she's cool?"

"Actually, I've never met my real sister, me being adopted and all, but I know her by reputation. Her name's Animalia. She granted a wish that caused the Black Plague of the 14th century that killed a third of Europe's population."

"Okay, okay, you win the 'evil sister' contest. But it doesn't change the fact that my sister thinks I'm a loser and wants nothing to do with me."

"So let's show her you're not a loser. Let's show all of them."

"Okay, I'll give it a try. It's not as if I'll fall on my face. Not as long as I can fly."

Will ducked to climb out from under the bleachers, but Tang grabbed him by the ear. "Don't forget: you can't do anything to reveal your powers. So however you handle this, be subtle, be smooth."

"If Will Cricket is anything, my friend, it's smooth," Will said, before banging his head on the bleachers as he made his way out.

"Cricket!" Diego yelled. Will had barely taken two steps toward the oak tree when the bully spotted him. "Where do you think you're going? This ain't got nothing to do with you, so unless you want me to beat you like an egg, you'd better scramble."

"Oh, um, hey, Diego. Nice day, huh?" Will said with a twitch.

"Nice day? Oh, yeah, it's a gorgeous day. You wanna go sit on a hilltop and watch the clouds go by, Willy?" said Diego. "Or better yet, how 'bout I just knock you up to the clouds instead?"

"How 'bout I just go climb that tree?" said Will, glancing up at the white oak. "Looks like Jensen could use a hand."

"You?" Diego blinked in amazement. "Cricket's going to climb that tree and help jock boy down? Yeah, right! When pigs fly!"

Will couldn't help but crack a smile.

"You think this is funny, Cricket?"

"Not as funny as when he lost the shirt off his back!" Jerritt chimed in.

"Yeah, that was funny. So funny, I'd love to see it again. Let's snatch his shirt and use it to tie him up to the tree. Maybe he won't laugh so much if we leave him there overnight!"

The shirtless incident from the previous day still made Will's cheeks burn. He didn't want to be that kid anymore—the one that let people run over him, who lost sleep every night because of bullies. Suddenly, something in Will's mind clicked, a memory from earlier in the day. Shirt. Sleep. Of course!

Will rubbed his hand across his shirt, the same area where he'd wiped it earlier after meeting Reverie. Her sleeping dust was still there—his hand tingled. The dust was working. Without a moment's hesitation, he flung the specks into Diego's eyes.

"What the?" Diego was stunned the moment it hit him. His eyes watered. He rubbed them, but it was too late.

"Hey, Deego, you okay?" Jerritt ran up behind his partner in crime and tapped him on the shoulder. Diego moaned softly and then fell backwards.

"Not again," Jerritt squeaked. He tried to scramble out of the way, but Diego fell, pinning Jerritt to the ground.

"Help! Help!" Jerritt screamed. As hard as he tried, he couldn't get out from under Diego.

The entire gym class huddled around the two troublemakers. Everyone was silent, barely breathing—in awe. Will wanted to bask in his classmates' adoration, but he had a more urgent job to attend to.

Will looked back up at Jensen, who was still clinging to the tree for dear life.

"Jensen!" Will yelled. "You can stop now. Diego's, um, down for the count."

Jensen looked down but apparently couldn't see through the leaves and branches, "Who ... who's there?"

"It's Will Cricket, Kaitlyn's brother. I'm going to help you down. Just stay put."

Will scrambled to the side of the tree away from all of the kids who were still gathered about Diego and Jerritt. He glanced around, made certain no one could see him, and then slowly levitated off the ground. He stretched out his arms and lifted his legs to make it look as though he was climbing the tree. Will was at the top in 10 seconds. He floated over to a branch that seemed solid, but he didn't dare turn off his power.

Pushing his way past a few reddening leaves, Will found Jensen desperately holding to a flimsy branch, sobbing quietly. His eyes were tightly shut. He didn't seem to hear Will's rustling noises or the creak of the branch when Will put some weight on it. Will moved within arms' reach as Jensen's eyelids hesitantly drew open.

"You actually got up here?" Jensen said, his voice trembling. "Wow, you're a good climber."

"I'm up here because of my sister, you know," said Will. "She likes you, Jensen. She thinks you're a sweet guy, believe it or not. Me, on the other hand ..."

"Kaitlyn?"

"Yeah, she figured you might need some help getting down."

"Help?" Jensen said with disbelief in his voice. "I don't need anybody's help. I can get down myself."

"Oh, yeah? Fine. I'll see you." Will took a step off the branch and positioned his hands to climb back down.

"No! Wait!" Jensen shouted. "Okay, okay ... I'll admit it, I need help. Please."

"I dunno ..."

"Look, none of my boys helped me out. But your sister, she stuck by me, even though she didn't have any reason to. I should probably be nicer to her ... you too, I guess."

"Honestly, I don't care. If it were up to me, I'd leave you hanging up here. Guess that would be kind of ironic, since you did the same to me yesterday."

"I'm really sorry about—"

"Come on, take my hand before Diego gets up," said Will.

Jensen was slow to let go of the branch and grab onto Will. When he finally did, Will hoisted him back to his feet on top of the branch. Jensen's legs wobbled like noodles.

With Jensen behind him, Will said, "Now put your arms around my neck and clasp your hands together. Try not to strangle me, okay? I'll do all the climbing, and you just hold on tight. And don't look down—"

Before Will could finish his sentence, Jensen looked down.

"Oh, jeez!" Jensen yelled. "We're up crazy high! Don't drop me, man!"

"I told you not to look down!"

"Oh ... man ... I'm dizzy ..." Jensen said, his grip loosening.

"Jensen! Hold on!" From below, Will heard gasps from his classmates. He couldn't see any of them through the leaves, and he guessed they couldn't see him either. They must have heard his shouts and assumed the worst.

The worst was exactly what was happening. Jensen wasn't just slipping, he'd fainted!

"Jensen! Wake up!" Will yelled. But it was too late. Jensen's unconscious body toppled over the branch and plummeted toward the ground.

Everything that happened next zoomed by in a split second. Will had no time to think. He just dove out of the tree, racing after Jensen. He dipped and swerved, dodging leaves and branches. He had no idea how he was able to fly like that, but it paid off. He was within a few feet of Jensen! Will poured on more speed and reached out, grabbing the quarterback's belt buckle. He slowed their descent, but not by much—Jensen was too heavy. Will had to do something else, and quick—they were almost in direct view of the gawkers below.

There was only one low-lying branch left, and with his free hand, Will grabbed hold of it. With a miniscule burst of inconspicuous flying power, he threw himself over the branch. He held tight to Jensen while Tang and Kaitlyn ran over to them.

Jensen's unconscious body hung down far enough that they were able to reach him. Will dropped the quarterback into their arms.

They laid Jensen down on the grass, and almost immediately he came to. Kaitlyn made a swipe or two at his cheeks, mostly between choking back tears. The students all gathered around Jensen, whispering back and forth to one another and gesturing at Will. No cheers, no congratulations, just the normal finger-pointing, as though Will had somehow been the cause of all this.

Will started to lower himself to the ground when Jensen called to him. "Dude, my watch. Lost it on the way down. You see it?" Jensen was back in "cool guy" mode, even though just a minute ago he'd been a blubbering wimp.

Will cocked his head and spied something shiny about 30 feet up. "Looks like it's caught on a branch."

"My mom's going to kill me if I don't come home with it."

No, Will thought to himself, *I'm not going to do it. Today's wish is granted, and I'm done. I'm not risking my neck for that good-for-nothing—*

"Will can do it," Kaitlyn said. "My brother will get your watch, Jensen."

Her … brother? "Okay," Will called out to his sister and Jensen. "I'll be right back."

"Um, hey, Will!" Tang yelled out.

"Be right back, Tang," Will said as he used his flight power to discretely pull himself back up on the branch.

"Would you just please wait, Will?"

"Just hang loose for a second." Will inched up the tree until he found the sterling silver watch dangling off the side of an empty bird's nest. He carefully unhooked it, stuffed it in his pocket, and then began to drift back down.

Tang was below, still yelling up at him, but Will couldn't make out what he said. He pushed off the tree and hovered around to the side away from all the activity and peeping eyes. The tree's trunk was so large that he could float down without anyone seeing a thing. He wanted to experience flight one last time before heading home. It had been the biggest rush of his life, and he hated to think that, at midnight, he'd lose this power.

That didn't seem quite right. He vaguely recalled something being said about how his powers came and went. Then it came to him, something Tang had told him last night.

After the wish has been granted, your powers for that day will fade away.

Wait a minute, Will thought. *I just granted today's wish. So that means—*

Will feverishly reached up and flung his arms around a small branch. But it was far too thin, and there was no way it could support a boy his size. The branch snapped just as the last of Will's power of flight burned itself out.

Will plunged to the ground.

"So you got off to a rocky start," Tang said as they approached Will's house. "Happens to the best of us. Tomorrow will be better, I'm sure. Just relax—"

"I nearly got myself killed, Tang! Any more rough of a start and it would've been a complete stop! If you hadn't seeded the ground with those quick-grow, super-spongy dandelions, I'd be a mashed potato."

"It's only your first day on the job, and you've already made a monumental difference for Jensen and his family and honestly the whole school—not to mention your sister. You did a splendid thing today."

"Yeah, I suppose," Will said, stopping at the lemon-yellow front door of his house. "It's just that this whole wish-granting deal isn't turning out to be as cool as I thought it'd be."

"Aw, come on, Will, you did terrific today," said a familiar voice coming from the boxwood shrub planted next to the front door.

"Thanks, Mr. Shrub," he said, his voice flat and monotone.

"Will, it's me, Hollywood." The wish agent popped his head out of the bush and gave the boys an exaggerated wink. "I'm incognito. The paparazzi have been hounding me all day. Apparently they took note of my appearance again this year in *Wish Time*'s list of most eligible bachelors."

Hollywood jumped from behind the hedge and landed in a strange crouch. "Coast looks clear," Hollywood said, peering up and down the street, at the roof and even under his shoes. He folded his body on the front steps and pulled Will down beside him. "Everything was new and crazy today, but tomorrow you'll be an old pro at this. It's still going to be hard, I won't lie. But I'd say you're going to come away from this experience not only a new young man, in accordance to your wish, but you'll be a hundred times happier."

"I dunno ... maybe ... I guess I'm just used to my routine. Not that it's been great or anything, but it's all I know."

Hollywood stood, brushed off his pants, and said, "It's a process, Will. Stick with it, and you won't believe the results. One day down, six to go. You can do it. We'll catch you later, partner!"

"Bye, Will. Good job today. I'll meet you back here in the morning," said Tang, reaching into his bag. He took out two of his life-saving dandelions—like the ones that broke Will's fall from the tree—except these looked different. They were ivory-colored, and they shimmered when the wind blew across them.

Tang handed one to Hollywood, and they both held them up to their lips. They sucked in enough air to fill a dozen balloons, held it for a few seconds and then blew out with all their might, just as a kid would when making a wish ... only the plumed seeds didn't detach and blow away from the stem like normal. Instead, Hollywood and Tang's bodies turned into a mass of dandelion seeds. They broke apart and blew off into the wind. The rays of the falling sun made the seeds glow like stars as they faded into the atmosphere.

"Those guys sure know how to make an exit," Will mumbled to himself.

At the dinner table, Nonnie was unusually quiet. She'd watched Will like a hawk ever since he'd come home from school. She'd silently joined him in the kitchen for an afternoon snack, accompanied him to the living room for an hour of Batman's latest adventures, and even attempted to follow him into the bathroom. The whole time, she didn't say a single word—she just stared.

Though he'd barely touched his food, Will was almost finished eating when Kaitlyn arrived.

"You're late for dinner again, sweetheart." Will's father kept his head buried in the newspaper as he slurped down iced tea. "Where were you?"

"Aw, Daddy, I beat Mom home, didn't I?" she said, plopping her books on the table. "What does it matter anyhow?"

"Alright," he said. "How was school today? Anything interesting happen?"

For the first time all afternoon, Nonnie's gaze left Will and switched to his sister. "Yeah, Kaitlyn, tell us all about your day. Do they teach rock climbing at that school of yours? You kids must have some wild adventures."

Will's fork slipped from his hand and clanged against his plate. As much as he wanted Kaitlyn to brag about his heroic rescue of her would-be boyfriend, he couldn't let anyone uncover the whole story. Hollywood and Tang had warned him against it many times over. For the sake of his mission and his wish, he'd have to stop his sister from bragging about his bravery and gushing over his selflessness.

"Today was completely embarrassing!" Kaitlyn wailed. "Will was the biggest meathead ever! He totally humiliated me in front of the cheerleaders and Jensen and practically the whole school."

Wait a minute, Will thought. He'd saved her Prince Charming and risked his life a second time to retrieve the guy's—

"Will stole Jensen's watch!" Kaitlyn collapsed into a chair and slammed her head against the table.

Will felt around his pockets—the watch was still there. His sister was right, sort of; he had taken Jensen's watch. "Huh," Will said as he fished it out and plopped it on the table. "I totally forgot

I had it. Slipped my mind. You want to give it back to him, Kait, or should I?"

Kaitlyn seized the watch and clutched it to her chest. "I'll find someone to get it to him. He's not speaking to me. He thinks I helped you take it from him."

"Will," his father said, putting down his paper. "Is this true? Did you steal this watch?"

"No way, Dad! You have no clue what happened today," Will said.

"So tell us." Nonnie inched her chair closer to Will. "I think we'd all like to see what fruit this tree has to bear."

"What? Uh ... no, there was no fruit, no trees, nothing. I just ... well, you see we were playing 'musical watches' and—"

"Weren't you just playing 'musical shirts' yesterday? Is that all you do at this school, play games?" Nonnie asked, scratching her pink hair. Will's father lost interest and picked up the sports section again.

"The point is," Will said, "I didn't steal anything. It was just a misunderstanding. Kait, I'm sure when you take it back to him and remind him what a terrific pal your brother is, he'll let it all slide."

"What brother? I don't have a brother. Because of you there's no way Jensen's going to ask me out now!" Kaitlyn shouted, leaving the table and stomping to her room.

"At least things are back to normal," Will whispered to himself.

"What was that you said, boy?" Nonnie asked.

"I said, 'I think Kaitlyn's been possessed by the paranormal.'"

"Yeah, I was thinking that too," Nonnie said, very gravely. "Think I'll go check on the little demon, make sure she's okay." Nonnie excused herself, put her plate and silverware beneath the table, and then wandered down the hallway toward Kaitlyn's room.

"At least she didn't confuse the dishwasher with the washing machine again and throw her plate in for a spin," said Will's father.

"But she always puts it on the delicate cycle, Dad," Will said, thinking he was rather funny.

"Hmm? Oh yes, right ... delicate." Will's father was taking notes on an article in the paper. In his own way, he worked almost as much as his wife, which in Will's opinion was entirely too much.

A car horn beeped outside in the driveway, but it didn't sound like his mom's Jeep. It was like a tambourine in the hands of a mad jingler.

"Who's that?" Will asked.

"Whoever it is, they must be doing okay to spend money on a custom horn." Will's father sprinted to the front door with Will in tow.

They opened the door to find Will's mom had indeed returned home. Just as Will suspected, she wasn't in her car. She wasn't alone either. A man with dark hair, graying at the temples and a light beard helped her out of the vehicle.

"That's a 1949 Rolls-Royce Silver Wraith!" said Will's father. "It's got the long wheelbase. They only made a few hundred of those."

Will's father made a mad rush to the car, and Will had to run to keep up.

"Oh, honey, hi there. Hi, William," Will's mom said.

"Hey, dear. Glad you're home." Will's father took his wife's hand and shook it vigorously, his eyes still glued to the fancy car.

"Sweetheart, stop shaking my hand." Will's mother snatched it away and snapped her fingers at her husband until she finally broke him of his vehicular trance. "I'd like you to meet my boss. He was kind enough to give me a ride home. The car didn't start again."

"Very nice of you, Mr. ..."

"Peach. Lincoln Peach. I can't believe this is the first time we've met. I feel like a part of the family, given how much time I spent with your wife's father back when he was a professor of archaeology." The words were polite enough, but they were accompanied by a sneer.

"Oh, please, call me Cal," said Will's father, shaking Mr. Peach's hand. "Pleasure to finally meet you. You have quite an incredible ride here. I never thought I'd see one of these in person. Is it really yours? I mean, they're so rare."

"I stumbled across the Rolls and immediately snatched it up three years ago in Egypt. I was there on an expedition for an artifact affectionately called Mummy's Dearest, which is a bracelet carved from ivory and set with onyx stones, said to have been buried with King Tutankhamen's mother. I found both the artifact and the car on a seedy used camel salesman in Alexandria."

"Sure is a beauty," said Will's father.

"Speaking of beauties, I do apologize for keeping your wife so late these days. It's been exceptionally busy around the office lately," said Mr. Peach.

Will's father chuckled and pulled his wife in for a quick side hug. "No need for apology. Emily loves working for you, and she loves the job. She's always carrying on about all of the exciting projects and acquisitions at Peach Preserves."

"Whenever she's actually home, that is," Will whispered, but loudly.

"Will! What did you say?!" Will's mom put her hands on her hips and craned over him. "I think you owe Mr. Peach an apology."

"Nonsense," Mr. Peach said, placing a hand on her shoulder. "The boy's right. I work you entirely too long and hard." He crouched and extended a hand to Will. "What might this fine young man's name be?"

"Will." He took Mr. Peach's hand, though reluctantly. He put all of his effort into a firm squeeze, but his mom's boss had none of that—Mr. Peach squeezed back even harder.

"A strong name for a strong boy. I see you have your grandfather's eyes. Don't worry, Will. I have your mother's best interests at heart. After next week, her schedule will be a lot more manageable."

"Oh?" Will's father said, suddenly snuggling closer to his wife. "This is the first I'm hearing about it. What's happening next week?"

"The last pieces of our Ancient Prophets collection finally arrive. We've been tracking them down for years. Thanks to some hard work and a lot of capitol, it's coming together nicely. I'll truly have something to be thankful for this Thanksgiving."

"If it means Emily gets to come home earlier, then I'll be thankful too. We all will, right, Son?"

"Yeah, sure, whatever," Will said, arms crossed. "If it happens ..."

"I understand you have your doubts, Will, but I will do my very best to get your mother's work schedule back to normal," Mr. Peach said. "Emily tells me your school is having a career day next Wednesday and that you'll be joining her in the office. You'll get to see firsthand what we do. I'd be happy to personally give you a tour of the facilities. Just wait until you feast your eyes on the Ancient Prophets collection! You may even be there for the arrival of the final piece."

"Wow! How 'bout that, kiddo!" said Will's father.

"Yep, great," said Will, rather less than enthused.

Will's father took Mr. Peach's hand and shook it up, down and sideways even. "Thanks, Mr. Peach, for helping Emily tonight and for taking such an interest in Will. We really must have you over for dinner; it's the least we can do. In fact, why don't we do it tomorrow night? Emily, is that all right with you?"

"Sure, Cal, but even though tomorrow is Saturday, I'll be working late. We may have to order in."

"Nonsense, my dear. You know what a terrific chef I am. I have this amazing new rice dish that I've been dying to try."

Mr. Peach rubbed his hands together with glee. "What a delight! Of course, I'd be honored to come. I do hope I'll get to see that lovely mother of yours, Emily. I haven't seen her since ... well, since her husband left us."

Will's mom nervously bit her lip and nodded gently.

"I really must be going. Have a fabulous evening, all. I am terribly eager to spend more time with all of the Crickets. I'll see you in the morning, Emily, bright and early."

Will's mother nodded, her rosy cheeks evident even with only the half-moon's light.

As Mr. Peach pulled out of the driveway, Will's mom and dad waved vigorously, as if he were a favorite relative they might never see again.

"What a breath of fresh air," Will's father stated. "You've always said you have an excellent boss, but you weren't doing him justice. He's really a swell guy. We're very lucky he knew your dad and came after you to work for him."

"Come on, honey, let's get inside. I wanna warm up some dinner and relax for a little bit," said Will's mother.

"Do you think we should talk about tomorrow night's menu? I was thinking something exotic, perhaps ostrich. Or maybe we should do a theme night, like Hawaiian vacation. I could dig a pit in the backyard and roast a pig."

Will's mom tapped her nose for a moment, but hesitated to say anything. "Let's worry about that later. I should say 'hello' to Kaitlyn first."

"Good idea. She's upset about a boy at school. Will? Coming inside?"

"I think I'll just sit out here for a minute." Will said, dismally slumping down on the front porch steps, propping his chin in his hands.

"Sure thing, champ."

As his father closed the door, just like that, Will was alone again, as usual. Just because he'd pulled off magnificent heroics today didn't mean he was any different. No one cared. He felt like the same old Will with the same old problems.

The sound of a twig snapping in the yard caused Will to fling up his head. Speaking of the same problems ...

"Cricket," Diego growled. "What a coincidence meeting you here."

Will jumped to his feet and backed up toward the front door. "Well, it is my house, Diego, so that's really not much of a coincidence."

"Ironic?"

"Nope."

"Then how about premeditated? You know, like premeditated murder."

Will reached behind him for the doorknob. "Look, Diego, don't do anything I'm going to regret."

A blast of cold wind blew up a pile of dead leaves from behind the bully. Diego cracked his knuckles, spit on them and rubbed it in. "Wouldn't dream of it. Not here, not with so many witnesses around."

"Then I guess you're out of luck because next week I start home-schooling. Yup, that's right, doing the learning-at-home thing. So don't even bother looking for me at school on Monday. If you see some kid who looks like me, it won't actually be me, of course, 'cause I'll be right here, y'know ... learning and stuff."

"Nice try, Willy. Do you think I'm an idiot?"

"Well ..."

"Listen up, Cricket, 'cause you're in for a world of hurt. I don't know how you pulled off that trick today during P.E., but you're gonna regret ever sticking your piggy nose where it don't belong. I'm gonna watch you 'round the clock. When the time's right, you're going down."

Will felt the cold brass doorknob in his hand. He turned it slowly. "Look, I'm sorry about today—"

"Shut up, dork! I just came by to tell you you're officially Diego Enemy Number One. Hope you've got your funeral planned out, 'cause you're not gonna survive another week."

Just as Will gave a tiny push on the door, Diego threw his arms in the air and barked like a rabies-stricken attack dog. Will jolted backward, shoved the door open and fell flat on his back on the foyer floor.

"See you soon, Willy!" Diego cackled.

He heard Diego tromp away, laughing and barking intermittently. As Will lay motionless in the doorway, he heard something else too: a wish from Diego Rouleau. *I wish I hadn't gotten cut from ballet class this afternoon.*

Will had no clue how to react to that.

Will looked over himself, wiggling his nose, twitching his fingers and crossing his eyes, hoping that something might trigger his new Mizm. Nothing happened. He even tried to walk through the wall—wondering if he might be able to turn intangible—but ended up with a sore nose.

His parents had tacked a note to the refrigerator, explaining that his dad had to drive his mom to work since her car was at the garage. A hastily written "love you" was at the bottom—Will imagined it as an afterthought.

He heard cartoons playing on the television in the living room accompanied by a shrill cackle—Nonnie was watching her Saturday morning shows and loving every second of it. Will kicked back at the table, opting for bran flakes. If ever there was a time he needed to be regular, this was it.

He chased down some vitamins with orange juice, grabbed his coat and headed for the door to begin his second day of wish-granting. He stopped at the foyer mirror and decided to try for one last power. "I wish I could turn invisible," he said.

"For once we agree on something," Kaitlyn said as she brushed past Will, slamming the front door behind her.

As he stepped outside, he noticed Kaitlyn had already disappeared. Instead, he found Tang napping under the family's mailbox. "Tang!" Will yelled.

Groggily, the half-Genie pushed himself up from the ground. "Guess I stayed up too late last night working on my ... um, project."

"Another work assignment?"

"Yeah ... I mean, no. It's personal. Can't really discuss it," Tang said, smoothing his curls back.

"Sure, okay. Say, your hair's a different color again. What is that? Banana yellow?"

"Yeah, I squeezed at least a dozen banana peels to get the dye right this morning. It just felt like one of those days when you should have fruit on your head, you know?"

"I'm not really sure what today feels like. I still haven't figured out my power yet." Will kicked at a rock as they walked toward the park, and nearly tripped over his own feet.

"That's not altogether unusual. Sometimes Mizms aren't apparent. You don't figure them out until you need them. They're a mystery even to us Arcanians. Somehow they always fit the need, even if we can't see how or why at first. Did you check to see if you have super-strength?"

"I could barely get the lid off the jelly jar ... and I saw Nonnie open it yesterday."

At the park, Will had to readjust to all of the wishes that whizzed into his head as dozens of kids and families raced around. He tried sifting through them but after hearing seven "I wish had One Direction tickets" and 10 "I wish it were Christmas" and 12 "I wish it were lunch time" (three of which came from Will), he was inclined to ignore them all until something urgent came along.

"You've still got, like, 10 hours before midnight," Tang said as they settled into a secluded section away from the playground and bustle.

"I've got to go home soon. Whose wish am I supposed to grant there? Maybe I'll get the power to travel through time so I can send Nonnie back to 1973 so she can finally catch that Led Zeppelin concert she's always whining about having missed."

"Wishing is a simple thing, Will. When the time is right, everything will fall into place."

"Are you sure? What if my Mizm is broken? Maybe we should have someone check it out. Who do you guys call in situations like that?"

"They call me," said a gurgly voice that sounded as if it was underwater.

A tremendous splash suddenly erupted from a nearby puddle of water—almost like a geyser. As the water continued to pour, it took shape. There were feet and legs and then the waist and torso and arms. When the water finally stopped gushing out, a woman stood before them. Or at least, it was the form of a woman. Her body was made up entirely of greenish water. Will could see right through her. The water woman opened her eyes and stretched out her arms—she was decidedly alive!

"Hey! Nixie, what's shaking, lady?" Tang flashed her the Hawaiian "hang loose" hand gesture.

"I've been on call for the last 72 freakin' hours, and I've sucked down 12 cups of coffee since noon—there's not a part of me that *isn't* shakin' right now."

"Will, this is Nixie. She's a water nymph. Born and raised in the toughest wishing well this side of Djinn City. Nixie works in the SCENE's compliance department. She makes sure everything's up to spec."

"Pleased to meet you," Will said, extending his arm.

Nixie grabbed his hand and thrust it up and down like a backyard water pump. "Good to know you."

"So are you here to, um, fix me?" Will asked.

Nixie tossed back her head, coughed up a storm and then spit at the ground. "That's right, kiddo! Hollywood turned up at my well earlier, worrying about your power maybe not kickin' in just right, so I told him we could do a complete overhaul, but I'd need to check under your hood first, of course. So then Hollywood said … hey, where is Mr. Fancy Pants, anyway? He was right behind me a second ago. Aw, geez, he must've forgotten to strap on his floaties. Hang on a second, rug rats."

Nixie's head spun entirely around on her wet shoulders and looked down over the puddle from which she'd emerged. She shook her head, muttered something under her breath and then stretched out an arm.

Like an enormous waterspout, her arm kept flowing. She plunged her hand into the puddle and braced her legs. She looked like a fisherman reeling in a huge catch. Her arm moved this way and that across the water until finally it came to a dead stop. Nixie gave her arm a tug and yanked it from the puddle. When her hand emerged, it was latched onto the sparkling but drenched Hollywood. She held him tight, flinging him overhead and depositing his limp body between the three of them.

Hollywood leaned over to the side and knocked himself in the head to force the water out of his ears. "Stand back, will you? You might wanna cover your eyes. This is one star who needs to let his little light shine."

Clinching his fists, Hollywood's entire body unleashed a wave of fiercely bright light. The burst only lasted a second or two, but Will could've sworn their shadows took five minutes to reappear.

"Now that's better. I just needed to dry off—" Hollywood stopped suddenly and jerked his whole body. He gave his jacket a tug and then chomped on a finger. "Oh, no. The jacket's dry clean only. It shrunk two sizes. It's ruined! How am I going to explain this to my fan club?"

"Don't freak, HW," Tang said. "I'll work on it when I get back to the office tonight. I'll have it good as new in no time."

"Be a pal and replace that button that's missing too. I think I lost it in a meteor shower last week." Hollywood squeezed out of the jacket and plopped it on Tang's head.

"You're welcome," Tang growled.

"Speaking of important things," he said, turning to Nixie, "What do you think?"

With a finger poked in her ear, she said, "I ran a spectro-analysis on the kid while I fished you out of the drink. I'm big on multi-tasking, you know. Test showed everything's in order. The Mizm is there, ready to be used whenever the need arises."

"What exactly is my Mizm, then?" Will asked.

"Can't rightly say. That power inside you don't originate with us Arcanians. We just help you tap into it. Beyond that, we're as clueless as you."

"That's comforting," said Will.

"Sarcasm will get you nowhere," Hollywood said. "Let's all keep thinking positive thoughts. I'm sure there will be some horrid emergency at home that will trigger your powers in order to save your family from impending doom."

"Disaster raining down on my family is a positive thought?"

"Hey, what does it really matter anyhow? You're the one who wants out of there. I'm just here to help you make that wish come true."

"Oh, yeah," Will whispered.

"Look, if we're all done here, I've got another seven or eight stops to make before heading home, which I'm sure will be a complete disaster. Can I give you a ride back to the office?" Nixie asked Hollywood.

"Um, thanks for the offer, but I think I'll starlight back."

After barely a nod, Nixie's body returned to its watery state, gushed back into the puddle and vanished without a splash.

Hollywood plucked a miniature star from his shrunken jacket and plopped it in his mouth. "I must be off. Don't worry, Will. Success is in the air—I can practically taste it!"

The wish agent moved between a throng of trees just as he began to glow. Once his body was entirely illuminated, he waved to the boys and shot off into the cloudy afternoon sky.

Will and Tang trudged back to the Cricket house, stopping only for serious matters like examining a cluster of tree frogs and antagonizing ants with long sticks.

"You're coming in, right?" Will asked Tang as he traipsed through a pile of fallen pine needles.

"I have some paperwork to file at the office, but I guess it can wait. I'm sure HW would want me to stick around and make sure today's wish happens. But as soon as that's underway, I have to scram."

"Cool, no problem. So come on in and meet the rest of the family ... just don't hold them against me."

"What do we have here?" said Nonnie, making binoculars out of her fingers and peering down at Tang. "Do you have a brother I've forgotten about, Will?"

He took a deep breath. "No, Nonnie, this is Tang. He's a new student in my class. He's from a far off place."

"Yeah, I'm a foreign exchange student," Tang said. "I'm from New Jersey."

Nonnie gave him the eye and scratched her chin. "New Jersey, huh? Yeah, I tried to visit there once, but my passport wasn't in order. Even tried sneaking into the place, but those sharpshooters at the gates are darn good shots. That's how I got my second belly button. Wanna see?"

"No!" shouted the boys in unison.

"There's something about you." Nonnie gritted her teeth and cautiously poked a finger at Tang's arm. "I know all about your kind, and they're nothing but trouble. You and your off-the-wall hair color."

"Nonnie," Will said, pointing to her head, "have you looked in a mirror lately."

Nonnie's head whipped back. "William Sherman Cricket, are you talking back to your old Nonnie? Why if Mr. Winston Churchill was here right now, he'd have a few things to say about how you're treating his lucky lady."

"You did not know Winston Churchill." Will felt his cheeks go flush. This was why he never brought anyone home.

Nonnie spun around on her heels as a soldier would and marched back down the hallway.

"What was that all about?" Tang pulled a strand of hair down to his face, checking to make sure it hadn't switched color on him during the confrontation.

"She's a crazy old woman."

"But you still love her. She's family."

"Not for long," Will huffed. "Come on. Time to meet the rest of the mental patients."

Tang trailed behind Will as they approached the kitchen. Will's dad was once again working hard to turn the area into a complete disaster. The refrigerator and freezer doors stood wide open, and Will's father peered inside jotting down the contents onto paper.

"Dad ... what's going on? I thought you were fixing dinner not taking inventory."

"A good cook must know what his kitchen contains lest he be surprised, or worse, have to improvise! Once you're intimate with your pantry, the menu practically writes itself. Do you think your mom's boss would—well, hello there. Who's your friend, Will?" His father brushed a bit of frost off his nose and closed the refrigerator doors.

"Tang, sir. Nice to make your acquaintance."

Will's dad sighed heavily. "What am I thinking? The dogs won't even eat my food! What kind of mess have I gotten myself into, inviting Mom's boss for dinner? Her job is so important to her. For her sake, I—" His voice trailed off, but he continued to think, *I just wish we'd be able to have a fantastic dinner this evening.*

Tang whipped his head around at Will, whose eyes had suddenly become enormous.

"Skewered four-cheese tortellini with red pepper pesto," Will said.

"What? What'd you say, Son?"

"Tonight, before dinner, we'll have four-cheese tortellini as an hors d'oeuvre. Yes, that'll be perfect." Will flipped a skewer into the air and caught it with extraordinary precision. "Dad, I'm going to need you to run to the grocery store for a few items. Tang and I'll start prepping while you're gone."

As Will wrote down his list of cooking needs, his father looked back and forth between the two boys, opened his mouth several times to speak, but words failed him. Finally, he said, "Sounds like a plan," grabbed the list from Will and ran for the front door.

"Will?" Tang stood in the middle of the kitchen and watched Will race around him. "Your Mizm?"

Holding up a steel-tooth meat cleaver, Will smiled and said, "I'm a super-chef!"

*

As soon as Will's mom returned home in her newly-repaired Jeep, she rushed into the kitchen. She had, no doubt, expected to find things in such disarray that she'd rather torch the kitchen than clean it up. But aside from a pot or two, everything was spotless.

Tang was pulling bread out of the oven, Will was stirring something on the stove, and Will's father sat on a stool, mouth wide open, staring in awe.

"I-I-I-" Will's mom stuttered.

"Don't try to talk, honey." His dad shook his head. "There are no words to describe what's going on here. The boys are on a roll."

"Will?" she managed to say. "Everything looks ... smells ... heavenly. What is all this?"

Tapping his spoon on the side of a pot, Will said, "Mom, this is Tang; he's the new guy at school. He's also been helping me throw together tonight's meal. Tang, I think now's a good time to grate some cheese."

The half-Genie gave Will an extremely serious salute and went about his assigned task.

"Well, thank you for your help, Tang. It's good to know Will has such terrific friends," said Will's mother.

Will said, "I went with an Italian menu for tonight. I hope that's okay."

"The first person who complains gets kicked out of the family," Will's father shouted.

Will lifted the coverings on a couple of pans to give his mom a quick look. "For appetizers, we've got tortellini with red pepper pesto and seafood cannelloni. The cannelloni's stuffed with lobster, scallops, shrimp and ricotta in a pink sherry sauce. I thought we'd go with a salad instead of soup, and for that we have mixed greens, gorgonzola cheese, cranberries, pears and walnuts in balsamic vinaigrette.

"The main dish is what I call Filet Cricket, which is perfectly cooked Angus beef with copious amounts of the most flavorful Maine crab available. It also has mozzarella and au jus, which adds a hint of juicy spice. We'll have horseradish-mashed potatoes on the side, and once you've tried them, you'll never have potatoes any other way. The vegetable will be gilded asparagus with a golden sauce made from egg yolks.

"For dessert, we've got tiramisu tortes with an assortment of flavored gelatos. The gelato is store-bought, I'm afraid ... didn't have the time to freeze it properly. When Dad picked it up at Mary's Gelato Pop Shop, he was assured this was the best in town."

"And I got free samples." Will's father waved a tiny pink tasting-spoon at them.

"Mom, are you okay? You haven't blinked in, like, three minutes."

Will's mom twitched a little and said, "I guess I was afraid that if I closed my eyes for even a second, all of this would just disappear. I really can't believe this. It's a wish come true."

"You're telling me," Will mumbled to himself.

"I can't thank you boys enough. You too, dear. After work slows down next week, I'm going to treat all of you to—"

The clanging doorbell interrupted Will's mom, and everyone jumped at the sound.

"Oh! Oh!" Will's father said. "The car's here! I mean, um, Mr. Peach is here."

"Please remember to be on your best behavior, sweetie," Will's mom said.

"Hear that, Son?" said his father.

"I was talking to you, dear," she smiled.

He gave her a sheepish grin, tucked her arm into his and together they raced to the front door.

Shoving the spoon back into the potatoes, Will said, "What happens when I go back to being a kid whose idea of hors d'oeuvres is peanut butter and jam on a Ritz cracker? They only like me right now because I'm doing something with food other than scarf it down. And let's not even talk about Nonnie's insanity and Kaitlyn's mean streak."

"Where is Kaity Kait, anyway? I've been hoping to run into her all afternoon."

"Kaity Kait? You're just sick, man."

"What? Sure, I'm old enough to be her great, great, great, great, great, great, great, great, great—"

"Tang, I get the point."

"What I'm saying is that we Arcanians age and mature differently. I think Kaitlyn and I would make quite the handsome couple. Too bad I can't stay to serenade her over the tortellini. My, uh, other project has a major deadline next week, and if I don't make it ... well, let's just say things will get ugly."

Will and Tang slid out of their aprons. "Thanks for all the help today. Even with my ability to bake building-high cakes in a single bound, I wouldn't have had the time to pull it all off if you hadn't pitched in. I owe you one."

"You haven't been keeping count, have you? You owe me like a dozen already."

"Yeah, whatever." Will laughed and gave him a friendly punch to the arm. "Race you to the door!"

The boys chased each other down the hall, zipping over furniture and laughing a lot. As they approached the foyer, Will and Tang rounded a corner, cut under a potted palm tree and ran smack into the guest of the evening, Lincoln Peach.

"Will!" his mother exclaimed, taking hold of Mr. Peach's arm to steady him.

Mr. Peach stroked his beard, but Will could still see that familiar sneer. "Now, Emily, no need to get excited. Boys are supposed to run around carelessly and knock over an ancient artifact or two, myself included! No harm done, not in the least."

Will's mom lifted a finger as if to speak, but Will cut to the chase, saying, "Sorry, Mr. Peach. Hope we didn't hurt you or anything."

"Yeah," Tang chimed in, "and it won't happen again, Scout's honor."

Mr. Peach raised an eyebrow at Tang and patted his back pocket as if he suspected his wallet had just been stolen. "Who is this young man? Not another of your children, is he, Emily?"

"This is a friend of Will's. His name is Tang."

"Tang? That's a mighty unusual moniker. Not from our lovely town of Corinth, I take it, young man?"

Tang's brow furrowed, and his smile broke. "Um, no, sir. I'm from New Jersey. Just moved here."

He scooted around the adults and snatched open the front door. He gave a quick wave and yelled, "See you tomorrow, Will!"

"Interesting boy," Mr. Peach said, squinting faintly out the window as Tang ran out of sight. "But I must say those enticing aromas wafting from the kitchen are certainly making it difficult to wait for dinner. If the food tastes as good as it smells, this evening will be most divine."

"We have Will to thank for that. He and his friend fixed everything."

"A budding chef, eh, my boy?" said Mr. Peach. "I can hardly wait to see what magical delights you've whipped up for us."

As everyone gathered in the dining room, Kaitlyn appeared and quietly slumped into her chair. Will's father opened his mouth, as if to tell her to sit up straight, but Mr. Peach spoke up first. "A charming young girl such as you could command an entire room with the right posture."

She immediately sat up straight, blushed a little and fussed with her hair. "I'm Kaitlyn."

Mr. Peach reached across the table, took Kaitlyn's hand and planted a kiss on it. "I've heard many incredible things about you, my dear. Your mother gushes about your beauty every day, but I see she hasn't done you justice. You're probably breaking the hearts of quite a few boys at that school of yours, aren't you?"

Kaitlyn giggled and buried her face in her hands.

"We're waiting on one more, yes?" Mr. Peach said, stretching his neck to look into the kitchen and then down the hallway.

Will's mom replied, "I should probably go—ouch!" Nearly knocking her chair over, she jumped up, favoring her left leg. "Something bit my ankle," she said, and everyone else at the table jumped back too. Together, they all craned down and carefully looked under the dining room table. Crouched on all fours and batting a ball of string back and forth was Nonnie.

"Mother!" Will's mom reached under the table and pulled Nonnie out by her blouse. "What in the world are you doing under there? Why'd you bite me?"

"Aw, come on, Emily, it's not like I had my teeth in." Nonnie patted down her pockets, but her dentures were nowhere to be found. "I was just feeling a little frisky is all. Smelling all this great cooking, well, I had to gnaw on a little something."

"Mother ... how could you ... we have company ... my boss ... oh!"

"No need to be embarrassed, Emily," Mr. Peach said, pushing his chair slowly away from the table. "I have an elderly mother, too, and she ... well, she thinks she's the ringmaster of a traveling circus. Besides, your mother is the whole reason you have your job. I learned all I know about antiquities from her husband when I was a student of his. It's just a shame how she's gone downhill since the ... incident in Paris. So please, no need to get upset."

Will's mom nodded reluctantly. "I suppose you're right. It's not as though she can help it. Let's just all sit back down and enjoy our meal. Mom, let's find your teeth."

"Already found 'em." Nonnie dunked her hand into Mr. Peach's glass of ice water and pulled out her dentures. "Forgot I had put 'em on ice before everyone came in. I like my teeth cold." She shoved them back into her mouth causing her body to spasm.

"Give me strength," Will's mom whispered.

Mr. Peach licked his lips, as if in anticipation of the meal, but he continued to glare at Nonnie. "You're quite a spitfire, young lady."

"Who're you calling a lady?" Nonnie shot him a cross look.

"I don't think she remembers me," Mr. Peach said, bowing and shaking his head. "I know it was ages ago, but my memories of those days are still so vivid. I was part of the dig Professor Labenski led all those years ago in Saudi Arabia, the city of Tayma. He left such an impression on me. He's the reason I started Peach Preserves."

Will knew his grandfather—Nonnie's late husband—had been a professor of archaeology. He would travel the world occasionally with a group of select students, hitting various archaeological sites for weeks on end. He'd always described his life as one fantastical adventure until he died unexpectedly two years ago while he and Nonnie were in Paris hunting down an old friend.

Will watched as Mr. Peach's eyes darted around the room. "I'm just glad Emily accepted my offer to work for me when I started the business. She reminds me so much of her father. The Professor was such an indispensable part of my life ... almost like family."

"You're not part of *my* family." Nonnie picked up her tortellini and squished it. The cheese filling splattered across her face, surprising her. A moment later, she was in tears.

"Oh, Mom, let me help you." Will's mother reached for her napkin, but Nonnie snapped up from her chair.

"This is all wrong. Don't you see what's happening, Pete? It's Paris all over again." Nonnie said, looking right at Will.

"It's me, Nonnie. It's Will, your grandson."

"I ..." her voice trailed off. Nonnie looked around and then dashed out of the dining room.

The rest of the family, however, remained as frozen as statues. Kaitlyn, surprisingly, was the first to speak. "If it's okay, I think I'll go make sure Nonnie's alright."

As Kaitlyn left to check on her grandmother, Will's mom couldn't stop shaking her head. "Oh, Mr. Peach ... I don't know what to say. My mother ... she's been on a downward spiral ever since we lost Dad. I'm just ... I'm at a loss."

Mr. Peach patted her hand and said, "It's not your fault, Emily. My mother suffers from similar delusions. No matter how much you love her, it takes more to solve these kinds of problems. You need help, and there's no shame in that."

Will's father said, "That's been a heated topic of debate around this house lately." He turned to Will and said, "Champ, why don't you eat in front of the TV, just this once, so the grown-ups can talk."

Will took his plate into the kitchen, but he stopped there so he could overhear the conversation.

Before Will's dad could continue, Mr. Peach said, "Emily has confided in me that you want to put her mother in a home. I know she's against it, but ... Emily, your husband has valid concerns. Nonnie's not exactly young anymore. Listen, I'm not sure if this helps, but when the Professor—your father—and I were digging up those old relics, he'd often talk about what he would do when he got old. He always told me he and his wife never wanted to be a burden on you. It was their choice, he said, and they did not want to live with you if it was going to cause problems. Emily, you know what I'm saying is true."

"I know you're right. I've just been fighting this for so long now. I don't want to give up on her. She never gave up on me," Will's mom said in a hushed tone.

"No one thinks that you're giving up, Em," Will's father said. "We just need some help. You and I can't do this alone."

Grabbing the hands of Will's parents, Mr. Peach said, "As I've told Emily numerous times at work, there's an excellent facility close by where my own mother stays. She absolutely loves the place, and it seems to have calmed her some. Listen, we'll have a look at it tomorrow. You'll see that it's a truly wonderful environment, the best place to help your mother. I'll be there with you. I'll help you through this. Tomorrow, alright?"

Peeking around the corner, Will scowled to see his mom slump over and hesitantly nod. Sure, he wanted to get away from his family and his crazy grandmother, but he didn't like this at all.

"It's going to be expensive," Will's dad said.

"Don't worry about that. If you and your wife can't cover it, I'll be there to help. What's the point of having a little money, a little power, if you can't use it to help people?"

You took the words right out of my mouth, Will thought. *I've gotta do something to help Nonnie. Until Tang, she's been the only friend I've ever actually had—crazy, but still a friend. She deserves my help one last time before I blow this joint. I'll use whatever power I get from the Arcanians to make sure that Nonnie stays with the family. I don't care if it violates every last line of my wish contract.*

DAY 3

Will didn't sleep much, so he was on zombie-mode as he climbed into the shower at the break of dawn—far earlier than on a normal Sunday. His entire night had been filled with crazy dreams of Nonnie as a psycho-slasher, running around the house with a hockey mask, razor fingers, and a talking bunny that sat on her shoulder.

He'd always thought of his grandmother as quirky and perhaps a little senile, but never unstable. It was only after Mr. Peach mentioned his grandfather that Nonnie seemed truly befuddled. Will also wondered why she'd called him by his grandfather's name. Nonnie rarely talked about Poppa anymore. She never mentioned the circumstances surrounding his death. No one in the family was quite certain what had caused him to die, especially given that he'd been in better health than men half his age.

As Will showered, he sent out a series of urgent wishes for Tang to discreetly meet him at his house right away. Not only did he have to figure out his Mizm and grant his third wish, but Will was determined to use any trick in the book to help Nonnie.

After Will toweled off and dressed in his bathroom, he opened his bedroom door to hear faint rustling in his room. "Tang!" Will exclaimed as he dashed out of the bathroom, expecting to find his newfound friend awaiting him with secret maps, camouflage outfits and maybe a couple of stun rays. But it wasn't Tang.

Sitting in the middle of Will's pile of comic books was an exact duplicate of himself!

The boy looked indistinguishable from Will: the same pudgy waistline, the same buzz cut, the same sword-shaped birthmark on his ankle. For all practical purposes, this boy could be Will's identical twin brother.

"I like your books," the boy said, grasping a near mint copy of *Fantastic Four* number one by a corner of its cover.

"No, don't hold it like that. It's very valuable. You have to handle it gently." Will reached to take the comic from the boy, but their hands brushed against one another. A feeling of ice ran up Will's arm, and he immediately pulled away, clutching his wrist. "Who are you?"

"Oh, I'm sorry. Where are my manners? My name's Will. Nice to meet you."

Backing away from the clone, Will tripped over his skateboard and crashed to the floor. "This is crazy!"

"You need a hand there, partner?" the other Will asked.

"No, don't touch me. I'm fine!" said the real Will. "What are you supposed to be? Are you some kind of shape-shifter? Why are you impersonating me?"

"I'm not impersonating you, Will ... I am you." He touched the real Will's forehead and a brief feeling of icy cold moved through Will's body, followed by a long-lasting warm and cozy sensation. Will felt himself in the mind of the other Will, and he felt the other Will inside his own head. They could read bits and pieces of each other's thoughts.

"Wow! You are me!" Will said as he jumped up from the floor.

"Told you so," said the other Will. "I wouldn't lie to you ... to myself ... or whatever."

"So, is this my Mizm for the day?"

The other Will rolled his eyes. "Guess I'm the brains in this duo."

"Sarcastic much?"

"Pot meet kettle," he said, pointing to Will and then himself.

Will stared hard at his duplicate, and then caught his own reflection in the dresser mirror. He punched at his leg. "We need to come up with a name for you."

"How about 'Will the Sequel?'"

"I don't think so."

"Will 2: The Revenge?"

"No, that's actually not what I had in—"

"Will 2: Bad Boys United."

"No! No more fake movie titles! We're going to call you 'Ditto' and that's final."

Ditto laughed and pointed at Will. "I totally knew you were gonna call me that. You're sooooo predictable."

"Oh yeah? Well, did you predict me saying this? Get to work on my chores!"

"Yeah, I knew you'd say that too, darn it." Ditto dragged himself over to the closet and started picking up Will's clothes. "Lazy, good-for-nothing ..."

For the next hour, Ditto did everything Will was supposed to do for the day. He hung up Will's clothes, cleaned a load of laundry, tidied up Will's bathroom and even finished three pages of his geography homework. Will, on the other hand, continued to attempt contact with Tang through wishes. Just when he was giving up hope that the half-Genie might arrive before the rest of the household awoke, his Telewishing picked up a thought: *I wish Will would come let me in his front door already seeing how he's responsible for dragging me away from bed and my favorite footie pajamas.*

Will ordered Ditto to remain in his room while he dashed out the back door to take his friend by surprise. Tang sounded exhausted, so maybe a little sneak attack would get his friend's blood pumping. Will needed him wide awake for the day ahead.

Rounding the corner to the front of his family's home, Will quietly dove into the bushes and crept along the front of the house until he was a few inches away from the nearly-asleep Tang. In the deepest, scariest voice he could muster, he called out, "Tangible!"

Tang's face turned ghostly white, and he hurdled backwards five feet. "Moloch?"

Will popped up from the hedge and gave an awkward smile. "Tang, it's me, Will."

"Will? Oh, thank Zorba it's you." Tang said clutching his chest.

"Who's Moloch?" asked Will. "And Zorba?"

"Zorba is the most ancient and powerful of all Arcanians. He's also the founder of the SCENE. Really swell guy. You should meet him sometime. Anyway, busy, busy day ahead. Let's get going."

"Wait, you mentioned another name ... Moloch. Who's that?"

"Hmm? Moloch? Oh, right, Moloch. Ah, well, he's my, uh, personal trainer. Right, that's it, personal trainer. I skipped out on my session with him yesterday, so I thought he might've tracked me down. He's a, um, wind nymph, you know, so you can't always exactly see him. Those wind nymphs are slippery chaps ... though I suppose water nymphs are technically more slippery."

"Tang, you're babbling."

"I'm just tired. Tell me what's going on with you. What's the emergency?"

Will and Tang settled on the front steps. "Things got mega-crazy last night after you left, and then having to deal with my Mizm this morning. I just ... this is all so much right now. Can you help me?"

"Of course I can," he said, patting Will's back. "That's what best friends are for, right?"

"Best friend, huh? That is pretty awesome. I've never had a best friend before."

Will explained Nonnie's dinner behavior, and the boys quickly hatched a scheme to save her from being sent away.

"How do I look?" Tang asked. He had morphed into a replica of Mr. Peach.

"Frighteningly accurate." Will stuck out his tongue and gagged.

"Okay, you go back inside, and then I'll ring the doorbell, pretending to be Mr. Pear—"

"Peach."

"Right. I'll tell your parents that I reconsidered my advice and that Nanny—"

"Nonnie."

"Yeah. What Nonnie really needs is some good ol' TLC right here with her loved ones."

Will sighed. "This has disaster written all over it."

"Oh, just wait, good sir. Prepare to be amazed. I think our ploy sounds like a—"

"Bad idea," said another voice. Two figures stepped out from behind the garage.

"Hollywood?" Will said.

His glowing jacket revealed the answer. "Yes, Will, it's me. Norv's here too. We've come to escort Tang back to Mythos."

"Mythos?" Will asked.

"It's where we Arcanians live," said Peske.

"But Tang was going to hang out and—"

"Enough!" Hollywood's face was piping hot with anger. "Do you two have any idea of the madness you're cooking up?"

Tang had shifted back to his regular form, but it was clear the adults had overheard everything. "We were just trying to help!"

"We've been keeping our eyes on you boys," Peske said with a click of his tongue. "You had intended to use your shape-changing ability, Tangible, for reasons that were neither approved nor necessary for your work with Will. It was a frivolous expenditure of power."

"That wasn't it at all!" said Tang. "We were protecting someone!"

"You guys don't understand," Will said. "We're just watching out for my Nonnie."

Peske waved a finger in Will's face. "The circumstances are unimportant. It was how you and Tangible were handling it. This was very poor judgment on both of your parts. We specifically warned you not to use wish power—yours or Tang's—for anything but wish-granting."

"So what're you saying?" A column of flames shot up from Tang's hair. "Are you pulling me off this case?"

"I'd suggest you calm down right now, mister," Hollywood said. "I don't know what's gotten into you lately, but we may have to take some disciplinary action. The inappropriate display of your wishcraft abilities is only the latest in a string of problems. Reverie found evidence that you've been using SCENE resources to work on an unapproved project and that you've been hiding the details surrounding it."

"This is ridiculous!" shouted Tang. "The only reason you guys are coming down so hard on me is 'cause I'm part Genie. This is totally unfair."

"Maybe, but that's not for you to say." Hollywood looked at Will and said, "You will continue your wish-granting as scheduled. Understand, Will? We've come too far to turn back now, and we're running out of options."

"Hollywood," Peske hissed. "That's enough! Watch what you say!"

"Oh, he doesn't know what I meant by that," said Hollywood. "Forget that last part, Will. Just pay attention to this: it is of the utmost importance that you continue to perform your duties and perform them well. I'm not sure what we're going to do with Tang, but you may not see him for a while."

"What?! No! Don't take him away. It was my idea! Honest!" argued Will.

Peske cut the conversation with a raised hand, and just like that, all three Arcanians vanished in a stream of luminosity that radiated from Hollywood. As they disappeared into the early morning light, Will was afraid he'd never see his best friend again.

*

"Was just trying to help Nonnie," Will mumbled to himself as he plopped down onto the parlor room's sofa.

"Did I hear my name?" asked Nonnie from the hallway. "Am I the next contestant on *The Price is Right*? I'll bid $33 for the recliner and love seat, Bob." Nonnie wandered into the parlor. She wore a raincoat and galoshes, and daintily sat next to her grandson.

"Hi, Nonnie," Will said, head down. "You look fabulous today."

"It's the water," said Nonnie. "I drink the recommended 18 glasses a day. Sure, I pee like a race horse, but it keeps the skin soft and supple."

Will just shook his head. "I wish Poppa was still here."

Nonnie stopped fussing with her galoshes and grabbed Will's hand. "Your Poppa was the bravest man I've ever known. He always went out of his way to protect me, even though I could handle myself. I wasn't named arm wrestling champion at the Senior Center for four years straight by blind luck, y'know. If only he had let me go to Paris alone, he'd still be alive today. But no, he had to get himself killed by that—" Nonnie looked at Will and quickly clambered up from the sofa.

"Killed?" Will said. "I thought he died from a heart attack or something. What were you about to say, Nonnie?"

"I'm not going to say another thing about it ... and you can't make me!" she screamed at the top of her lungs.

Five seconds later, Kaitlyn burst into the room. She stood armed with a water pistol in each hand. "What's all the yelling about in here? Is it real trouble or is it just Nonnie freaking out again?"

Will couldn't believe it. Had his sister heard the commotion and come to check on them out of concern?

"No ... she's, um, okay," said Will.

"Good. Then I want you dorks to listen up. By some miracle, Jensen asked me to go study with him this afternoon. I've only got four hours to get ready, so I don't have time for any interruptions. If anything happens again, I'll assume it's all thanks to you, Will," she said, squirting one of her water pistols at Will's eye. "Next time, I'll tie you up, cover you in dog food and fetch the neighbor's Rottweiler."

"That reminds me—I'm hungry," Nonnie said, wandering off toward the kitchen.

Exhausted from the morning's events, Will passed out on his bed as his duplicate dusted his action figures. Just as Will had fallen asleep, his television set flipped on. "Aw, Ditto, turn it off, man. Can't you see I'm, uh, concentrating on important stuff?"

"I didn't do it," said Ditto. "It came on by itself."

"Will Cricket!" announced a booming voice from the television.

Ditto and Will both leapt into the air. Ditto covered his eyes while Will hid under his blanket.

"Will, it's just me, Hollywood," said a voice emanating from the TV.

Will peaked out from his blanket, and Ditto uncovered his eyes. "Hollywood?" they both said.

The picture on the TV went from static to a close-up shot of the wish agent. "Yeah, sorry about that," said Hollywood. "I didn't mean to yell, but your television doesn't have the best reception. I was just—" The screen went fuzzy again.

Will jumped up and pounded on the set, but nothing worked.

"Aw, nutters." Hollywood's voice came through, but his picture was scrambled. "Stand back, I'm coming through."

Will backed away from the TV as Hollywood's arm reached through the screen. Out popped Hollywood's head, and he flashed the boys a gigantic smile. "Small television set you've got here, Will," he said. "Good thing my waistline's the same size it was when I was 1001. Got to stay in tiptop shape for all of my starring roles." With his other arm free, Hollywood braced himself against the edge of the monitor and forced the rest of his body out. "Now I know why they call it the 'small screen.' I'm not sure how Heiko's going to make it through."

"Hi-who?" Will said.

Before Hollywood could answer, a sound like the clip-clop of a racing horse echoed from the TV. Hollywood grabbed both boys, pushed them to the floor and then flopped down to cover them. "Heads down!" shouted Hollywood.

A split second later, something barreled out of the TV. Will looked up to see horse hooves sail overhead. They landed on the floor in front of him with a soft thud. "Greetings, lads."

Will gazed up, expecting to find a talking horse, but instead saw much more. The creature was humanoid—two arms, two legs and all that, but his feet were hooves and his face had the snout of a horse. His hair was a brilliant curly black mane that ran down his back, hidden by the shirt he wore. "What ... what are you?"

"I am Heiko, last of the noble Equine."

"Heiko's people are ... were a race of humanoid horses. Brilliant outdoorsmen, they were. Now Heiko is the SCENE's senior vice-president of remagination," Hollywood said.

"Don't you mean imagination?" said Will.

"Hardly!" Heiko stomped a hoof into the carpet. "My task is to ensure the mysteries of the Arcanians remain hidden from the human world. To fulfill my sworn duties, I use the ancient art of remagination. It's truly ironic that an Equine—the most honest of all creatures—has been given charge to protect through deceit."

"What it boils down to," Hollywood said, "is that Heiko is a remaginator. He makes people who see wishcraft think they imagined what they saw. They come away thinking it was just a daydream. It's an extraordinarily intriguing and precise technique."

Will outstretched a hand to brush Heiko's shiny brown coat.

"If you don't want to lose that hand, you should remove it swiftly," said Heiko. He stared down imposingly at Will, who quickly pulled away.

"Very sorry, Mr. Heiko. I had no idea that there were wish creatures like you."

"You've heard the saying 'if wishes were horses?' Well, we are."

"Wicked cool," said Will and Ditto at the same time.

"Anywho, Heiko tagged along today because he and I are concerned about you, Will," said Hollywood. "You know we're keeping a close watch on you. After what happened earlier, I would think you of all people would make every effort to avoid abusing your power. But this morning, Reverie came to me—talking in her sleep, of course—and said that you've had your duplicate doing all of your work for you today. What's worse, this dupe you've named Ditto has been interacting with the rest of your family, putting our confidential work in jeopardy!"

"What?!" Will had no clue Ditto had even seen his family, let alone talked with them.

"Yeah," Ditto said. "I think they like me better than you, too. They even invited me to a family outing this afternoon."

"They only want you to go because they think you're me!" shouted Will.

Hollywood just shook his head. "Boys, boys, boys. You're missing the point. Will, you must learn to use your Mizms more responsibly. The abilities are not to be taken lightly. You know this. They are a privilege, not a right ... and we will revoke that privilege if necessary, meaning no wish for you."

Will didn't know what to say. After what happened to Tang, he thought the wish agent might be as serious as he looked.

"Hollywood speaks the truth," said Heiko. "We dare not encroach upon another Frost Epidemic, yet such would be our fate if the humans learned of our existence. When last the Frost took hold of Mythos, it slew the whole of my kindred. I buried 1200 kinsmen in a span of time no greater than the life of an insect. I tell you this, young William, not to garner your fear or pity, but to strengthen your resolve. Your brother-in-arms Tangible seems to have let this knowledge slip from his mind. You would be wise to hold to it tighter."

"I ... I didn't know," Will whispered.

"Of course you didn't," Hollywood said, giving him a pat on the back. "But now that you do, you'll be more careful, right?"

Will nodded assuredly. "What about Tang? You're not going to punish him or anything are you?"

Hollywood and Heiko gave each other uneasy glances. The wish agent cleared his throat and said, "Since it's Sunday and you're not around as many people like when you're in school, you probably won't need much supervision, but I'll pop in and out to keep an eye on you."

"But—" said Will.

"As for tomorrow, we'll have someone in place at your school to assist you should the need arise," said Hollywood.

"Hold on a sec. I wanna know if Tang is okay."

"Will, we would never do anything to harm Tangible. That's not how our society operates. But, unfortunately, we don't exactly know where he is right now. He sort of ... vanished."

"Vanished?"

"Yes, as we were on our way to Mythos. He seemed rather miffed about being disciplined. Don't worry ... I'm sure he'll show up in a day or two."

Will rapped a knuckle against his forehead. "Why? Why would Tang just disappear like that?"

"We're honestly not sure. This isn't like him. He usually does an admirable job of keeping that Genie temper under wraps. But they are an unpredictable lot, even the half-bloods."

"Hollywood, you said this morning that he was involved in some other secret project that no one knew anything about. Do you think that might have something to do with him disappearing? Maybe it was something dangerous. Honestly, Hollywood, do you think Tang might be in some kind of trouble?"

With a heavy sigh, he said, "Yes, Will, I do."

As much as Will tried to prod information from the two Arcanians, neither Hollywood nor Heiko would say more about Tang. They squeezed back through the television set with a reminder for Will to be doubly cautious, especially today since there was two of him.

Two of me. How is having two of me gonna fulfill any wishes? He thought to himself.

"Will, are you ready to go?" called Will's mom.

Will ordered Ditto to stay out of sight while he found his mother. She was in her bedroom, wrapping a bracelet around her wrist. "There you are, but look at you! You're not dressed yet. I told you earlier we had to leave at three o'clock sharp. Go finish getting ready."

"Sorry ... I lost track of time, I guess. So where are we going again? And why doesn't Kaitlyn have to come?"

"We'll tell you when we get there. Kaitlyn has school work to do, so she gets a pass."

"But Nonnie's coming?"

Will's mom stopped fumbling with the clasp on her bracelet. She yanked it off her wrist and shoved it back into the jewelry box in a huff. "No. Nonnie's staying here."

"I thought she wasn't supposed to stay by herself."

"Mrs. Pinskey from next door is wrapping up a project and then coming over to sit with her. We'll only be gone for a couple of hours. Now stop goofing off and get ready. I'm not telling you again."

Will flinched at his mom's harsh tone. "But Mom—"

"Listen to your mother, Will," Nonnie said, suddenly behind him. "Mothers know best, after all. Daughters, on the other hand ..."

"Nonnie—Mom, please not now." Will's mom said. She wouldn't look at Nonnie.

"Of course, Emily. Didn't mean to bother you. I'm just a lonely old woman who should be grateful she hasn't been taken into the backyard and shot like some useless animal."

"Oh, Mom, don't be so dramatic. Is this because we're not taking you with us?"

"You're darn tootin' it is! You kids are all I've got these days."

I really do wish one of us could be here today to keep Mom company, Will's mother thought.

"Too bad you can't be in two places at once, kiddo," Nonnie said, shooting Will a sideways glance.

Without a single word, Will raced back to his bedroom. "Ditto, I've got something critical for you to do—a wish for us to grant. My Nonnie's stuck here for the next few hours by herself, but she doesn't want to be alone. So you get to stay and keep her company."

"What?!" Ditto stomped his foot. "That's not fair. I wanna go with the family and do fun stuff. I don't wanna be stuck with Nonnie all day, and you can't make me!"

"Oh, come on, man! You have to!"

"I'm not doing it."

"I'm the boss here, mister, and unless you want to go back to Clone World or wherever it is you come from, you'd better do as I say."

Ditto crossed his arms defiantly. "You should be the one to stay with her. It's your wish to grant, after all."

"Look, stop being selfish. This isn't about you, it's about me. So ... oh." Will paused, blinked and looked down at his hands.

He shook his head. "No, I'm better than that. I'll stay with Nonnie today. You go with my family."

"You're sure?" Ditto asked cautiously.

"Yeah, definitely. Nonnie deserves to have the genuine Will keep her company."

*

When Ditto and his parents left, Will called Mrs. Pinskey and informed her that she wouldn't be needed to watch Nonnie. After he had hung up, he found his grandmother in the parlor room, sitting on the couch, staring out the window.

"Hey, Nonnie!"

She slowly, casually turned to Will, as if she'd been expecting him. "Didn't I just see you leave?"

Will shrugged. "Nope. Wasn't me."

"Huh, that's funny. Although it could've been an alien dressed up to look like you, y'know. Aliens are known to do that."

"Sure, Nonnie, whatever you say."

"Is that awful Mrs. Pinskey still coming over?" asked Nonnie.

"No, I called her and told her I'd be here with you."

"Good! She smells like toe jam and mangoes." They both laughed.

"I say we hit the road and get some fresh air." Nonnie looked out the window again and traced the outline of a tree against the glass. "You able to drive yet?"

Will shook his head.

"I've still got my old license ... of course, it expired 10 years ago. Haven't done much driving lately, but I'm sure it'll come back to me. You'll just have to remind me which pedal makes it go and which pedal makes it stop. Deal?"

Tugging uneasily at his shirt collar, Will said, "Maybe we should just take a taxi, instead. I'll give them a call."

"No need," Nonnie said, tapping on the window. "There's one outside, already."

Will peered out the window. The driver in the cab extended his arm and waved to them. "That's weird. I've never even seen a taxi in our neighborhood before. I'll run ahead and check it out. Can you lock up behind us?"

Nonnie pushed herself off the couch. "No problem. I'll be outside in two shakes, provided I don't break anything while I'm doing my shaking."

As he rushed outside, Will already had a decent idea who was behind the driver's seat in the taxi. Halfway down the driveway, the cabbie stuck his head out the window and yelled, "Yo, Mac, need a ride?"

Will grinned. It was Hollywood, and he sported a fake mustache large enough to cover the faces of three men.

"Nice disguise," said Will. "Look, my wish today involves hanging with Nonnie, and she's about to come out, so—"

"No problemo, Will; I'm a star, remember? I was born to act!"

Will didn't think it would take much of an actor to pull the wool over Nonnie's eyes. Will had a hunch she would be focused on a strawberry shake from Beanie's Old Fashioned Malt Shop. It was her favorite place in the city, and Will was certain that's where she'd want to go.

"Are we ready to ride?" Nonnie asked as she climbed into the cab.

"You bet," Will said. "Off to Beanie's?"

"No, sir!" said Nonnie.

"Where to then, ma'am?" asked Hollywood.

"Boone Cemetery. We've got a date with a dead man."

Will looked over his shoulder as he walked just behind Nonnie. Hollywood waited in the cab for them to finish whatever business Will's grandmother had in the graveyard. Will had been here a couple of times before, but his skin still had goose bumps. There was an uneasy silence that blanketed the cemetery. The wishes that had continually moved through Will's head over the past days fell absolutely silent now, for there was no life in this place and no one around to make a wish. The silence of the cemetery should've been a welcome respite for Will, but all he felt was cold.

"I know your Poppa's headstone is around here somewhere," Nonnie said as she peered out over a sea of graves. "It's marble, and it has words written on it."

"That should narrow it down," Will mumbled.

"I know you don't like it out here. Can't say I blame you. Not really a place for kids. I hated it when my great grammy brought me here to visit some long dead relative like her great grandpappy Solomon. I'd wish and wish that I was anywhere but here. Then she'd take me home, and I'd wish to be anywhere but there too."

"Sounds like you used to wish a lot, just like me."

"Oh, I wished every hour of every day. I wanted a lot more out of life than what I had. It took a long time before anyone heard my wishes, though. Took even longer for me to seriously listen to my own wishes. I was such a stupid kid."

Will grabbed her hand and squeezed. "Don't say that, Nonnie. Kids have it pretty rough, y'know."

"Yeah, kids do have a terrible time of it. Course, so do us old fogies. People treat me like I don't know anything. Nobody ever tells me nothing, especially your mother. She always thinks she knows better than me, but she ain't seen a pinch of the things I've witnessed in my lifetime. Why, sometimes I have to pretend to be asleep just so I can get the scoop on what's going on.

"When I first moved in with you kids, I told your mom and pop I wanted to paint my bedroom, make it feel like my own place. Well, they just worked themselves up in a tizzy, afraid I was going to color the room citrus orange with green polka dots. So I sacked out on the couch, took a fake snooze, and listened as they called a painter to do the job instead. They wanted him to paint it beige, and they weren't even going to tell me about it. *Beige*, for cripes' sake! Good thing I bribed the paperboy the next morning to run to the hardware store and pick up some paint for me. By the time your folks figured out what I had done, it was too late. I had my room just the way I wanted it."

"I think your room's awesome," said Will. "It looks just like the sky, clear blue with fluffy, white clouds. Sometimes I look at the walls and see a lion or elephant shape in the clouds, and then the next time I see something entirely different. I think you did a fantastic job."

"Thanks, my boy. I like it too. Makes me feel like I'm flying ... hardly anything better than that."

"No kidding," Will whispered.

"Well, looky here." Nonnie came to an abrupt halt and pointed down. "Here he is!" They stood over a headstone that read:

Peter Ethan Labenski

1929 - 2012

This is not the end

"Had it been any closer, it would've bitten us," said Nonnie. "But what in the world is this?"

She stooped over and swiped a bouquet of bright sunflowers from the grass in front of the stone. "Now who in their right mind left these here? Pete had horrible allergies, and everyone knows allergies only get worse after you die." She tossed the flowers over her shoulder and brushed off the top of the tombstone.

"Nonnie, how did Poppa die?"

"That question again? How about I tell you how Poppa lived, instead? Oh, I know you remember him, but you were too young when he died to genuinely know him. He was rock solid, always dependable. He was the practical one, you see, while I had my head in the clouds. When I first met him, I thought he was such a stick in the mud, but I was wrong. Even though I was the dreamer, he taught me something crucial about dreaming. He showed me how to do it with purpose, how to fight for my wishes and for those of my loved ones. That's what he did, every day of his life ... right up until he died."

Nonnie clutched Will's hands in her own and pulled them up to her face, kissing them. "I've been granted many amazing wishes in my day, and I don't mean to be greedy. But if I had another, I'd wish that you grow up to be the kind of man your Poppa was, the kind of man who doesn't just make wishes, but one that makes wishes come true—for yourself and for others."

Will forced a weak smile. He didn't know what to say, but he didn't want to let his Nonnie down either. "I'll do my best," he said meekly.

"I know you will, my dear, I know you will," Nonnie said with a tear in her eye. "Now let's get the heck out of this graveyard. If I'm out here too long, they might think I want to stay permanently!"

Once they were home, Nonnie insisted on playing a game of Monopoly. Will set up the board in the parlor room so he could keep an eye out for the return of Ditto and his parents. An hour later, Will was in mortgage up to his eyeballs, and Nonnie had all but three properties. Just as he landed on the "Go to Jail" spot for the ninth time, Will saw his father's car pull into the driveway.

Will jumped to his feet. He couldn't let his family see him, not as long as Ditto was still around. His duplicate was likely to vanish very soon, given that the fulfillment of Nonnie's wish was almost complete, so he had to time this perfectly.

Opening the closet door adjacent to the foyer and the parlor room, Will said, "I'm going outside to meet the folks. Um ... maybe we shouldn't tell them about our afternoon together. They'd be super jealous that they missed out on all the fun."

Nonnie tapped her nose and nodded. "You bet, my boy. But why are you walking into the closet? You can't get outside that way."

"Oh, uh ... no, I'm looking for my coat." Will jumped into the closet and shut the door behind him, leaving it open just a crack to keep an eye out for Ditto and his parents. Barely a minute later, his mom came through the door followed by the others. They'd apparently picked up Kaitlyn on their way home, and all of their faces matched the weather outside—gloomy and cold. They glanced toward Nonnie in the parlor room, but none of them looked directly at her.

Nonnie stared right at Ditto, who just nodded uneasily. "Well, how in the heck did you get outside so fast?"

Ditto gritted his teeth and scanned the room and hallway.

"Mom," Will's mother said, "where's Mrs. Pinskey? Don't tell me she didn't show up. When we left, she said she was on her way over."

"Don't you worry about me. I had the best company an old woman could ask for. And you see I won at Monopoly again. Will may be a smart boy, but he has to get up pretty early in the morning to beat me."

"But ... he wasn't even here, Nonnie," Will's father said, shaking his head and giving his wife a sad look.

"Oh, Will was so right about you kids!" Nonnie threw back her head and cackled. "He said you'd be jealous, and he was right. Don't worry, I won't mention another peep."

"So you had a good afternoon, then?" Will's mom asked.

"Yup. Got to see your dad, which is always nice."

Will's mom collapsed on the couch next to Nonnie and grabbed her hand. "Oh, Mom ... I just ... I just don't know what to say anymore."

While the rest of the family was distracted with Nonnie, Will took an umbrella from the closet and, stretching as far as he could, used it to tap Ditto on the back. When his duplicate turned around, Will let out a giant gasp. Ditto's body was disappearing from sight!

Will motioned for Ditto to join him in the closet. Silently and quickly, the duplicate stepped away from the family and crept inside with Will. Pulling a flashlight from the bottom shelf, Will shined it on Ditto. He was almost completely vanished now—Will could see right through him.

"We don't have much time," Will whispered. "Since Nonnie's wish has been fulfilled, my Mizm for today is fading ... so that means *you're* fading. Tell me what happened today. Anything important I need to know?"

Ditto looked down at his body; his feet had entirely disappeared, and his knees were almost gone too. "We didn't go anywhere near Disney World as I'd expected. Went to some ammonia-smelling place with lots of old people. Your mom and dad were—"

"Oh no. They're still looking to put Nonnie in a nursing home?"

Everything below Ditto's waist had vanished. "No, Will, they aren't looking ... not anymore. Your parents signed the papers today."

"What? What papers? What are you saying?"

As the last of Ditto faded from sight, he managed to say, "They're getting rid of Nonnie, Will. They're moving her into that place in just a few days!"

With those last words, Ditto was gone.

Will had never been angrier with his parents. He sat at the breakfast table with them, but he refused to speak. He'd been giving them the silent treatment since hearing of Nonnie's fate yesterday from Ditto, and he planned to keep it up as long as possible. He wouldn't break his vow of silence, even to ask for lunch money, and that was saying—or, in this case, *not* saying—a lot!

"I'm hoping to get that interview this afternoon, the one with the archaeologist who recently uncovered an extremely rare artifact near the Sudan-Ethiopian border," Will's father said as he scanned his newspaper. "Fascinating find, from what I hear, though I suppose you would know more about that, Em."

Will's mother nodded, almost imperceptibly. "His name's Dr. Horatio Donnatelli. He's a professor here in Corinth at Dad's old school. Mr. Peach just acquired that rare item you mentioned. From what I hear, he paid a fortune for it."

"Do you think Mr. Peach would put in a good word for me? This Donnatelli fellow is a hard man to get a hold of. Maybe I'll go with you to work this morning and see if that generous boss of yours might—"

"No!" Will's mom yelled. Everyone jumped, even herself, at her tone. She took a deep breath and calmed down. "Sorry. I meant to say, there's no point coming to the office. Mr. Peach isn't in today. He's on a business trip until tomorrow."

"Aw, nuts!" said Will's father. "Tomorrow will be too late. My contacts at the paper say the good Doctor is flying out this evening for another dig, so if I'm going to get this interview before he leaves, I'll have to use some of the old-fashioned Cricket charm. Maybe I'll whip him up some of my famous delectables. Can't go wrong with your pop's cooking, can you, Will?"

Will blinked at his father and continued eating his cereal.

"Alright, then. Son, I'm going to pick you up from school this afternoon. Your mom is taking Nonnie to a doctor's appointment, and Kaitlyn said she and Jensen would be studying at the library. You're probably still a little too young to stay at home by yourself."

Will blinked again, this time at double speed. *I'm most certainly not too young to be home alone*, he thought. *Why are they always treating me like a five-year-old? Don't they know how responsible I am?* He was, after all, granting wishes, making people's lives better, for Pete's sake! He wished he wasn't *not* talking to his father so he could tell him a thing or two.

"If I get that interview this afternoon," Will's father continued, "you'll have to come with me after I pick you up. Okay, Will?"

Will shrugged almost imperceptibly.

"William!" said his mother, her face changing from pale to bright pink. "You better start treating us with more respect around here! We're your parents, like it or not!"

"Are you even listening?" said Will's father. "I want you to repeat what your mother said about respecting us."

Angrily, Will opened his mouth and said, "You better start treating us with more respect around here! We're your parents, like it or not!"

His father stared quizzically at Will. His mom's face changed to an even paler shade than before. Their expressions were contorted in disbelief, not because Will had perfectly repeated what his mom had said, but because his normally squeaky voice had sounded exactly like his mother's.

Oh boy, Will thought. *How am I going to get out of this mess? What's my freakin' Mizm for today anyway—to sound like Mom?*

"Will? You okay? Got a frog in your throat?" asked his father.

"No," Will said without thinking. His eyes went big as he listened to the single word trip out of his mouth. But it was okay. He sounded like himself again. He breathed in and sighed deep.

"Oh, man!" Will's father tapped his wristwatch. "I need to get to City Hall to pick up some documents. I'll see you this afternoon, okay, Will?"

Reluctantly, Will nodded.

As Will's father pulled his car out of the garage, he rolled down the window and yelled something to Will's mother who stood in the doorway. He gave her a wave and then drove away.

"What'd he say?" she asked.

"He said, 'Try to have a good day, honey. Love you.'" With that, Will slapped a hand over his mouth. His mother looked back at him, puzzled again. His voice sounded exactly like his father's this time.

"Uh, gotta go!" Will said in his normal voice and ran out the door for school.

Once at Lamone Pledge, Will tried to push the concern for Tang and Nonnie out of his head to focus on his daily wish-granting. He was so intent on keying into his Telewishing that he didn't even look up when he entered Mrs. Griswald's classroom.

"Take your seat, William, it's time to get started," said an eerily familiar, yet out-of-place voice.

"Peske," Will muttered in astonishment.

"That's Mr. Peske to you, William. Now take your seat. Should I have to tell you again, you and I will be spending a long afternoon together in detention."

The books in Will's hands slipped from his grip and crashed to the floor.

Peske approached Will, bent down and picked up one of his fallen books. Will snapped out of his haze and joined him near the floor. "What are you doing here? Where's Mrs. Griswald?" Will whispered.

"Your teacher developed a rather debilitating phobia last evening and decided that she needed to take a few days off. I'm filling in."

Norv Peske, SCENE lawyer and general curmudgeon, was his substitute teacher today! At least he wasn't in a dress this time. He actually looked fairly normal, except that the bowtie he wore slowly spun around in a circle. It was almost hypnotic, and Will wondered if that's why the other students were so quiet, so exceptionally well-behaved.

"A phobia? So she's afraid of something? What kind of fear could possibly keep her away from school?"

"The fear of children."

"What'd you guys do to Mrs. Griswald?" asked Will.

"You, of all people, William, should see the poetic justice of instilling the fear of children into a woman who has, herself, instilled fright in many a child. Don't worry; it's only temporary. It was necessary so that I might be placed here at the school as your new daily contact, given Tangible's ... disappearance."

"I can't believe I even care, but as long as Mrs. Griswald is okay, I guess that's fine. What about Tang? Have you heard anything more? Do you know where he is?"

"I'm afraid that topic's not up for discussion, William."

"But Peske—"

"That's Mr. Peske, William!" The lawyer waved an angry finger at Will. "To your seat, now, or you'll have a full week of detention!"

Will slumped off to his chair and, despite himself, couldn't help but miss cranky, old Mrs. Griswald.

By the time lunch rolled around, Will was more than ready for a break from Peske. He'd already assigned four times the usual amount of homework, covered the first three weeks' worth of material for the next year's advanced English class and given the longest lecture ever on the American legal system.

As he headed for the lunchroom, Will overheard a conversation between Benji, Connor and Mason.

"The guy's completely lame," Benji said.

"And he won't shut up," said Connor.

"Won't let a dude take a nap either," Mason said with an enormous yawn.

"That legal crap was the most boring stuff ever," said Benji. "I think he maybe said one interesting thing, but I was too tired to pay attention."

Will couldn't help himself. Standing behind the boys, he cleared his throat and did a spot-on imitation of Peske. "Even though most laws should always be followed as strictly as possible, there is the occasional edict that was instituted many years prior and never removed, despite changes in time and culture. For example, in Georgia there is a city where it is actually illegal for a chicken to cross the road."

The three boys froze. After a few seconds they turned, and, as their jaws dropped, saw Will instead, who grinned from ear to ear. Benji's face immediately soured, but the other boys burst out laughing.

"That was great!" Connor said. "I didn't know you could do voices."

"Very cool," said Mason. "Can you do Mrs. Griswald?"

Will touched a finger to his chin, thought about it carefully, then in Mrs. Griswald's voice said, "If you brats even breathe, I'm going to string you up from the ceiling by your toes and smack you like a piñata!"

"Whoa! Awesome, man," said Mason, gasping for breath between laughs. "You sounded just like her. Pretty cool, huh, Benji?"

The diminutive jock shrugged. "Yeah, I guess."

"Treat the guy with a little more respect, dude," Connor said. "His sister's hanging out with Jensen now. But, I mean, who even cares about that ... the voice thing, man, it cracks me up. Say, Will, you want to sit with us at lunch and do more impressions?"

Will did a double take, examining Connor for a long moment, as if his classmate might be an impostor. The four boys rounded the corner next to the bathrooms just as Will opened his mouth to answer. He was interrupted when an agonizingly familiar voice called out, "Come here, ya wimp!"

Will flinched and nearly jumped out of his shoes at the sound of Diego's coarse voice. Benji and his friends sped off toward the cafeteria, but Will froze as he looked this way and that for the bully. He quickly realized the sound came from behind the closed door of the bathroom. Will listened at the door to hear Diego taking out his frustrations on some poor soul he'd trapped in there. *Oh well*, Will thought. *Not my problem. No wish involved here, and at least Diego's not coming after me. Not like I could do much anyway.*

"Help!" exclaimed a teeny voice from inside.

Will recognized the voice. It belonged to Duncan Sapp, a petite boy who had skipped a grade this year.

"Please! Someone help!"

"It's not a wish," Will mumbled to himself. "Why should I put my neck on the line when it won't do me any good?"

Will forced himself to take one, two and then three steps away from the door, despite Duncan's continued pleas. He pushed the thought of it out of his mind—who was Duncan to him anyway? He'd barely said two words to the kid the whole time he'd been in his class. Nobody talked to him much—he was different, after all.

Just like Will.

He stopped, turned on his heels and went back. Will opened the door to the boys' bathroom, but only a little. He couldn't see in, but they couldn't see out, either. He cleared his throat, decided on the perfect voice, then said, "Diego Rouleau! What are you doing in there?"

The ruckus in the bathroom came to a halt.

"Principal Shimerman?" Diego said, his voice cracking.

"That's right, young man! I've had enough of your shenanigans! You're about half a step away from being sent to juvenile hall. At this school, you're a big slob of a bully in a sea of pipsqueaks. There ... well, you'll still be a big slob of a bully, but

128

you'll be surrounded by even bigger bullies. They'll tear into you like the last piece of pizza at fat camp."

"But—but, sir." Diego's voice trembled. There were few people in the world Diego feared, and the principal was unquestionably one of them.

"I'd be willing to forget this incident on three conditions. Number one, you send little Mr. Sapp out here right now. But you—you stay put."

Will could hear Diego give Duncan a shove. The small boy's feet shuffled across the floor as he raced out. As soon as he hit the door, Will put a finger to his lips, signaling for him to stay quiet. An enormous grin covered Duncan's small face, and he nodded over and over again.

"Now, Diego, the second thing I want you to do is to leave Duncan and other kids like him alone. That includes Will Cricket."

"Aw, but—" Diego protested.

"Last slice of pizza, remember that," Will sang out.

"Whatever. He's not worth my time anyway."

Will gave Duncan a wink. "Good, very good. The last thing I want you to do: take the lid off the trashcan in the corner, turn the trashcan upside down and place it over your head. I want you to stand there like that until I tell you you've served your punishment."

"No way!" Diego huffed. "There's all kinds of disgusting junk in that trashcan. That's gross. They'll all laugh at me."

Exactly, Will thought. "Fine, just come out then, and we'll go to the office and call your mother. I'm sure she'd be terribly interested to know what you've been up to."

"No! Not my mom! I'll do whatever you say! Please don't call my mom!" *Actually, I kinda wish you would call my mom ... but I bet she still wouldn't pay attention to anything I say. I wish she'd listen to me about ballet class.*

Duncan covered his mouth and snickered while Will listened at the door. His brow furrowed as he heard Diego's wishes. But any concern vanished as a trashcan lid clanged against the floor. Will waited a few seconds more and then slowly stuck his head inside the bathroom. There was Diego, trashcan covering his ugly mug, standing in the middle of the room for anyone to see.

"Perfect," Will said, still mimicking the voice of his principal. "Now you wait right there, young man. I'll be back shortly, but you're not to go anywhere until I say so."

Diego said something, but the trashcan muffled his words.

Closing the door, Will said in his normal voice, "You okay, Duncan?"

"I sure am, thanks to you, Will." Duncan's wavy blonde hair bounced up and down as the boy shook with excitement. "I thought I was a goner, for sure, back there. Never in a million gazillion years did I think you'd come and save the day. I mean, I didn't think you'd even care ... you being so much cooler than me."

Will's mouth hung open as he blinked in disbelief.

"Maybe you'd like to come sit at my table for lunch today. It's just me and the other guys from the chess club, but we'd be honored. I know you usually like your space at lunch, just to hang out by yourself and show the others you're too cool for them, but if you'd like some company, we'd be glad to have you."

Twilight Zone. That was the only possible explanation. Will thought he'd fallen into some crazy alternate dimension. People were laughing with him instead of *at* him. The smartest kid in his class thought he was cool. He'd gotten not one, but two lunch invitations in the last half hour. What in the world was going on?

"So about lunch—" said Duncan.

"William is going to have to wait for lunch," said a voice from around the corner. It was Peske. He had a pained expression, like he'd just been stung by a dozen bees. "Duncan, please move on to the lunchroom. William and I have something to discuss."

"Course, Mr. Peske, sir. See ya, Will!" Duncan took off down the hallway, leaving the lawyer and Will alone.

"William," he said plainly, but with a hint of disdain. "Is it your goal to break every rule we've set up for you?"

Will glanced at the bathroom door. "But I—"

Peske clapped his hands. "No! There will be no more excuses. Once again you purposefully and blatantly used your powers for a non-wish-granting situation. This must be stopped immediately. Have you given any thought to what will happen tomorrow when someone asks you to do another impression?"

"I ... I guess I won't be able to."

"Precisely. And that will raise people's suspicions. Granted, in our line of work, a few eyebrows are always raised, but we like to keep that to a minimum. So, unfortunately, I'm going to have to ask you to cease all of your impressions until the proper time."

"I'm really sorry ... I was just trying to help Duncan. He was gonna get beaten up if I hadn't stepped in."

"What you did was admirable; no one denies that. But using your power in this situation was the equivalent of setting off a nuclear bomb to rid a house of a few ants. It's not only overkill, but the after effects could be deadly for everyone involved. Will, you could have gone to a teacher for help. You could have even come to me. Instead, you risked the future of my people so you can play the hero to some child."

Hanging his head, Will said nothing. *I wish he'd just forget about this so we could move on already*, he thought.

"Well, I'm not going to forget about it, William." Peske tapped a finger to his forehead. "Telewishing, remember? I hear wishes too. Apparently you don't realize the seriousness of what you've done. So there's only one thing left to do. If you don't consider me a viable authority figure, then I'll send you to one who might frighten you a bit more. You should be very familiar with him, given your recent imitation of his voice."

"The principal? You're sending me to the principal's office?" Will blinked in disbelief.

"Indeed. I'm going to make sure you keep your nose clean, young man. As for that boy in the bathroom with the trashcan on his head ..." Peske glanced at his watch. "Well, I suppose we'll find time to come back for him later."

"William Sherman Cricket! What is the meaning of this?!" Will's father barked through the telephone.

Will held the phone away from his ear and looked across the desk at the principal, hoping to find a sympathetic face. He didn't. Principal Shimerman actually smiled.

"Son, are you listening to me?" his father continued through the receiver. "I can't believe you're in the principal's office! And because you were disrespectful to your substitute teacher? There's just no excuse for this!"

"Dad, it's not what—"

"I said 'no excuse!'"

Principal Shimerman kicked his legs up on the desk and put his hands behind his bald head. He got comfortable in his chair and closed his eyes as if settling in for a peaceful nap on some sun-drenched beach.

"This is the last thing your mother and I need right now, young man. Do you have any idea how exhausted we are? Nonnie's behavior has taken a terrible toll on us, especially your mother, who's already under an enormous amount of pressure at work. Now we have to deal with you getting in trouble at school? I really expected better from you. You've always been the stable one, Will."

Stable as a bag of Mexican jumping beans, Will thought.

"I … I really didn't need this today. I just got off the phone with Dr. Donnatelli, and he refuses to let me interview him. I'm at my wit's end here."

Will turned in his seat, away from the principal. "Dad, I'm really sorry. I didn't mean to cause problems."

"This interview today—it's a big one, and if I got it, I know it would open the door for me at the paper. Maybe then your mom wouldn't feel like she has to work so hard to support us." *I wish I could get that interview to help ease Emily's burden.*

Will felt a pulse of adrenaline pound through his body. Even over the telephone, his Telewishing allowed him to hear his father's wish. "Maybe there's still hope, Dad."

"That's about all I have left." His father's voice was low, not sharp at all, as it had been earlier. "Look, I'll pick you up this afternoon as planned. We can talk more about what you did then."

"Then we'll go to that interview."

Will's father sighed. "I wish, kiddo, I wish."

When Will hung up the phone, Principal Shimerman was back on his feet. The principal thumbed the lapels of his suit jacket, smiling broadly. He opened his mouth to speak, but was interrupted by a buzz from his phone.

"Yes? ... You're kidding me! ... They tied up Ms. Gaynor? Again? ... Just stay put, I'll be right there."

The principal slammed down the phone and shot toward the door. "Don't move a muscle, William. I'll be back in five minutes."

As soon as Principal Shimerman closed the door, Will flew into action. He didn't know how long he'd have until the principal came back. And even though Will was alone in the office, there were people just outside. He had to be quick.

Will yanked the phone book from the bookshelf and flipped to the D's. He skimmed through the listings until he came across Donnatelli, Horatio. There was only one listing.

He got an outside line from the principal's phone and dialed the number. One, two, three rings, and finally an answer!

"Yes ... hello ... who's there?" said a raspy voice.

Will focused on the voice he wanted to imitate, that of his mom's boss, Mr. Peach. "Donnatelli, how are you, old man?"

"P-Peach? Is that you?"

"Of course it is. Who else would it be? Listen, about that recent transaction—"

"What? Is something wrong? The artifact's authentic ... genuine ... real, I swear! You know I'd never cheat you! I wouldn't!"

Will pulled back and eyed the telephone. This Donnatelli character sounded a little off his rocker. "Nor would I ever think such, my dear man! No, this has to do with the media and a certain newspaper."

"I haven't talked to any of them. Hate ... despise ... loathe them all, just like I'm supposed to!"

Oooookay, Will thought. *I can see why Dad was frustrated after talking with this guy. He's a complete nut!* "Doctor, the media are our friends. Imagine yourself on the front page of our prestigious paper—why, you'd be getting call after call from people wanting to fund your archeological digs. You could spend the rest of your life doing what you love without ever again worrying about finances."

"Slow down, Peach. Are you telling me you want me to talk ... chat ... converse with the press?"

135

"Most certainly. Well, one of them in particular, a Mr. Cal Cricket of the *Corinth Chronicle*. He's the goods."

"He called ... talked ... disturbed me several times this morning. I'm familiar with him, yes, yes."

"Then you won't mind calling him back, arranging for a meeting this afternoon?"

"If you insist ... persist ... won't take no for an answer."

"I do... er, won't ... um, just do it, okay?" said Will with a scratch to his head.

"Okay ... fine ... agreed," said Donnatelli.

Will hung up the phone, returned the phone book to the shelf and settled back into his chair with a smug grin. He never would've thought being sent to the principal's office could be this rewarding. Wish number four was well on its way to being granted.

When Will's father picked him up from school, he was in a considerably better mood than when they'd talked on the phone. He tapped his fingers to the music on the radio and whistled along.

He told Will about his surprise call from Dr. Donnatelli and how they arranged for a brief interview this afternoon. Even though the news came as no surprise to Will, he still smiled seeing his father in such a pleasant mood.

When they arrived, they were both a little hesitant to get out of the car. Donnatelli's house looked like it belonged in some old horror movie. It was about 20 years overdue for a paint job. There were more shingles on the lawn than on the roof. Each shutter swung back and forth on no more than a single screw.

"He's just eccentric, that's all," Will's father said as he braved a smile for his son.

As the two Cricket men climbed the wobbly and half-broken porch steps, Dr. Donnatelli came rushing out the door. He was as thin as a rail but with a bulbous nose that looked out of place on his small face. He wore a baseball cap that had so much dust on it, Will couldn't make out what team it represented. Dr. Donnatelli lugged a shag green suitcase and seemed very much in a hurry.

"Crap ... phooey ... balderdash. I was hoping to be gone before you came around. You're Cricket, I assume?" Donnatelli set his suitcase down on the flooring and plopped himself on top of it.

"Um ... yes, sir, I'm Cal Cricket, the reporter. Why were you trying to leave? You're the one who called me to arrange the interview, remember?"

"Just because I dig ... excavate ... uncover ancient artifacts doesn't mean I'm one of 'em! My memory suits me just fine. Twerp."

"Well, if you have a few minutes, maybe we could still do the interview." Will's father flashed his recorder. "If you don't mind, I'll record it so I can quote you correctly."

"Quote ... recite ... retell this: buzz off!" Donnatelli jumped back up, yanked his suitcase and barreled past Will and his father. He made it down to the last step when his foot crashed through the rotten wood. His suitcase went flying from his hand into the yard, but Donnatelli wasn't going anywhere. His leg was stuck.

"Are you all right, sir?" Will's father asked as he carefully stepped down.

"Blasted steps! I just repaired ... renovated ... overhauled these things not more than 25 years ago. Cheap wood."

Once on solid soil, Will's father examined the step. "Doesn't look like you'll be able to pull your foot out the same way it went in—the angle of entry's all wrong for that. I think I can pry this piece off, and then it'll be a simple matter of breaking through some rotten wood. Shouldn't take long at all."

"Just long enough for an interview, eh?" Donnatelli said, crossing his arms and snarling in disgust.

"Sir, I plan on doing what's right whether or not you feel you should do the same. I don't turn my back on someone in need." Will's father grabbed a baseboard and gave it a hearty pull.

"Fine ... dandy ... okay! I'll give you your interview, but you'd better make it quick." Donnatelli dropped his arms to his sides and seemed to relax a little.

"Okay," Will's father said as he clicked on the recorder, "Would you tell me about the piece you sold to Mr. Peach's antiquities company, Peach Preserves?"

"It's called the ring of Candrissa. She was a priestess of sorts at a place called Tophet, in the valley of Geennom, we're guessing around eighth century B.C. It's said that Candrissa was the one foolish ... daft ... illogical soul who opposed a particular ritual sacrifice practiced by her priesthood."

"What were they sacrificing?"

"Children. Hard to believe she wouldn't go along with that, isn't it? For her troubles, she was put to death by stoning ... hanging ... being cut in two."

"Wait ... which one was it?"

"All of the above. As a reminder to any other would-be-traitors, the chief priest fashioned a ring from the bones of one of Candrissa's fingers and placed her own eye in the center as its jewel ... bauble ... adornment."

CRACK! Will's dad ripped the step's baseboard loose. The loud noise combined with the creepy story made Will leap into the air.

"Rumors ... legends ... whispers say that the eye still blinks for its master."

"Rumors?" Will's father stopped and looked up at the archaeologist. "What do you mean by that? You're the one who recovered it. You of all people should know whether that's true or not."

"Do you think me a moron ... buffoon ... imbecile? I realized what the ring was when I saw its band sticking out from the dirt at the dig site. I covered it immediately and didn't dare look at it fully. That ring is a symbol for one of the worst atrocities committed by ancient man. It is pure evil ... hatred ... sin. And it contains powerful magics. Anyone who covets to wear it is out for only one thing: blood ... blood ... blood."

Donnatelli's leg smashed through the rotten wood. Will and his father were too stunned by the story to move, let alone stop him. He grabbed his suitcase from the lawn and tossed it into the back of his pickup truck. The clang of the suitcase against the metal bed of the vehicle seemed to bring Will's dad to his senses.

"Dr. Donnatelli," he said, "please, don't go. There's more I need to ask. My wife ... she works for Mr. Peach. If that ring's as dangerous as you seem to think—"

Donnatelli slammed the door to his truck, turned on the engine and high-tailed it out of the driveway. Will and his father, though, didn't move for some time.

Will didn't say a word the entire ride home. Donnatelli's story had made his stomach flip upside down. A week ago, the tale of Candrissa's ring would've fascinated him; but that was before he'd learned that supernatural forces were exceedingly real, making Donnatelli's far-fetched story highly possible.

Will's dad tried striking up a conversation, but the confrontation with the archaeologist had disturbed him too—he didn't stop biting at his fingernails once during the 10-minute drive.

When they arrived home, they were alone in the house. Will marched into the living room and plopped down in front of the TV, hoping that the magic box might take his mind off his worries.

Kaitlyn came home a few minutes later, and she immediately honed in on her brother. She sat down right next to him on the couch, far closer than normal. Will flipped the television stations until he found the Discovery Channel, hoping that something educational might scare his sister away. No such luck.

"So, Will," she said, twisting around to stare him in the face. "Kids at school were talking about you today."

"So what's new?" he said unblinkingly.

"Not in the 'Will's a loser' kind of way like usual. There were rumors going around that you got sent to the principal's office."

Will clicked off the television. "True," he said.

"Wow. So they were right. Well, I told everyone that if you had been sent to the principal's office, it was probably because they caught you in the kitchen eating all the desserts for tomorrow's lunch."

Will narrowed his eyes. "False."

"You accidentally sat on some kid and suffocated him to death?"

"False. And you're just plain mean."

"So it didn't involve food or another student? How about a teacher? I heard Griswald was out today. Did you get in trouble with your substitute teacher?"

"True."

"Whoa ... for real? Some kids said you were making funny voices, but I didn't think you'd actually do anything to tick off a teacher. Will—my brother, Mr. Goody-Goody—a troublemaker? Why ... I'm so proud of you!"

Kaitlyn held up her hand for a high-five. Will looked around the room, expecting a practical joke. Reluctantly he raised his hand, and his sister slapped it.

"Maybe you're not the complete loser I thought you were. Maybe. Speaking of losers," she said, quickly changing the subject, "where was that weird kid who was hanging around last week? Tongue?"

"Tang," Will said. "He's, um, sick, I guess."

"Seems like your stranger-than-normal behavior started when he showed up. Hope he hasn't been too much of a bad influence on you."

Will was just about to jump to Tang's defense when his mom burst into the room. Will's dad and Nonnie were right behind her.

"What's going on, Emily?" her husband asked. "You didn't even say 'hello' when you ran through the door. Why are you in such a panic?"

"We were on our way back from the doctor's office when she got some call on that little pocket calculator she's always carrying around," Nonnie said. "We were just a few blocks away, but she stomped on the gas like she was racing the Daytona 500."

"Will, put the news on," his mother commanded.

"What station?" asked Will.

"Any station!" his mother yelled.

He quickly followed his mom's orders. Will knew better than to tarry when his mother was in rampage-mode.

"Emily, please," Will's father said. "An explanation would be nice."

"I got a call from work," she said, not taking her eyes off the television. "Like I told you this morning, Mr. Peach is out for the day, so they called me first. I knew I shouldn't have left the office this afternoon!"

Nonnie shrugged. "Would've been fine by me. Don't like doctors no how. They put those Popsicle sticks in my mouth, but they always eat the Popsicle before I get there."

Will finally turned to a channel covering local news. "Mom? You're kind of freaking us out. Dad and I heard some crazy stuff today about that ring of Candrissa, and we've been worried that—"

"The ring! That's the problem precisely." Will's mom sat on the couch, stared at the screen as the weatherman covered tomorrow's forecast, and then jumped back up again. "Candrissa's ring was being stored on-site at our warehouse."

"So you haven't seen it, then?" Will's father asked.

"No, but—"

"Thank goodness, honey. Like Will said, we got the scoop on this ring of yours today, and I have to wonder why Mr. Peach wanted it. It's supposed to be bad news."

Will's mom shook her head. "Lincoln's just a middleman. He finds artifacts like the ring and sells them to buyers. He told me himself that the ring is purported to have some sort of curse on it. He wouldn't let anyone look at it, and he said he couldn't wait until the ring's new owner claimed it. That doesn't matter now, does it?"

"Honey?"

"The ring of Candrissa was stolen!" shouted Will's mother.

As if on cue, the local news flashed a picture of the offices of Peach Preserves. Will's mom snatched the remote and cranked up the volume.

> *Breaking news from the local antiquities dealer known as Peach Preserves. Details are still sketchy, but police have issued a statement that a recent acquisition by the company was stolen this afternoon. The item in question is supposedly the ring of Candrissa, which is rumored to be worth upwards of $300 million. Unfortunately, police and company employees do not currently have a description of the stolen ring. Police are speaking with Peach Preserves owner and founder, Mr. Lincoln Peach, to put together a sketch of the item, but even Mr. Peach had limited dealings with the ring and, therefore, may not be able to provide much more information.*

> *The one break in the case comes in the form of surveillance video footage captured from a security camera inside the warehouse. Unfortunately, the video only shows the suspect from the back, but police have still asked that we share it with our viewing audience in hopes that one of you might recognize the suspected thief.*

The screen flashed to a black and white view of the warehouse. Will had been there once with his mother. It was a well-guarded facility with only one way in and out. There was always a security detail of at least two men, and entry required a particular key card only held by Mr. Peach and Will's mom. Will couldn't imagine how anyone could've broken inside.

The voice of the newscaster continued as the video played.

>*You'll notice this is the point where the thief enters. From the clothing and height, it would appear to be a young man, just over five feet tall. We're unable to determine the color of the hair, however, because as you can see, there were some problems with the video feed. For some odd reason, the suspect's hair color keeps changing.*

Will's eyes bulged out in horror. *Hair that changes color? That can only mean one thing: the person who stole the ring of Candrissa was Tang!*

DAY 5

Groggily marching into his bathroom at 7:00 a.m., Will checked himself out in the mirror—he could already tell it was going to be a rough day. He turned on the hot water, stepped into the shower, and dozed off three times just standing there. He thought there must've been something wrong with the water because the stream barely trickled out of the showerhead. When he got out, things didn't go much better. Will exhausted himself trying to find the neck hole in his sweater, so he lay back down for a quick nap.

When he woke, he felt a little more refreshed. Amazing what a 15-minute nap could do for a dog-tired boy. Will looked back at the clock to see if he stood a chance of making it to school on time.

7:03 a.m.

"What the?!" Will snatched the alarm clock off the nightstand and gave it a shake, but everything seemed to be working. He rushed over to his dresser, picked up his secret decoder watch. It read 7:03 a.m. too. Then he flipped on the TV. He could see it warming up, but it took almost a minute for a picture to come on screen. Even then, the people moved and spoke in extremely slow motion.

That's when it hit him. "They're not moving slow at all. I'm moving so fast that everything around me just seems slow! I've got super-speed!"

Once Will realized what his Mizm was, he mastered it in no time. He raced out of his room and into the kitchen. His sister was about to sit at the table, but Will moved so fast that she appeared to be frozen in time. Will rushed over and plopped down in her chair.

Kaitlyn kept moving, unaware that her brother was anywhere nearby. Even though it seemed to take forever to the fast-moving Will, she sat down a split second after him. As soon as Kaitlyn felt Will's cushy lap, she jumped back up. "Will, you jerk!" she screamed flailing her arms and knocking over a glass of orange juice.

Will watched the glass fly into the air in slow motion. The juice poured out like thick syrup. Little drops sprinkled in several directions. This was going to be a colossal mess, and Will would get the blame. He couldn't risk getting in trouble again so soon after yesterday's visit to the principal's office.

Moving at speeds unseen to the human eye, Will shot out of the chair, raced around Kaitlyn and grabbed the glass in midair. He scooted around the room, scooping each individual drop of juice in the glass. There must have been hundreds, but Will retrieved every last one before Katilyn had a chance to shout, "Mom!"

"Whoa! You almost knocked this over," Will said, back at regular speed so his voice would be heard normally. He'd returned to the chair and handed Kaitlyn her seemingly undisturbed glass of orange juice.

"What the ...?" Kaitlyn inspected the table. "How did ... what in the ... oh, just give me that!" She snatched the juice from Will and sat across from him, glaring.

"What's all the yelling about?" Will's mom fastened an earring as she entered the kitchen. "This isn't exactly the best time for the two of you to start a screaming match."

"So when would be the best time?" Will asked, getting a smirk out of Kaitlyn.

"Don't be such a smart aleck, mister," said Will's mom. She joined her kids at the breakfast nook, but with her briefcase instead of cereal. She poured through papers and charts, clipping stuff together and making an occasional note.

"You really shouldn't wait to do your homework at the last minute, Mom," Kaitlyn said, shaking a finger at her.

Will's mother didn't look up from her paperwork, but said, "Aren't you a bundle of support? Actually, I have an offsite appointment this morning so I won't be going into the office until later. I'm meeting with another antiquities dealer just outside of town. She's a lovely woman named Mrs. Spots. She's been helping us locate the final—hey! Where are my notes? I could've sworn I put them in here last night." Will's mom tore through her papers in search of the missing document.

"Mom? What's wrong?" Will asked.

"I jotted down some questions Mr. Peach wanted me to ask at my meeting today, but I must've left them at the office. Now I have to drive all the way out there, and I'll never make my appointment in time. How totally unprofessional." Will's mother shook her head and sighed.

"Wow, Mom," Kaitlyn said. "If I could help, I would." *She's been so crabby lately, but I really do wish she could find that paper in time for her meeting.*

Will's mom sighed. "I'm afraid I just won't be fast enough today."

Jumping up, Will knocked his chair back to the floor. "Oops. Sorry about that. I thought I saw your papers in your bedroom last night, Mom," he lied. "I'll go get them!"

Will raced out of the kitchen at his normal pace, but as he headed down the hallway, he cranked up his super-speed. He made a quick turn, and instead of going to his parents' room, he shot out the front door and down the street.

Yes! Will thought to himself as he ran past the neighbor's yard. *This is going to be the easiest wish to grant so far. Wish number five, here I come!*

Barely a minute after leaving, Will was at the offices of Peach Preserves. The front doors were unlocked, and several haggard-looking employees congregated in the coffee room. Will zipped past them and ran straight to his mom's office.

Once inside, Will closed the door, but left it open just a crack so he could hear if anyone approached. He moved to his mom's desk and poured over her paperwork at top speed. Her office was in total disarray with papers strewn everywhere, and Will wondered how she dared to be critical of his messy room.

Will turned to a stack of papers with a sticky note on top that read, "To be shredded." He suspected he might find something interesting in this pile. He did, but not what he expected. At the bottom of the mound of papers that were to be destroyed, he found a framed photograph of him and his family.

He rolled his eyes, but quickly returned to shuffling through the stacks of paper. Pretty soon Will had run out of places to look. He was just about to give up when he noticed something wedged between his mom's desk and the filing cabinet next to it. "What's this?" Will bent down and managed to get his fingers in far enough to pull it out. At the top of the paper, it read, "Q's for Mrs. Spots."

"Voila," Will said. "Now to get my speed on and—"

Will froze in mid-sentence. Someone was just outside the door, walking toward the office. He ducked down and squeezed under his mom's desk. He peered underneath to see two pairs of men's shoes stop in the hallway. One of the two men gave the door a push and stepped inside the office, while the other waited inside the doorway. Even with his super-speed, there was no way Will could escape as long as his exit was blocked.

"Emily's not here," said a familiar voice Will knew all too well, considering he'd just imitated it yesterday. It was Mr. Peach. "Blast! I forgot she was seeing Spots today!"

"Excuse me, sir?" the other man said.

"Spots, Mrs. Spots. She's the key to acquiring the final piece of the Ancient Prophets collection."

"No offense, sir, but isn't that sort of moot at this point? Now that the ring of Candrissa's been stolen, the collection will never be whole."

Mr. Peach swung around to face the other man. "My dear Charlie, in your two years as my assistant, how many times have you heard me use the word 'never?'"

"I really couldn't say, sir." Charlie's feet nervously danced back and forth.

"I *never* use the word 'never!'"

"Except just now, that is, um, sir."

Mr. Peach stopped moving, and Will wondered if he might haul off and deck Charlie. Instead, he burst out laughing. "Right you are, Charlie! Now I remember why I keep you around. Ah, good man. But listen, my point was that I don't give up. I created this company with lots of sweat and blood, and it's going to take a lot more than a petty thief to do me in, I guarantee you that."

"Do you think the police might be able to find the ring, sir?" Charlie asked.

"Hardly. This is out of their league. But I'll find a way to turn this run of bad luck to my favor."

"Speaking of bad luck, sir, did you see this morning's paper? Right next to the headline story about the missing ring, there's an article about its history. Apparently Donnatelli talked with some reporter ... a Cal Cricket."

"Indeed." Mr. Peach faced the office again and pounded a fist on the desk. Will let out a tiny gasp and then slapped a hand over his mouth to keep quiet. "That interview should have never happened. The last thing I need is for the town to think I'm hoarding evil artifacts here at Peach Preserves."

"Should I ask the PR department to work on a press release to counter the story's negative portrayal of the ring?"

"No, we'll worry about that later. The most important thing is getting the ring back. Believe me when I say, I will personally find this boy who stole my belonging. When I do locate him, he will regret ever having stepped foot on my property." Mr. Peach moved toward the door. "Come. We have lots to do. This is going to be our busiest week ever."

As soon as the men left, Will crawled out from the desk. With his mom's paper in hand, he had everything he needed to complete today's wish, leaving only two more before his own wish would be granted. Right now, he couldn't concentrate on how great his life would become; all he could think about was how much trouble Tang was in.

"Look what I found," Will said as he rattled the paper in his hand.

"Oh, thank my lucky stars!" Will's mom snatched her notes, gave them a quick glance and tossed them into her briefcase. "Thank goodness I thought to have you look in my bedroom."

Will's jaw dropped in disbelief.

"Looks like I'll still be able to make it on time. See you kids later!" She scooted out of the house, moving almost as fast as Will had earlier.

"You have a great day too, Mom," Kaitlyn said snidely as she gathered up her books and headed for the front door.

Will gave his sister a few minutes head start and took off. On his way, he cut through the park where he and Tang had goofed off. They'd played hide and seek, hunted tree frogs and hung out on the swings. Will couldn't believe his friend was the thief everyone was after.

Crossing through a grouping of trees, Will noticed their shadows lengthen as he passed. He looked up at the sun, but nothing seemed out of order. Still those dark shadows edged across the ground like water spilling over the side of a bank. This wasn't normal or natural, and Will had a bad feeling about it in the pit of his stomach.

He picked up the pace, but so did the shadows. In fact, they were quickly catching up to Will. Hoping there was some reserve of super-speed left inside despite having already granted his daily wish, Will took off in a run. For a split second, he moved like the wind, but then any remaining vestige of power dried up and vanished—he was just Will again, and running was not something he did extremely well.

Will forced himself to keep going, but as he looked back, he saw the shadows snap up from the ground and travel through the air. They looked solid, like they could choke the life from him! He pushed his breathless body forward, but it was too late. One of the shadows caught him by the arm, and then another latched onto his leg. He pulled with all his might, but it felt like an anchor weighed him down. Other shadows whipped around him, and, a moment later, he was ensnared. The darkness that bound him grew, covering more and more of his body. Despite his flailing, soon every last inch of him was covered. When the amorphous shadows had swallowed him whole, they simply vanished from sight. Even though everything else in the park returned to normal, Will Cricket was nowhere to be found.

When Will awoke, he immediately realized he was no longer in the park. He was still outside, but from where he lay, he could only see a single tree. The sky wasn't clear and crisp like before—it was warm and cloudy, and it felt like a summer rainstorm approached.

Will tried to push himself off the ground, but he was still so drowsy. He wished he could get back to his feet, and suddenly he felt his body lift up. When Will stood once again, he looked down and found he'd been lying in a field of dandelions. These weren't the ordinary run-of-the-mill flowers he was used to—these dandelions waved their leaves at him and bowed to one another, as if whispering secrets. Will tried to rationalize it away, but not even a stiff breeze could make flowers move like this—these dandelions were as animated as people!

Will stumbled backwards and away from the flowers. He didn't know where he was, but he suspected wishcraft was involved.

He raced to the solitary tree, thinking a higher perch would allow him to see his surroundings. Sure, he'd never actually climbed a tree—his experiences had consisted solely of flying up or falling out of them—but he was willing to give it a try. Then as he looked up to the tree's branches, he noticed the odd fruit growing on them.

Reaching a low-lying branch, Will plucked a piece of fruit. It had the shape of an apple, but it was covered in dark chocolate, caramel, marshmallow bits and chopped nuts. Even though he had no clue as to who had brought him here or why, he couldn't resist a bite. He sunk his teeth into it and discovered it was precisely what it appeared to be—a candy apple!

Will stepped back from the tree to get a better look at it. "How do I get one of these for my yard?"

Suddenly, the sound of thunder crackled directly overhead. The storm clouds darkened. The wind picked up. A roll of thunder barreled from the clouds, and it began to pour. Will covered his head in anticipation of the deluge. The rain didn't rush down, however; it took its time, almost wafting to the ground. When the first drop finally plopped on Will's head, it wasn't wet at all. It was light and solid, like confetti.

Will turned his gaze skyward and felt his heart pound up to his throat. There were no droplets of water, and even though it felt like confetti, it was anything but. The sky was filled with green. It was raining money!

Leaping into the air, Will grabbed handfuls of 50 and 100 dollar bills. His heart raced—a few more minutes in this storm, and he'd be set for life! He couldn't believe his luck. The money was all his. It was practically calling his name.

"Will!" The voice was Hollywood's. "Will!" he called again, stepping out from behind the candy apple tree. "Don't you have enough sense to come in out of the rain?"

"Oh, that's all right," Will said, turning his attention back to the falling money.

"William Cricket. Over here. Now."

Will turned up his lip in disgust. He stuffed the dollar bills he'd captured into his pocket and stomped over to Hollywood beneath the tree. "I'm a little busy here. Can we make this quick?"

The wish agent shook his head. "Those slips of paper won't do you any good, my young friend. Watch."

Hollywood pointed up to the storm cloud and a ray of starlight shot from the tip of his finger. As soon as the light hit it, the rain came to an end and the cloud dissipated, revealing golden sunshine.

"Hey! Why'd you do that? I was only a few bills away from being a millionaire!" Will pulled a wad of cash from his pockets and shoved them into Hollywood's face. As soon as they were in the light of day, the bills melted into a green goo that oozed over Will's hands and plopped to the ground. "What in the ... ?!"

"The moneydrops you collected wouldn't have done you a lick of good in your world, Will. As you can see, they melt at the first sign of sunlight."

Will threw his hands in the air. "Aw, man, that's not fair ... hey, what do you mean they won't do me any good in *my* world? Where are we?"

"You're in the land of the Arcanians, Will. Welcome to Mythos."

"What? I'm on your home world? So you brought me here through those shadows? You know, you could've sent me a text or something telling me what you were up to. Why do you guys always have to freak me out?"

"Sorry, sorry, sorry about that, Will. I wasn't thinking straight. So much on my mind these days. It won't happen again. I promise."

"There's no way to keep that money, huh? What's the point of having gobs of it rain down on you if you can't do anything with it?"

Hollywood's face tensed. "Moneydrops didn't come from we Arcanians, Will; they came from you humans. You see, while my people grant thousands of wishes for your kind every year, there are millions more that go ungranted. Ever hear someone wish it would rain money? Or that candy would grow on trees? Obviously we could never bring those wishes to life on your world;

they would cause mass chaos. But some wishes have a life of their own; they have to go somewhere, so they take seed in our world."

"Wow," Will said, thinking of the possibilities. "You guys must get all kinds of crazy stuff happening here. I bet you never know what to expect."

"It's our way of life, so it's not so unusual for us. Besides, you'd be surprised by the lack of originality of humankind. If I had a dollar for every moneydrop that fell in Mythos ..."

"What about wishes that aren't so nice? I mean, you guys grant selfless wishes, and these wishes that pop up here seem pretty innocent. What about the wishes that are meant to hurt people?"

Hollywood faced away from Will, staring into the sun. "Those wishes go to a place I won't speak of in front of you. The name alone makes the ears of children burn. The other place is like an echo of Mythos, only twisted and perverse. I wouldn't wish for even the Genies to be banished there."

When the wish agent turned back around, Will let out a gasp. Hollywood's perfect face was as wrinkled as an old man's.

"My face, is it? Scarred or elderly-looking perhaps?" Hollywood asked. He placed his hands against his cheeks and molded his features like clay until he was back to normal. "That's what happens at the mere thought of the echo world. So let's get moving toward SCENE headquarters and change the subject to something less disfiguring, shall we?"

Hollywood shuffled Will to a path paved with gold coins. "Where exactly are we?" Will asked. "I mean, I know we're on Mythos, but where is that? Is it a hidden continent in the Bermuda Triangle? Are we on a planet identical to earth that rotates on the opposite side of the sun?"

"No, although I've been to both of those spots. They're quite lovely vacation getaways. Mythos, however, actually resides in conjunction with the human world, but on a different plane of existence. We're all part of the same big cosmic soup, but Mythos is just slightly out of sync with your world, like on a different wavelength you can't see or hear. It's kind of like a peanut butter and jelly sandwich."

"Come again?"

"When you're eating peanut butter and jelly, what do you taste?"

Will rubbed his tummy. "Well, I taste peanut butter and, um, jelly."

"There's a lot more than that. You can't taste them, but there are calories in the sandwich that affect you."

"You guys are calories?" Will put his hands on his belly. "I don't really want more calories."

"You're missing the point!" Hollywood popped Will on the back of his head. "You need calories to fuel your body, but you can't see or taste them. Nevertheless, they're still there, working for you. Just like Mythos."

"But I can see and hear you just fine."

"Only when we crossover into your world. Or, as is the case right now, when you crossover into ours. It's really not a difficult concept, Will."

"Yeah, I s'pose. I just want to make sure there aren't any surprises coming my way. Can't stand surprises. They make me nervous, give me hot flashes."

With a reluctant sigh, Hollywood said, "Then you'd better prepare yourself, my boy, because what I've got to tell you is so shocking, you just might spontaneously combust."

Inside the offices of the SCENE, Will nervously glanced around the building. It appeared to be just like any other workplace—only with the most outrageous-looking employees he'd ever seen.

Down one hallway, there was a pale-skinned girl who wore a dress made entirely of four-leaf clovers. Will spotted an Asian woman with fingernails the length of a ruler having a conversation with a bushy-eyebrowed koala bear. There was also a set of bright yellow-skinned male triplets who took turns finishing each other's sentences. A creature that looked like a tree but spoke with an Indian accent sidled past Will, leaving a trail of sap in his wake.

"Oh, Will," said a dreamy voice from down the hall. It was Reverie. Her hair streamed all over the place, and her eyelids were barely open. "Everyone's in the meeting room. Time to get ..." Her head plopped onto her shoulder as she dozed off.

Even though he knew Reverie should have finished by saying, "started," Will was hesitant to join. She and Hollywood had gathered several SCENE higher-ups for a meeting specifically centered on Will. He wondered if this had something to do with him speeding around the house this morning and goofing on his sister. Or maybe they thought he was secretly hiding Tang, keeping him out of sight until the heat died down. Whatever the case, Hollywood wouldn't look him directly in the eye.

"No point putting this off," Will said to himself. He marched toward the meeting room, ducked under Reverie and scooted inside.

At the center of the room was a long shiny table, surrounded by several cozy-looking chairs. Most of the attendees were already sitting, flipping through notebooks and typing on laptops. Norv Peske was at the back of the room, staring at Will from a distance. Nixie gulped down a bottle of water while her feet were propped on the table. Heiko paced back and forth along a wall made entirely of glass that opened up to a plush pasture below. The strange tree-looking fellow was there too as was the koala.

Hollywood pulled the snoozing Reverie from the doorway and led her to a seat next to his. He sat her down and propped her head up with one of her arms. "Reverie," he said, "be a dear and keep notes, would you?"

She nodded, but her eyes remained shut. Her arm slipped and her head slammed down onto the table.

Hollywood slid a notepad under her hand and placed a pen between her fingers. "Don't worry," he said to Will, "she's excellent at taking sleephand notes."

As he passed around a series of documents to everyone in the room, save Will, Hollywood said, "Before we get started, there are a couple of introductions to make. Will, the gentleman with the receding leaf-line is Kalpatharu. He's the SCENE's vice-president of research and development. He's always on the lookout for ways to improve the wish-granting process, Telewishing and that sort of thing."

"It is a pleasure meeting you, Mr. William." Kalpatharu nodded, and a few of his leaves broke free and fell to the table.

"The koala is head of security for the office," Hollywood said. "His name is Hiroshi—born in Japan, but has what some of us consider an unhealthy obsession with the North American Old West. And please do something with that cigar."

Hiroshi shrugged and flipped his cigar into the air. He leaned back and opened wide, catching it in his mouth and swallowing it whole.

"Now then," Hollywood said, his voice more somber than usual. "On to business at hand. You've all had a chance to review the notes, so everyone should be up to speed. Who'd like to start?"

"That would be me." Heiko click-clacked to the table. "William, you and I met just two days prior, correct?"

Will nodded, but wondered if he should have a lawyer present.

"And what was the subject of our gathering?"

"You, uh, warned me about the, um, dangers of abusing my powers," Will gulped.

"Precisely!" Heiko stomped a hoof and then marched toward the window.

"What I think he's getting at," Hollywood said, "is that you seem to have ignored our warnings yet again these last two days. We heard all about your escapades with the voices yesterday— you did a superb Peske impersonation, by the way. I had tears I was laughing so hard. Just brilliant, absolutely—"

"Could we get on with it?" Peske hissed.

"Right, right, right. So there was that funny but totally inappropriate voice thing, and then just this morning, we found you tormenting your sister with those super quick feet of yours. Will, we're very concerned about your behavior."

"Yeah, and not just 'cause your stunts are puttin' us at risk," said Nixie. "We got us a seriously big issue, and it's about to clobber us upside the head."

Hollywood tapped a pencil against the table and stared at Nixie. "Okaaaaay ... I wasn't exactly ready to head down that path, but sure, let's go there. Will, we're concerned that your erratic behavior may be the influence of Tangible."

Hiroshi slammed down a fist. "Cut to the chase, already! Kid, are you joining forces with that traitorous half-Genie? Are you gonna sell us out to the forces of evil?"

"What?!" Will had no clue what they were talking about. He felt his jaw move, but he could barely speak. "Me ... sell ... evil ... huh?"

Reverie's pen stopped moving. Without opening an eye or raising her head, she said, "He's innocent. His dreams are pure." Then she fell back to sleep again.

"As I knew they would be," Hollywood announced, puffing out his chest.

"I don't understand," Will said.

Hollywood looked around the room, as if seeking their approval to speak, and was met with a few nods. "Okay, it's like this. Long story short. We think Tang may have joined up with a rogue Genie who's bent on subjugating your entire world."

"No way!" Will stood up, fully prepared to walk out, until he remembered he had no idea how to get home. "Tang would never do that."

Peske crossed his arms and snarled. "Oh no? Then why did he vanish when we tried reprimanding him for his abuse of power?"

"He was just upset, that's all," said Will.

"That was two days ago, William," said Peske. "Why hasn't he returned? He hasn't even contacted you, his supposed best friend. That in itself is suspicious enough, but then he was seen stealing the ring of Candrissa!"

Will narrowed his eyes at Peske. "I thought you were supposed to be the lawyer here. That robbery videotape is circumstantial evidence—you can't see the thief's face!"

"But you can see his hair. How many boys do you know whose hair changes color?"

"Okay, that may not look good, but it doesn't mean he's joined forces with this bad guy you're talking about."

"Bad guy?" Hiroshi laughed. "He's no simple bad guy, kid. We're talking about the worst Genie to have ever had his lamp rubbed. He hates humans. Feels like he's been forced to grant their wishes all these years. He once tried to enslave the whole dad-blasted African continent. Heck, he was almost single-handedly responsible for the Frost Epidemic that killed all the Equine. Took a darn-tootin' miracle to trap him. And we had 'im imprisoned in his lamp until a few years ago. He broke free, and the lowdown varmint's been on the down low ever since. But we've heard whispers the last few months that he was gonna make another stab at conquering your planet. He gets his claws into humanity, and it's over for your people and ours. This Moloch character is the worst of the worst."

Moloch? The name sounded familiar to Will. Where had he heard it before? "Oh no," Will gasped. "That name—Moloch—I ... I heard Tang say his name that day just before you guys took him away. I snuck up on him and scared him. He jumped a mile high and said 'Moloch,' like that's who he thought I was."

Hollywood's face fell into his hands. Peske turned away from the group, and Heiko just stared blankly out the window. Reverie woke up again.

"This is bad, very bad," Kalpatharu said, his leaves trembling as he spoke.

"Not Tangible," Reverie whispered.

"I just can't believe it," Will said to no one in particular. "I know Tang was always miffed about how badly Genies were treated, but I never thought he'd do something like this. I guess this explains that secret project he was working on. It's just … he was my best friend."

"That's what he wanted you to think." Hollywood finally raised his head, revealing tired, glassy eyes. "He must've befriended you in hopes of turning you to Moloch's cause. But then he realized we might be on to him, and he disappeared."

"But why? Why would Tang and Moloch want me to help them? I'd never do it in a million years, of course, but what kind of help would a boy be to two powerful Genies anyway?"

Everyone in the room turned his or her attention to Hollywood. Even Heiko looked back at him from the window.

Clearing his throat, Hollywood said, "I think it's time we were honest with you about the details of your contract." He paused and stood up, then began to pace. "Don't worry; we still have the same deal in place: you help us grant seven wishes and then we grant your wish. But there is a clause in the contract that allows for the possibility of an eighth day."

Will blinked. Eight days? That wasn't the deal. He had two more wishes to grant, and he was done.

"It's not something we can force you to do, but we're hoping that after your time as a wish-granter, you might agree to assist us once more.

"Friday—the day *after* you grant your final wish—is what we Arcanians refer to as the Day of the Divine. This is the most powerful day for those who practice wishcraft, when entire worlds can be changed and remade. Such a thing has never been done before because it requires more power than any one Arcanian possesses. To complete such a task, one would first have to be a wish master, which Moloch is, of course. Next, he'd have to acquire a source of unimaginable power to fuel his mad quest. Finally, he would need three ancient artifacts known as the Tokens of Tenet to manipulate the power and funnel it into himself. The ring of Candrissa is one such Token. We believe Moloch to be in possession of a second one, as well. We have no idea where the final Token might be, but it's likely he has it also.

"On the Day of the Divine, as long as Moloch has his vessel of power and the Tokens of Tenet, he'll be able to do the one thing no other Arcanian has ever been able to do. He'll be able to grant his own wish. No one here doubts what it is he wants: he'll wish to be master over the entire human race. As a result, he'll also get his next wish, which is to see our people destroyed."

Will's stomach bubbled with nerves. "The guy sounds awful, for sure. But I don't get where I figure into all of this. You said my contract mentions this additional wish day, but what does your Day of the Divine have to do with me?"

"As I said, that is the day when Moloch will strike. The Vanguard, our wish enforcers, is essentially helpless to stop him. They were useless the last time Moloch ran amok. We had to call in extra special help. I was there then, and, as a result, the Vanguard has left the burden of Moloch's apprehension in my hands this time, as well. We want ... we *need* your help to stop him."

"Me? But you guys have all the power. You're the ones who gave me the super-skills I've been using, the ones I can barely manage, I might add."

"That's where you're wrong, Will. We never gave you anything. We merely tapped into what was already inside of you. Will, you're what we call an Omni—that is a human who, under the right circumstances, can draw on the limitless power of man's heart, mind and soul to do the impossible. That's the real reason we came to you to grant your wish last week, in hopes that you might actually grant *our* wish to stop Moloch. I'm not sure we can do it without you."

Will's mind raced. He shook his head over and over again. None of this was possible. The Arcanians were so powerful—how could they need him? "But why me? I'm a nobody. How could I be an Omni?"

Peske took over. "We're not exactly sure what makes an Omni an Omni. Some Arcanians theorize that it could be genetic as there have been multiple Omnis within the same bloodline. Others think that a firm belief and steady faith in wishing attract the power of an Omni to the human vessel. Either way, you are one, Will, whether you like it or not—whether *we* like it or not."

"Peske, that's really not necessary," Hollywood scolded. "I'm sure Will's going to make the right decision and help us."

"And if I don't?" Will asked.

"Then it is very likely that, in three days, our two worlds will die." Hollywood choked on the last word, his eyes locked on Will. "Look, I know it's too much to ask. I'm perfectly aware that you don't owe us anything more than you're already giving. But Omni or not, I know you feel the connection between yourself and the wishing world. Humans are the recipients of our wish-granting abilities. Wishing gives them hope, keeps them from buckling under the pressures of everyday life. But we are equally reliant on your people. Mankind possesses the fertile imaginations and passionate desires that give our world life, our lives meaning. Without humans we have no purpose ... without humans we wouldn't even exist. We need you Will, now more than ever."

Will wanted to say "no." He wasn't brave or strong or anything a hero should be. All he wanted was to be liked, maybe even popular. But if Moloch had his way, he might not even be alive. "Not really much of a choice, is it?"

Will carefully examined each of their faces—Nixie, who'd sprung a leak in her cheek; Heiko with head bowed low; Kalpatharu, who nervously plucked his own leaves; Hiroshi, giving the tree a bark rub; Reverie, whose fingers held her eyes wide open; Peske with eyes welded shut; and Hollywood, giving Will an almost imperceptible reassuring nod.

"Can't believe I'm doing this." Will sighed and shook his head. "Go ahead and sign me up. Just tell me what I have to do."

There was a huge sigh of relief from the Arcanians. "If only we knew," said Hollywood. "We don't know when or where or how he'll launch his plans to conquer humanity. We have to be ready for anything."

"Will I get a new power on the Day of the Divine that I can use to help?"

"We're actually not sure how that'll work either," said Hiroshi. "That day is filled with so much raw power that anything could happen. The ability to tap into those gifts lies within you. The key is to believe in yourself, kid."

Believe in myself? Will thought. *They might as well ask me to run a marathon.*

"So is that everything?" Hollywood asked the room. They didn't say anything, just nodded and stared blankly. "Good. Then everyone back to work, and I'll send Will home and on his way to school."

The meeting room cleared out quickly. A few of them produced weak smiles, but no one looked Will straight in the eye.

"You'll have to forgive them," Hollywood said. "They're frightened, and they're not sure that one boy will be enough to turn the tide."

"What do you think?" Will asked.

Hollywood bent down and put a finger under Will's chin. "I've believed in you from the moment I heard your first, fervent wish so many years ago, and I believe in you now. You need to believe it for yourself."

"I'll try," he said with his eyes closed.

"That's the spirit! Now, we're going to send you and Peske back to earth so you can get to school. Don't worry about being late—I'm sure Peske won't give you detention for being tardy ... well, hopefully not. Just remember, be cautious over the next few days. Peske, the others and I will keep watch, but be on your guard should Tang appear. Tomorrow when you're at your mother's office for career day, be on the lookout for any clues concerning Candrissa's ring. If we could find it or either of the other two artifacts, we could bring Moloch's plans to a screeching halt. But don't worry—we'll stop him no matter what."

"No one's going to get hurt, right?"

Hollywood stared into Will's eyes for a long moment. He bowed his head and spoke softly, "The last time we dealt with Moloch, the Equine—an entire race—died. I don't mean to scare you, but I want you to understand the power we're up against. The truth is we might all be facing our last days."

After his visit to Mythos, Will spent the rest of his Tuesday at school jumping at shadows. He thought he saw Tang around every corner. Even though he had no clue what Moloch looked like, he suspected the Genie to be hiding behind every locker, inside every lunchbox and underneath every desk. When Will wasn't looking over his shoulder, he avoided all human contact for fear that someone might be a Genie in disguise. He couldn't stop his mind from running over what might happen on Friday. Could the world as he knew it actually come to an end? Were the Arcanians seriously hoping he'd be their hero? Were they out of their collective minds?

The stress of it all made Will so exhausted that he crashed immediately after he got home. He slept fitfully through dinner and then through the night. He might've slept Wednesday away too if not for a dream about Nonnie going missing.

Will woke with a start, even though it was just dawn. He threw on his robe and darted out of his bedroom. He made a dash for the kitchen when he heard stifled pleas for help. Will turned the corner to find Nonnie there and, just as he'd imagined, she did need help ... opening the pickle jar.

"Look at you," she said, "flying in here with a cape on."

"It's a robe, Nonnie," said Will.

"I think you look like a superhero off to save the world. Could you open my pickle jar first, though? I can't eat my cereal without something tangy on top."

Will forced back a gag but took the jar anyway. He tried prying the lid loose, but it wouldn't budge. Obviously, it wasn't his day for super-strength ... or even normal strength. "Won't ... open," Will said, his eyes bulging from the strain.

Suddenly a hand reached from behind and snatched the jar. Will heard a twist and a pop and then smelled the aroma of pickle juice.

"There ya go," Kaitlyn said, handing the jar to Nonnie. She flashed an enormous smile at Will and then stuck out her tongue at him.

"You loosened it for her," Nonnie said to Will, and then shook her head and mouthed "no way" to Kaitlyn. Nonnie shuffled out of the kitchen with her bowl of Lucky Charms and pickles. It was hard to imagine life without her insanity.

"Oh, man!" Kaitlyn said as she examined the fuzziest sweater Will had ever seen.

"What's wrong? Did that thing just bark at you or something?"

"Very funny. This button just fell off. I was totally going to wear it today. It's bad enough that your class gets to skip out for career day while the rest of us have to go to school, but now I can't even wear my favorite sweater. Life just absolutely sucks."

"Yeah, that's the definition of suckage," Will said as he took the sweater from her hands. "War and famine are for amateurs; real problems come in the form of wardrobe malfunctions."

"You wouldn't understand what it's like trying to look cool. It's a full-time job. You ... you just do your own thing and don't care what people think. I'm not like that."

Will laughed in her face. "Just get me some thread and a needle, okay?"

Kaitlyn pulled open a few drawers and sifted through, finally finding a spool of thread with a needle sticking through it. "Here," she said, tossing it to him, "I think that matches the sweater. But you can't possibly know how to sew it back on."

"Watch me."

Will threaded the needle without even looking at it. He tied the ends with a double-knot, placed the button back on the sweater and went to sewing. In less than two minutes, the button was on and looking better than ever.

"I don't believe it," Kaitlyn mumbled. She gently lifted the sweater out of Will's hands, as if it were an infant. "Thanks, Will!"

Couldn't be super-strength, could it? Really? I'm a seamstress? Ugh and I didn't even wait until someone made a wish ... I did it for free! I'm totally losing it. Maybe I should go make a dress pattern.

"Oh, man!" It wasn't Kaitlyn this time, though the tone was similar. Will's mom was hunched over the coffeemaker, flipping the on/off switch over and over again. "No, I must have coffee! I can't go without it, not today, not when I have to deal with—Will!"

Will had slinked up next to her to see what the problem was. "Hey, Mom."

"Sorry, you scared me. Almost ready to go with me to work?" she said.

"Um, sure, I guess. The coffeemaker's not working?"

"No, and I can't figure out what's wrong with the stupid thing."

"Huh, that's strange. It worked fine yesterday. Can I have a look?" Will unplugged the unit from the electrical outlet and removed the coffeepot and basket. He closed off the water reservoir lid and flipped the whole thing upside down. He pulled a screwdriver out of the junk drawer and quickly took the coffeemaker apart. A glance in the control cavity revealed the problem. "Disconnected wire," he said and reassembled it in the blink of an eye. Will put everything back together and turned it over. He hit the switch, and coffee immediately started dripping into the pot.

"How did you know to do that?" Will's mom clutched her coffee mug to her chest and sighed longingly.

"Will fixed my button too," Kaitlyn said as she munched on Corn Flakes. "He's Mr. Fixit today."

Mr. Fixit! Now that sounded a lot better! Will's Mizm wasn't an extraordinary ability to sew—it was the power to fix anything broken.

"Well thank goodness," Will's mom said. "A cup of coffee is just what I need to keep my day from dragging. Not that having you there is going to be a drag, pumpkin."

Why would she even say that? Bet she really doesn't want me there. I'll just get in the way of her precious work, Will thought.

"Thanks for fixing the coffeemaker, Will, and for helping Kaitlyn too. What would we ever do without you?" said his mother.

You'll find out soon enough. Once my wish is granted, I'm outta here. Will just smiled at his mother and didn't say a word.

During their drive, Will tried to bring up Nonnie several times, but his mother didn't want to hear it. Will assumed his parents would move Nonnie out over the weekend, so that gave him a few days to come up with a plan—he just hoped he wasn't going to be too busy battling the forces of evil to come to his grandmother's rescue.

After arriving at Peach Preserves, they stopped by Mr. Peach's office to say "good morning." The boss took one look at Will and slammed a notebook against his desk. "Pesky insect," he said, quickly switching to a smile. "Career day already?"

Will nodded and stepped behind his mom.

"Welcome aboard, then, young man! There are lots of exciting happenings around here, so I'm sure you'll have a terrific time."

"What ... um, what about my tour?" Will asked.

"Pardon?" Mr. Peach had a bewildered look on his face.

"Remember you promised to show me around?"

"Now, Will, Mr. Peach is terribly busy today." Will's mom shook her head and frowned.

"I'm afraid that is true, my good boy. Our final shipment for the Ancient Prophets collection arrives today, and everyone's running around like mad. You'd think it was the end of the world the way we're carrying on around here!"

Speaking of the end of the world, Will thought. "Any luck tracking down that missing ring?"

"Ah, it's not a missing ring, my lad. *Stolen* ring! Alas, we've had no solid leads yet. I am confident it will turn up soon. Hopefully that rapscallion who took the ring will be made to pay for his crimes. If only the security camera had captured his face so we could make a positive identification. Still, even from behind, there's something familiar about that boy. The way he moves on camera looks so familiar. Of course, that's just not possible. The only boys I even know would be you ... oh, and that friend of yours I met last week. Tang I think it was? Strange name for a child, don't you think, Emily?"

Will's mom and Mr. Peach chatted for a few minutes, mostly about their meetings for the day. As they droned on, Will explored Mr. Peach's office. For a guy whose life revolved around old stuff, he had a lot of high-tech gadgets. In the midst of it all, there was a shoddy, old toy crown. It looked like something a kid might get from a fast food restaurant. It was wrapped in tin foil that was peeling, and fake jewels were glued onto the side. The crown undoubtedly looked ancient, but it was hardly an antique and couldn't have been worth more than a quarter.

"What do you think of my old coronet?" Mr. Peach interrupted his conversation to ask Will.

"Oh, the crown? It's, um … different."

"Huh," Will's mom said, tapping her nose. "I don't think I've ever noticed that."

"Your father—Will's grandfather—gave it to me," said Mr. Peach.

"Really?" they both said, suddenly wide-eyed.

"It was a silly trinket he picked up during one of his visits to Paris. He said that beneath the gaudy exterior was a great story, which made the worthless crown priceless … to him, at least. It took me a long time to learn that lesson, and sometimes I still need reminding of it. In a way, this crown is representative of that and other mistakes I've made in my life. I keep it nearby so I never forget them. I have no intention of repeating the past." Mr. Peach picked up the crown and polished one of the jewels.

Will had a near uncontrollable urge to hold the crown, but Mr. Peach shoved it into a desk drawer.

"Oh, by the way, Emily, your assistant called in sick this morning. Today of all days. I had a temp come in as I'm sure you'll need the help."

"Thanks for thinking about me. You're right—I've got mounds of papers to get through," she said.

"Don't thank me just yet," said Mr. Peach. "I haven't met the girl, but rumors are floating around the office that she's an odd bird."

*

The temp was at the desk just outside his mom's office. Her skin was a dark mahogany instead of blue, and her wild silver hair was pulled back into a bun, but it was clearly Reverie.

"Good morning, Mrs. Cricket," Reverie said in her throaty, sultry voice. "I'm your temp, Gladiola Jones. But everyone calls me 'Rev.'"

"'Rev', is that short for something?"

"It's short for Gladiola. Obviously." Reverie reached out to shake hands with Will's mom. Remembering the effects of Reverie's handshake when he first met her, Will gave his mother a shove toward her open door. "No time for pleasantries," he said. "Lots to do! Right, Mom?"

She gave him a nasty look. "Will, you're being rude! Fortunately for you, I do have tons of work. Otherwise, I'd take you out back and—"

"Sure, sounds great. Hey, let's do lunch, 'kay?" Will slammed the door on his mom, hoping for a few minutes alone with Reverie. Will's mom didn't come back out, and he soon heard her listening to voicemail messages.

"I have clean hands today, Will," Reverie said, holding them up for Will's inspection. "Nothing would've happened."

"I can't be too careful around you people." Will situated himself on top of her desk. "What're you doing here?"

"They needed someone to keep an eye on you today ... I got the job. Norv and Hollywood are, as you might imagine, working nonstop to find Tangible and Moloch. I don't think they've gotten a wink of ..." She yawned and said, "sleep."

"Speaking of sleep, how are you going to make it through the day without passing out? No offense, but you usually can't make it through a whole sentence without a nap."

Reverie tugged at her earlobe. There was a tiny earpiece inside. "I'm listening to a recorded speech Norv gave at last year's Mythosian Lawyers Association convention in Chicago. It lasted eight hours. Talk about boring."

"Just what you need to keep you on your toes," said Will. "So listen. While Mom's locked away with her work, I was hoping you could fill me in on a few details."

Reverie's eyes drooped a little. "Details? I'm afraid I don't know anything more about Tangible than what you've already been told."

"Not that ... I've been thinking about Moloch. I totally get how he plans to use all that power to take over my world ... but how exactly does that affect *your* world? I mean, everybody keeps talking about the Frost Epidemic and how the Equine died, but I don't understand how it happened. Would you mind telling me about it?"

"No, I won't tell you."

"Oh. Well, I didn't mean to offend—"

"You don't need to be told. You need to be shown." Reverie stretched out her neck and looked down the hallway. "Doesn't look like anyone's around."

"Yeah, they're probably all at the warehouse getting ready for that delivery."

"Good. This should only take ... five minutes." She pulled a compact from her purse and flipped it open but not to touch up her makeup.

"Hey! That's sleeping dust!" Will said in a hushed whisper.

"I said I didn't have any on my hands; I never said I didn't bring any with me."

"What're you gonna do? How's taking a nap supposed to show me anything?"

"Dreams are a pathway to all times, William—past, present and future. Don't worry. I'll be with you the whole way." Reverie pulled out her earpiece and her eyes immediately went heavy. She took a single spec of sleeping dust and flicked it right into Will's eye. Four seconds later, both Will and Reverie were laid out on the desk sound asleep.

"Where are we?" Will asked.

"You've been here plenty of times before, Will. This is the world of dreams." Reverie's skin was not only blue again, but it shimmered like the remnants of a shooting star. "Dreamworld connects all places to all times, allowing us to travel as far as our souls will afford."

They were alone on a white-sand beach. Quiet waves washed up a seashell, and a hot but welcome sun blazed overhead. If Will didn't know better, he'd have sworn they were in paradise ... or at least the Bahamas.

"We're in Africa," said Reverie, staring off into the ocean. "We're still in Dreamworld, of course, so this is more like a recreation of Africa ... but it's a very accurate recreation. It's 1802, and this is a British colony called Sierra Leone. Its population was made up of freed slaves, and its capital was, appropriately enough, called Freetown. As you might imagine, this was a bold time of change for the entire world. Then, Moloch came."

Reverie waved her fingers, and the air suddenly rippled. The beach transformed before Will's eyes—the sand turned gray, and the waves stopped all movement. There were no sounds of birds squawking or fish splashing, but there was noise, and it was horrible. There were backbreaking moans, terrified screams and pained pleas for mercy ... hundreds of them.

Reverie ushered Will up a large sand dune. "Moloch had allied himself with seven powerful Genies. Together they found the three long-lost Tokens of Tenet, including the ring of Candrissa. But Moloch betrayed the seven, slaying them all and siphoning off their rich wishcraft energies. With it, he was able to cast a spell over the entire continent, making himself ruler over nearly everyone who lived here."

Will and Reverie came to the top of the sand dune, and Will's stomach lurched. There were hundreds of people—all of them subject to some manner of torture. Several were buried up to their necks in the sand as fire ants inched their way within biting distance. Others were suspended in midair. They spun this way and that, only being allowed to stop when they were so sick they had to vomit. A few children were out in the water surrounded by dozens of frenzied sharks.

"We've gotta do something, Rev." Will started to march down the hill, but Reverie grabbed his arm.

"It's only a dream, William. You and I are like mist to them as they are to us. Besides, this is all in the past; we're here to change the future. To do that, you must learn."

Amidst the tortured crowd, a young man appeared. He wasn't one of them—his skin was lighter and olive, and his hair was down to his shoulders. He was older than Will, but still a teenager.

"Who's that?" Will squinted as the boy approached those buried in the sands.

"His name is Sol. He was an Omni."

"Like me?"

"More than you know." For the first time since entering the Dreamworld, Reverie had a hint of a smile. "He's here to stop Moloch."

Sol outstretched a hand, and the buried Freetowners suddenly sprung upward, as if catapulted out of the ground. The creatures surrounding them were flung high into the air, and Will never saw them come back down. Sol turned his attention to the frantic children in the water, and with his power he plucked them from the ocean and safely deposited them back on land. In turn, he gave the heavens a stern look, and those tossed around in midair slowly drifted back to solid ground. In barely a minute's time, they were all out of harm's way.

"He did it!" Will exclaimed. "He saved them all!"

"They were safe but only for the moment. He had to go on to face Moloch. The outcome of that battle would determine the fate of these people," said Reverie.

"You guys helped him fight and learn how to use his powers?"

"At this point in history, Sol had learned to cultivate and control the Mizms on his own. We had been there when they first developed as we've been with you. As for the actual war against Moloch, Hollywood and a few others did stand alongside young Sol. But most Arcanians were busy with another kind of battle. Come. It's time to see the effects of Moloch's ravaging on my world." She grabbed Will's hand, took a leap off the top of the sand dune, and together they vanished.

Reverie and Will reappeared on a snowy landscape. A frozen lake lay before them, and mounds of snow several feet high surrounded them in almost every direction. Enormous hail rained down but fortunately passed right through their dream-bodies.

"Reverie?" Will clutched his torso. "I thought this was only a dream. The snow isn't touching me, but I feel so cold."

"Such is the nature of the power Moloch unleashed here."

"Where are we exactly? And when are we going to Mythos?"

"We're in Mythos, William, well, at least the Dreamworld's version of it. This was Mythos 200 years ago, a veritable wasteland of ice." Reverie led him through a wall of snow. On the other side, Will saw the SCENE building. It was covered in giant icicles that stretched from its roof down seven floors to the ground.

"So this is the Frost Epidemic? The one that killed the Equine?"

" ... Yes." Reverie looked westward, the same direction in which Heiko had stared during yesterday's meeting.

"Is that where they lived?"

"Equine are ... were woodland creatures. The Frost overtook our world so quickly that they didn't have time to seek shelter. They died almost instantly."

A stiff wind blew by and cut through Will's body, intangible as it was. "What caused this to happen?"

"Oddly enough, it was the wishes themselves that created all of this. As I'm sure Hollywood explained, most excess wishe+s that we can't or won't grant come here and take root. When Moloch demonstrated to the people of Africa that he was a Genie bent on revenge for all of the wishes he'd been forced to grant by human masters, all of those people suddenly believed in the power of wishcraft. They *all* started making wishes; granted, most were pleas to be rid of Moloch, but there were still an overwhelming number of them. Everybody wanted something. We Arcanians couldn't handle the bombardment; the wish energy overflowed into Mythos causing the biggest ice storm in our history."

"That's why Peske and Heiko kept telling me to be careful with my power, to make sure that no one found out about your people." Will inched closer to Reverie for warmth, and continued, "But if letting people know about Mythos and the Arcanians is all it takes to hurt your world, why doesn't Moloch just go around telling everybody?"

"You humans are a strange, cynical lot. You can't simply tell them something and expect them to buy into it. They have to see to believe. And even then, most humans will find some way to dismiss it. Unless they experience it firsthand.

"In the present, Moloch's power isn't strong enough to convince such a large group of people of the existence of wishcraft today—especially not before alerting us to his whereabouts, which is the last thing he wants to do. After all, the destruction of Mythos is not Moloch's main goal. He may despise my people, but he absolutely abhors humanity. He wants your entire world under his thumb. If Mythos is destroyed in the process, all the better for him, but that's only secondary."

"If he's so weak and the Arcanians are so powerful, why are we worried?"

"As before, he plans to absorb enough power to grant his own wish. After that, we Arcanians will be insignificant in comparison. That leaves only one person to stop him, Will: you."

Will gulped. "So no pressure, then."

"We have every confidence you'll succeed. Omnis are a hearty bunch." Reverie swiped her hand through the air, and the snowstorm halted. She twirled a finger round and round, and suddenly the landscape changed. It was like standing in the middle of a movie on fast forward. The ice rapidly melted, revealing a dried up, near-dead world. Even that disappeared in a split second, making way for the vibrant Mythos Will knew and loved.

"Looks like your world recovered pretty quickly after Moloch was defeated."

"What you just saw took 30 years to accomplish in real time. To this day, Mythos still hasn't completely healed."

Blades of grass rustled from a gentle breeze and a herd of winged cougars flew overhead. Mythos seemed like a happy place again ... except for the dead patch of land to the west. "If so many people knew about the wishing world, why didn't they keep making wishes after Moloch was stopped?"

"We got lucky. When Sol defeated Moloch, the Tokens of Tenet were hidden in such a way that even those who hid them didn't know their locations. Moloch was imprisoned in his lamp, but first we siphoned the excess power he'd stolen. Removing wish-energy from an Arcanian has never been a stable process, especially when it wasn't theirs to begin with. There was an explosion that caused a backlash of wishing energy to sweep across most of Africa. The memory of the entire event was wiped from their minds."

"Even after all of that, he might have the three items again."

"It seems terribly likely, yes. In point of fact, we don't even know how Moloch escaped his lamp. Perhaps that's where Tangible came in to play. He did steal the ring, after all."

Will couldn't help but shake his head. "Are we absolutely sure? Tang was my best friend. I can't believe he'd—"

"Genies are masters at hiding in plain sight—that includes hiding their true personalities. I'm so sorry he betrayed you ... and all of us. But you have to be prepared. You may very well face him again before this is all over. You must be ready and wide awake."

"You're sleeping?!" shouted Will's mom.

Will jolted at the sound of his mother's voice. He was awake, back in the real world. Reverie woke up too, though much more slowly. Will checked his watch—they'd been out only five minutes, just as Rev had promised.

"Oh, hi, Mom. We were just—"

"You were snoring so loudly, the third floor called to complain."

Reverie popped back in her earpiece and immediately livened up. "It was an innocent power nap. It helps one get through those sluggish times of the day."

"It's barely nine o'clock in the morning!" Will's mother's ears turned beet red. "What's going to happen when three o'clock rolls around? Are we going to have to bring out cots and sleeping bags?"

"I'm scheduled 'til three?"

"Until five!"

"Oh boy." Reverie slumped over her desk and stuck out her bottom lip.

"Look, Rev," Will's mom said as she took slow deep breaths. "You can start on some filing I have in my office. Will, I need you to run this paperwork to Mr. Peach. Do you remember how to get there?"

Will grabbed the papers from his mom and said, "Sure, no problem." He gave Reverie a reassuring wink and took off down the hallway.

When he got to the office, Mr. Peach and his assistant Charlie were giggling like schoolgirls. Will quietly peeked around the corner to see what had them so excited.

"This is it! The last piece of the Ancient Prophets collection! After all of these years, we've finally found it!" Mr.

Peach held something in his hands, but with his back to the door so that Will couldn't make it out.

"It's amazing, sir," said Charlie. "Have you contacted the buyer? I'm sure he can't wait to take possession of it."

"He's anxious, to put it mildly." He held the item at eye-level, and Will could see an orange glow surround it. Mr. Peach placed it on his desk and took several steps back, his eyes wholly focused on it.

Finally, Will could see it. The artifact was a shiny crystal in the shape of a flame. It was fire orange and pulsed, as if it really burned. It was mesmerizing.

"Everyone said this treasure was lost in a sea of sand. I can't believe we found it." Mr. Peach rubbed his hands together with glee.

"It's hard to fathom that the opal was shaped like this when it was first discovered, sir."

"It is a phenomenal oddity of nature. You can almost feel the power coursing under its crystalline surface. It's even warm to the touch."

Charlie extended a hand toward the artifact, but as soon as he grazed it, he yelped and pulled away, as though he'd been burned. The jerking motion sent the artifact into a spin. It tipped over the side of the desk. Mr. Peach dashed for it, but it slipped past him and crashed against the concrete floor. There was a cracking sound. From even the doorway, Will could see a tiny fracture now ran down its side.

"You fool!" Mr. Peach threw a hand in the air, as though he might strike.

Charlie immediately dropped to his knees and scooped up the fire-like opal, only he didn't wince at its touch this time. "Mr. Peach, sir, I'm terribly sorry. It was an accident. It was so hot before ... I don't understand why it's cold now. Please, sir, don't be angry."

"Anger doesn't begin to describe how I feel. If you had any idea of the potential catastrophe you have unleashed, you would be groveling for your job and even your life! I should—" Mr. Peach raised a hand at Charlie but stopped. Out of the corner of his eye, he caught Will's spying gaze.

Will gasped and jerked his head out of sight. He heard Mr. Peach say, "Find a way to fix that crack immediately, or you'll find yourself immediately unemployed!"

Mr. Peach stomped out of his office but stopped in the hallway and stared down at Will. He glared beadily at the boy, and Will thought for a moment that he might get yelled at too; but Mr. Peach turned up his nose and marched out of sight.

Will heard Charlie half-sobbing, half-talking to himself. "Can't afford to lose this job ... got to find a way to make Mr. Peach happy. This fracture ... I'll never fix it ... I wouldn't even know where to start." *I ... I wish there was someone who could help me repair the opal ... for Mr. Peach.*

This is a job for Mr. Fix-it! Will thought. *And this time there's an actual wish. If anybody deserves a helping hand, it's this poor guy. Mr. Peach was a complete jerk to Charlie.*

Will poked his head around the corner. "Hey. You're Charlie, right?"

"Yeah," he nodded, wiping tears off his cheeks. "You're Mrs. Cricket's son?"

"That's me. My name's Will. Sorry to bother you, but it looks like you've got a problem on your hands."

"You can say that again."

"Looks like you've got a—"

"I didn't mean for you to literally say it again."

"Oh, right, sure. Well, anyway, I'd be glad to lend a hand if you like."

Charlie rubbed his eyes and shook his head. "No offense, kid, but I don't think an Elmer's glue stick is going to do the job."

"Ouch, Charlie. That really hurt. And it's still hurting." Will walked over and ran his finger along the opal's crack. "Actually, I thought we'd place a thin gold plate in the fissure and bond it to the opal. After that, polish up the area with a fine abrasive, and it'd be as good as new ... good as gold, even."

Charlie did a double take at Will. "You ... you really know what you're talking about, don't you?"

Will grinned and gave him a thumbs-up. "What are we waiting for? Let's go take a crack at it! Get it? Crack!"

Charlie didn't laugh.

For the next few hours, the two worked in the Peach Preserves' laboratory. All of the necessary equipment was on hand, so the process couldn't have gone more smoothly. They toiled away through the noon hour, and by the time Mr. Peach had returned from lunch, Will and Charlie were ready to unveil the new and improved opal.

Hesitantly, Charlie knocked on Mr. Peach's open door.

"Come in and that thing better be fixed, or you're dead meat," he said without looking up from a stack of papers.

Charlie walked in cautiously, as if he expected the office floor to be booby-trapped. "Sir, Mr. Peach, sir. The opal—it's been repaired."

Mr. Peach shot up out of his chair. "Really?"

"Y-yes, sir. No flaws at all. You'd never know that the opal had been damaged." His hands shook, but Charlie carefully passed the opal to his boss.

"Remarkable!" Mr. Peach held the opal to the light. It glowed again, just as it had before the accident. "I thought I was going to have to call in a specialist. Charlie, you've surprised me, and that never happens."

"Th-thank you, sir. I didn't do it alone. Mrs. Cricket's son lent a hand. Actually, it was his idea altogether." Charlie stepped aside and waved for Will to join him in the office.

"William," Mr. Peach said, as if his name was the answer to a riddle. "You fixed this yourself?"

Will fumbled with the buttons on his shirt and said, "I'm not sure I'd put it quite like that, but yes, um, sir, I helped Charlie put it back together."

"I can't tell you how much I appreciate your ingenuity and take-charge attitude, William. Rest assured, your mother will hear of your excellent performance, and perhaps we'll even put you on the payroll this week." Mr. Peach grinned at Will, bearing all of his perfectly white teeth. "And Charlie, my dear boy ... you're fired. Clean out your desk and leave immediately."

"What?!" Will and Charlie said in unison.

"You heard me." Mr. Peach's nose flared. He was talking to Charlie but staring right at Will. "I had hoped you'd redeem yourself of your earlier incompetence, but instead you turn to a boy to do your work for you. I need an assistant, not an infant who must be coddled and looked after! Now get out before I have security remove you!"

Charlie tore out of the office and could be heard bawling as he ran down the hallway.

"That's not fair," Will said, but meekly.

Mr. Peach was sitting again, already back to work. "You're still here? I'm rather busy, William, so please run along and raid the candy machines ... or whatever it is that boys of your size do."

Will took a step backwards. His obligation to Charlie was over. Will had granted the guy's wish; it wasn't his fault Mr. Peach was a mean, old goat. He couldn't afford to make his mother's boss cross, after all. That wouldn't be exactly smart, now would it?

"He did what you asked him to do, though, and you still fired him. I ... I know it's not my place to say so, but it just doesn't seem right what you did to Charlie." The words unexpectedly spilled out of Will.

Mr. Peach put his pen back in the ink well and looked thoughtfully at Will. "You're right, my boy, you're absolutely right ... it's *not* your place to say so."

"But, sir, he's a really nice hard-working guy who was doing the best he could."

"His best clearly wasn't good enough. Now kindly leave my office before—"

"Please, just give him one more chance, Mr. Peach."

"Enough!" Mr. Peach pounded a fist on his desk, and the opal lit up like a bonfire had ignited from inside. The light quickly faded, but Mr. Peach's anger didn't. "I will not suffer insolent children to tell me how to run my business! As highly as I think of your mother, I will tolerate no further disrespect from you, young man!"

Will was on the verge of tears when a familiar voice said, "What's going on in here?" It was Will's mom.

Thank goodness, Will thought. *She'll make Mr. Peach listen to reason. She definitely won't let him talk to her son like that.*

"William Sherman Cricket," she said, "how dare you speak so disrespectfully to Mr. Peach?"

Will blinked at his mom. "What?"

"I raised you better than to back talk to your elders. And my boss, of all people. Will, I'm really disappointed in you."

"Mom, you don't understand. Charlie and I—"

"Charlie isn't your concern. This is Mr. Peach's company, and he runs it extremely well. I'm ... I'm so sorry about this, Lincoln. Believe me when I say Will is going to be severely punished."

Any reprimand Will's mom may have cooked up was nothing compared to the harsh news Will found awaiting him when they arrived home from Peach Preserves that evening.

"What do you mean 'Nonnie's gone?'" Will said as his dinner fork became increasingly heavier in his grip.

"Your mom and I thought it would be easier if I took her to the nursing home while you and Kaitlyn were away during the day. We'll go see her this weekend, so don't worry about that. We got her all settled in with almost no drama." The icepack Will's father held to his forehead implied otherwise.

After a painfully quiet dinner, Will wandered outside to wish on the first star he saw. When he stepped into his backyard, another type of star awaited him. Hollywood stared off into the distant night, maybe looking for a cousin or a sibling. There was no light in his face, however. He flinched as Will approached, but he didn't look down at the boy.

"Hollywood?" Will said. "My parents are right inside. If they see you out here—"

"Your folks will be getting a call in a few minutes. I wanted to tell you first. Prepare you." He closed his eyes, took a deep breath and broke his gaze from the heavens. "There was a fire tonight at the nursing home."

Will's body suddenly froze. He couldn't move or speak, but his hearing seemed amplified.

"I personally went to investigate. They had no clue how the fire started, but it was rather odd given that they'd just installed a state-of-the-art fire suppression system last week. I asked about Nonnie—Sylvia—but she was the only person unaccounted for. So I sprinted into the smoldering building to check out her room for myself."

"Wait a second," Will said, finally able to speak. "You knew her room number? You already knew she was there, and you didn't tell me?" Will tightened his fists. His heart thudded in his ears.

"It's not like that, Will. Yes, I knew Nonnie was there, but it's my job to know everything about you and yours. I also know the old girl can take care of herself."

"But *I* didn't know! I should've stopped this, but I thought I had more time, and now she may be hurt or even worse all because of me!" Will sniffled.

"None of this is your fault. Unfortunately, it would appear you're indirectly involved, though. When I got to the room, I found five long burn marks along the wall, and the floor was covered in ash."

"You don't think she's ..." He couldn't bring himself to finish the question.

"No, we don't think that at all. Unfortunately, it might be worse. You see, those five marks looked like someone had clawed through the concrete. That's the mark of the ring of Candrissa. It was used in your grandmother's room."

"Tang?" Will asked, almost hopefully.

"Our instruments recorded a spike of high-level Genie activity in that area around the same time the fire started. It was too powerful to be Tangible. We think it was Moloch. From the looks of it, he's kidnapped your Nonnie."

When Will signed his SCENE contract a week ago, he'd imagined that on the morning of his final wish-granting day, he'd be the happiest boy alive. Now that Thursday was finally here, he felt even worse than he had before the whole mess had started.

Nonnie was missing, kidnapped by a malevolent Genie bent on subjugating all of mankind. Will hadn't heard from Hollywood or any of the others since the wish agent had left Will yesterday evening with reassurance that the SCENE was redoubling its efforts to find Moloch. He had no idea why the Genie would want to kidnap his crazy grandmother, but he had a strong suspicion that he'd done it as an assault on Will. Moloch must've learned from Tang that Will was an Omni being trained by the SCENE to help in the Genie's takedown. Worst of all, Will couldn't tell anyone about it—not the police who were looking for her or his parents who were worried sick.

Moloch had made a serious mistake. Before, Will had agreed to help the SCENE because the freedom of the entire planet was at stake. Now it was personal. Nonnie was family—at least for another day or two—and he owed it to her and his parents to bring her home safely.

Will turned over in bed, and an arm belonging to Kaitlyn crashed against his face. He and his sister had spent the night in their parents' bed, something neither had done in years. Kaitlyn was still asleep, though he was sure she hadn't slept more than an hour or two all night. Will's dad was still in bed too, but he thrashed around.

Will didn't remember his mother ever coming to bed. Gently lifting Kaitlyn's arm off his head, he quietly crept out of the bedroom in search of his mom.

He found her in the kitchen, hunched over a laptop and a legal-sized notepad. She was talking on the telephone when he came in the room.

"So there's no one there matching her name or description?" she said. "Yes, I realize I just called an hour ago, but I'm going to keep calling you and every other person I can think of every hour until I find my mother ... Yeah, thanks."

"Hey, Mom," he said as she hung up, cautiously stepping toward her. "Did you get any rest last night?"

"Too much to do," said his mother. "I've called all the hospitals and police stations in Corinth and the surrounding areas. I've been on the phone with the nursing home, coordinating the search."

Will noticed a set of keys on the breakfast nook. "You've been out looking? Why didn't you tell us? We would've come too."

"You kids need your rest. Besides, none of this would've happened if not for me. It's all my fault." Will's mom buried her face in her hands. She didn't cry, but she looked like she might shatter at the slightest touch.

"No, Mom, don't blame yourself." Even as he said it, Will blamed her and his father and himself too. Mostly himself.

"I thought she'd become too much of a burden," said his mother. "I'm so stupid. She's family, my own mother. How could I so easily write off someone I love? What was I thinking?"

Will's stomach did cartwheels. "Don't worry, Mom. We'll all be out looking for Nonnie today and hanging signs and doing everything we can."

Will's mom pushed herself out of the chair and lugged over to the coffeemaker. "You and Kaitlyn have school today."

"But, Mom—"

"Don't argue with me. Not right now," she snapped. "Mr. Peach gave me the day off, so your Dad and I will take care of everything."

"That's great and all, but I really think I could help."

"William, please. I have enough on my plate without a tantrum from you. Do as I ask, okay? I'll feel better knowing you and Kaitlyn are going about your regular routine. Nonnie wouldn't want you missing school. She wants the two of you getting a good education. Now please, if you never do what I ask again, at least do this for me today."

"Fine," Will grumbled. He marched to his bedroom to appease his mom, but he had no intention of going to school. He'd start his own search, or—better yet—he'd hook up with Hollywood and see what they'd discovered. If his parents thought he was going about life as usual, they were nuts.

As soon as Will closed his bedroom door, his television set blinked on. "Hello? Hello? Is this thing on? Can anyone hear me?" It was Peske's voice. An image of the back of his head faded in and out.

"Peske, turn around, I'm over here," Will whispered to the TV set.

The lawyer turned around and smashed his nose into the glass. "Oh, there you are, William. I hate this contraption of Hollywood's, but none of us has time to meet you in person."

"So you're not going to be at school today?" Will asked, hopeful.

"No ... but *you* will be."

"Aw, come on, not you too! I can't go to school today. Nonnie is missing, and we know that creep Moloch took her. I'm supposed to help you guys with him, remember?"

Peske waved a finger. "Yes, William, we all know you're the vaunted Omni, here to save the world from the big bad Genie. But his plans won't come to fruition until tomorrow, the Day of the Divine. Since we're relying so heavily on you, it's a necessity that you grant your seventh wish today. You need the experience, of that I'm sure."

"I could grant a wish somewhere other than school. I could do it while I search for Nonnie."

"We need you to fully concentrate on your wish-granting and the mastering of your Mizms, William. If you're not prepared for tomorrow, then it won't even matter if your Nonnie is found. The whole planet may be doomed. So you're to stick to your contract ... and remember, it is binding."

"I have to go to school today, but you don't?"

"William, I'm helping Hollywood search for Nonnie. We're *all* searching for her, every last SCENE employee."

"Oh." Will stared blankly into the TV screen. The SCENE's vast resources and personnel were being funneled toward finding Will's grandmother. With hundreds of Arcanians on the job, she'd probably be found by noon. Maybe Peske was right for a change. Maybe Will could do the most good by learning to better control his powers. Goodness knows he needed all the help he could get. "Okay, fine," he said reluctantly. "I'll go to school, grant my last wish, and then I get to help."

"I'm sooooo looking forward to that," said Peske.

Will flicked off the TV before Peske could say anything more.

*

On the way to school, something happened to Will that he thought would never take place, not in a million years: Kaitlyn walked beside him.

They didn't talk or even look at one another, but it still felt nice to Will. The quiet walk to school gave him a chance to think about his Mizm as the crisp November wind reddened his cheeks. He tried all sorts of things: reading Kaitlyn's mind, telekinetically lifting a stray cat into the air and traveling out of his own body, but nothing clicked.

Not only was Will still stumped when he got to school, he had a special welcoming party waiting for him on the steps to the front entrance.

"So, girls," Cheerleader Penelope Petrillo said as Will and Kaitlyn walked by. "Did you hear that they were finally able to feed all those starving kids in Ethiopia? Apparently Will Cricket skipped a meal yesterday, so there was enough food left over for an entire country!"

Oddly enough, Will's pulse didn't race. His face didn't go flush. He had real problems to worry about—their words meant nothing to him. Even as he shrugged it off, his sister jumped directly in front of Will, like she was ready to take a bullet for him.

"Leave him alone," Kaitlyn suddenly said. Her freckles flared up, but her head was raised high. She stuck a finger in Penelope's face and stared into her beady eyes. No one said a word or moved a muscle for a long moment. Finally, the cheerleaders blinked and took a collective step back.

Kaitlyn snatched Will by the arm and marched up the school steps. A few kids clapped and whistled. Will rubbed his eyes and stared at his sister.

"What?" said Kaitlyn.

"Hi, I'm Will," he said. "I don't think we've met."

"Oh, shut up." Kaitlyn tried her best, but she couldn't suppress a smile.

★

Since Peske was occupied with the search for Nonnie, Will had high hopes that a normal substitute might fill in. No such luck—Mrs. Griswald was back! If the scowl that covered her face was any indication, it was going to be a long day.

Her eyes locked onto Will as soon as he crossed the threshold. "Take a seat. We're almost ready to get started."

Will did as he was told. He'd just pulled out his Green Lantern Trapper Keeper when Connor, Mason and Benji surrounded him. Will bowed his head and cringed in anticipation.

"Hey, Will," Connor said, "we heard about your grandma on the news."

"Yeah," said Mason, "we just wanted to tell you that we're sorry and that we hope they find her soon."

From behind the other boys, Benji waddled up and said, "Yeah, man, if there's anything you need ... I mean, just, uh, let us know."

Will didn't know how to react. He tried to say something, but the words got caught in his throat. He gave them a nod and a quiet, thin smile.

"It's okay, man," Connor said. "You don't got to say nothing."

"We all got grandmas. I wouldn't want anything to happen to mine," said Mason.

"We don't want anything to happen to yours either," said Benji.

Finally, Will cleared his throat and said, "Thanks. Everyone's looking for her, so we'll find her. Just ... thanks for saying that."

"Back to your seats, boys," Mrs. Griswald ordered as she fidgeted with her chair.

"We'll catch ya later, Will," said Connor, giving him a nod.

As Will sat in amazement, the rest of the class quieted down. After a few days away, Will expected Mrs. Griswald to have thought of at least a dozen new ways to make everyone miserable—especially him.

"Everyone, please get your geography books and turn to page 172. I've got a handout to go along with the reading." She shuffled around her uncharacteristically disorganized desk for the papers, taking a long minute to find them.

Will scratched his head. No pop quiz over something they hadn't studied? No threats of bodily harm? Since when did she use the word "please?"

"Excuse me, Mrs. Griswald," Will said, "I just wanted to make sure you were feeling okay, you know, since you were out all week. You're not still, um, sick are you?"

Mrs. Griswald shook her head. "No, Will, no, I'm just fine."

It suddenly hit Will—Mrs. Griswald was still at least partially suffering from a fear of children. The SCENE had probably intended for her phobia to last the whole week since Peske was supposed to be undercover at the school through at least today. Given the way her hands shook every time a student asked a question, Will guessed she wasn't quite recovered yet. He could have so much fun with this.

Will jumped from his desk and approached the front of the room. Mrs. Griswald clutched at her heart. Will thought he'd give her a big hug under the guise of welcoming her back. He could hardly wait to hear her squeal in terror. But as he got closer, he thought less about revenge and the pleasure he'd take from it, and more about the cold fear in her eyes.

He continued to approach Mrs. Griswald but more slowly. As he reached her desk, he said, "I'll hand those papers out for you, Mrs. G. Don't worry. I'll help with anything you need today. You don't even have to leave your desk."

Without a word, the hard and ancient walrus-like woman turned the handouts over to Will. Her mouth quivered, and she tried to say something but nothing came out.

Will whispered, "You're welcome."

Even though loads of kids were being unusually kind to Will, he didn't feel like being surrounded by people at lunch. Any other time, he'd welcome the opportunity to make new friends, but he needed to concentrate on a plan to rescue Nonnie—that, and grant a wish, of course.

Will walked the lonely hallway toward the principal's office in hopes of using a phone to check the progress of the search. But he never made it to the office. His Telewishing ability kicked into high gear, and his mind was flooded by a single thought: *I wish somebody would keep Duncan from getting clobbered!*

"Oh jeez," Will said to himself. "Not again. Can't Diego take off one day?"

Will tried to ignore the wish, but the guilt pangs in his chest drove him batty. He turned on his heels toward the locker rooms. Thanks to the Telewishing, Will knew the precise location of the wish. He jutted down a side hall and headed for the indoor basketball court. As he approached the outlying locker rooms, he heard more commotion, so he picked up the pace and actually jogged the rest of the distance.

When he arrived, there was a fairly large crowd huddled around the entrance to the boys' lockers. Some chanted, others laughed, but most simply watched with expressions of dread. In the center of the madness, Will could make out Diego manhandling scrawny little Duncan Sapp.

Will still had no idea what his power was for the day. He tried moving his legs forward, but they shook so badly he couldn't budge. He gulped hard and backed away from the scene. He slowly put one foot behind the other—he didn't want any part of this, not without the benefit of a super-enhancing Mizm.

As he stepped backwards, the same wish as before entered his mind. *I wish somebody would keep Duncan from getting clobbered!* This time, however, he could tell who was making the wish. Will's jaw dropped. His eyes blinked furiously in disbelief. The wisher was Diego!

Will watched the bully's gaze dart around the crowd. He could see beads of sweat rolling down Diego's forehead. Will had no idea what his intentions were, but the wish didn't lie—Diego wanted someone to stop him.

Hoping that reason might have a chance of winning the day, Will suddenly found himself right behind Diego. The bully had lifted Duncan almost four feet off the ground. Jerritt was right there too, cheering on Diego and laughing his usual horse-like laugh. The whole crowd went silent when they saw Will reach up and tap Diego on the shoulder.

"Excuse me, Diego. How about letting Sapp run?"

The bully lowered Duncan to the floor and spun to face Will. "Well, well. This must be my lucky day. Two dorks for the price of one." Diego kept one hand on Duncan and grabbed Will with the other.

It wasn't the reaction Will had expected. "Whoa, hang on, big fella. I really don't think you want to do this!"

Jerritt snorted, "Forget it, Willy! You're barking up the wrong side of the bed."

"Shut your mouths, the both of you," Diego said. "It's too late. No turning back now." *I wish ... I wish I hadn't gotten myself into another mess.*

"Diego, you should listen to me," Will said, taking a deep breath.

"Sure, fine, whatever. This should be interesting. You gonna beg for your life, worm?" *Stupid ballet—I wish I wasn't so thick and clumsy—makes me so angry!*

Will leaned in close to Diego and whispered, "I know why you're mad all the time, why you pick on everyone."

The bully's grip on Will tightened. "You better shut up."

"No one else can hear me," Will said, his teeth chattering. "Your secret's safe with me. I know you love ballet. I know they kicked you out of your class."

Diego turned Duncan loose and wound up his free arm. He shook his fist in Will's face and yelled, "Shut up, you stupid loser! You don't know nothing!"

The crowd gasped and climbed over one another to get a look at the impending action. Will shut one eye and braced himself for a pounding, but nothing happened. Diego's fist was still in Will's face, but it shook nervously.

"I know what it's like," Will said softly. "Getting rejected or ignored or picked on—believe me, I know. But you're only making things worse."

Diego gave the crowd a hard stare and slowly dropped his fist. In a hushed tone, he said, "So what—are you blackmailing me? You keep your yap shut about the ballet, and I lay off you and the Sapp?"

"I just need to do what's right."

"You're insane, Cricket. Why are you being nice? And how in the world could you help me? Think you can wave a magic wand and grant all my wishes?"

Will laughed to himself. "It's not that easy. I thought I could be your friend. It helps to have one when things get rough."

"You? My friend?" Diego scoffed. "Having a friend isn't going to get me out of this. Look, I admit I don't wanna hurt the pipsqueak. I don't even wanna hurt you ... much. I'm just so mad. It's not fair."

"Just walk away. No one's going to make fun of you. They might even respect you a little." Will nodded encouragingly.

Diego squinted at Will for a long moment. He looked at his fists and back at Will's face. Finally he said, "Sorry, I'm not like you, Cricket. I gotta do what's best for me. I won't be dancing lead in the Nutcracker, but I'll always be the biggest and baddest Lamone Pledge has ever seen."

Diego's fist soared through the air so quickly, Will didn't have time to brace for impact. There was a swishing sound as the bully's knuckles cut through the air. Then BAM! Will's jaw took the hit, and it was enough to land an elephant in the hospital ... but all Will felt was a tiny sting.

Suddenly Diego let out an enormous wail. The bully dropped to his knees, tears rolling down his face. Diego clutched his limp punching hand while Jerritt ran circles around him in panic. The other kids gasped in disbelief, too shocked to say anything.

Duncan was half puzzled and half ecstatic. "Will, are you okay?"

There wasn't a scratch on Will, not a drop of blood. "Um, yeah, I'm ... yeah."

Just as Will began to wonder how he survived the blow, he felt a tingling sensation run from his ears down to his big toes—his Mizm for the day was fading. *Invulnerable,* Will thought. *All day long, I've been impervious to harm, but didn't know it. Nothing could've hurt me, not even—*

"My hand!" Diego wailed. "You broke my hand!"

His knuckles were ballooning, and his fingers were all twisted. It looked painful, but Will doubted it was broken; his body had been invulnerable, not made of steel.

"You're gonna be in so much trouble when we tell on you," Jerritt said, waving a finger at Will. "You can't just go around hurting people like that."

"Will didn't throw a single punch!" Duncan yelled.

"Yeah," called out someone from the crowd. "We're all witnesses!"

Another said, "You guys are wimps! You can't threaten us anymore!"

"Will don't take your crap and neither will we!" shouted a squeaky voice.

"Will's da man!" said another.

Jerritt took a step back from Diego. "Will is kinda cool," he muttered.

"You moron!" Diego yelled. "Forget about Cricket and get me to the nurse's office. Be careful with my hand—you know I'm the delicate type."

Jerritt put the bully's arm over his shoulder and together they moved away from the crowd. As they walked down the hallway, Jerritt turned back and gave them a cheery wave goodbye.

As soon as they disappeared around the corner, the crowd went wild. Kids chanted Will's name, gave him pats on the back and asked if he might play for the football team next year. Other kids from the lunchroom flooded into the locker area as rumors of Will's victory spread like wildfire around the school. Everyone wanted to congratulate the boy who brought down Diego.

Will's grin grew by leaps and bounds with each congratulation. Not only had he saved the day, but he'd granted his seventh wish. Will was certain it didn't come together as Diego would've preferred, but mission accomplished! Nonnie would be mighty proud of him.

By the end of the school day, Will's face was sore from smiling so much. But as soon as he hit the exit doors, his outlook on life took a nosedive back into reality. Hollywood stood at the bottom of the steps waiting for him.

The agent looked haggard, not like himself at all. He hadn't shaved in a couple of days, and his hair was tussled. Even the stars in his jacket looked dim.

Will had just taken a step toward Hollywood when Kaitlyn brushed into her brother. Jensen was by her side, holding her hand. "Hey, Bro, how's the big celebrity?"

He didn't take his eyes off Hollywood, saying, "I'm no star."

"I heard some kids wanted your autograph," Jensen said with a chuckle. "No one's ever asked for *my* autograph!"

"I'm sure all the fuss'll die down next week by Thanksgiving. Even if it didn't, I'd trade it all ..."

"I know." Kaitlyn pressed her face into Jensen's jacket.

"Yeah, I'm really sorry about your grandmother," Jensen said. "I hope they find her soon."

"Kait," Will said, "do me a favor, okay? Tell Mom and Dad that I went over to Tang's house to check on him. I may even spend the night."

"Your friend's been out all week," Jensen said. "He must be one sick, little dude."

"Yeah, he's really sick," said Will.

"Sure," Kaitlyn said. "I'll tell 'em that. Whatever you want. But ... you're not going to his house, are you?"

"I have to go look. I have to at least try."

There in front of Jensen and the entire school, Kaitlyn wrapped her arms around her brother and squeezed with all her might. "I want you to know how proud I am of you," she whispered in his ear. "I'm sorry I haven't been a better sister."

When she pulled away, all Will could do was nod. Kaitlyn and Jensen moved to the sidewalk and toward home. As he watched them leave, Will thought for the first time in a long time that he was exceedingly glad to be her brother too.

"Any luck?" Will finally asked Hollywood when his sister was out of sight.

"I'm afraid not." Hollywood's head hung, and his eyes drooped. "We're not giving up hope, so neither should you. By the way, congratulations on granting your seventh wish. From what I hear, you did an impressive job."

"That doesn't matter right now. Besides, I didn't even know what my power was until it was too late."

"Which makes what you did all the more impressive. I knew I was right about you." Hollywood produced a feeble smile and then said, "Ready to head back to Mythos? We need all the help we can get searching for Nonnie."

"Of course. I'm all for it. I owe it to Nonnie to find her. I mean, if not for me, Moloch would've never kidnapped her in the first place."

Hollywood took a deep breath. "Actually, that's not really true. You see, since you and I haven't spoken since Nonnie was taken, I haven't been able to fill you in on everything just yet. I didn't tell you this before because of the confidentiality clause in her contract, same as the one in yours. I mean, very few SCENE employees even knew."

"Wait. What in the world are you babbling about?"

"Your Nonnie, Will ... she's just like you. She's an Omni."

DAY 7.2

Hollywood refused to answer any of the questions Will threw at him until they made it to Mythos. When they arrived in the SCENE offices, the wish agent took Will to a section of the building he hadn't seen during his previous visit. Hollywood led him down a murky red corridor that had doors scattered across the ceiling and walls. He took Will's hand and floated up to a door with a glass knob that looked like the sun. "We call this room the Trench. It's a room we all hate. In here, we prepare for war," he said as he opened the door.

"W—war?" said Will.

Even though they entered through a door in the ceiling, everything was right-side-up in the Trench. Hollywood released Will's hand and scurried over to one of the many computers that filled the room. There were maps covering nearly every wall, and a massive table in the middle filled with toy-like figurines that were engaged in a battle simulation. There were 25 other people shuffling around, each reviewing documents or monitoring the computer systems. All of them looked as exhausted as Hollywood—so weary, in fact, they didn't seem to notice Will in the room.

"There's been movement in the Genie quadrant," Peske said to Hollywood.

"You don't think they'd actually trust Moloch again after he betrayed them when he conquered Africa, do you?" Reverie asked.

"Trust him? No," Hollywood said. "But they might be willing to play along to see where it takes them. You know how bent they are."

"Moloch don't need no dagnabit Genies to do what he wants anyway," said Hiroshi. "Not when he's got—"

"Nonnie." Will's tiny voice carried throughout the room. Everyone stopped mid-motion and looked over.

"HW, why didn't you tell us the munchkin was here?" Hiroshi said.

Hollywood ran a hand through his disheveled hair. "Sorry, sorry, sorry. Don't worry. Will already knows the truth about Nonnie."

"He what?!" Peske said.

"Now don't get your legal briefs in a bunch, Norv. Desperate times, desperate measures, remember?"

Peske opened his mouth, but Will cut him off. "Could you guys stop arguing and just tell me what's really going on with my Nonnie?"

Hollywood signaled for most of the Arcanians to return to work. He and those Will knew gathered around. "We've treated you lousy, Will. We really had no intentions of keeping things secret from you. I'm sorry for that. As I already said, your grandmother is an Omni, just like you. Also like you, Nonnie discovered her ability when she was young, when I came to her one night and agreed to grant her wish in exchange for her helping me grant seven other wishes. Of course, Nonnie's relationship with the SCENE extended well beyond those initial wishes. She went on to be one of the best Omni agents we've ever had."

"Whoa," Will said. "So Nonnie's got funky super-powers like me, and she's been helping you guys grant wishes all of this time?"

"She worked with the SCENE on and off for many years, yes. She retired some time ago. Said she wanted to relax and travel the world with your grandfather."

"Did ... did Poppa know about you guys?"

Peske rolled his eyes. "Despite your Nonnie's contractual obligation to keep her yap closed, she did tell your Poppa about us and her Omni abilities. That woman nearly sent me to an early grave."

Hollywood cleared his throat and said, "Speaking of graves ..." Several of the others shook their heads at him, but he raised his hand to quiet them. "Two years ago, well after Nonnie had retired, we called on her for a mission of the utmost importance. One of the Tokens of Tenet—the crown of Manasseh—had been spotted in the Parisian underground. She and your Poppa went there to recover it for us."

"Paris?" Will said. "Two years ago? But that's when ..."

"Moloch had just escaped his prison. He got to Nonnie and Poppa before we could. There was a struggle and ... Poppa didn't make it. Nonnie tried to save him, and that's when things went terribly south for her. She did two things a wish agent should *never* do: she tried to grant her own wish, and she tried to raise someone—Poppa—from the dead. I know she did it out of pure grief, but there are consequences for crossing such boundaries. Her brain couldn't withstand the onslaught of the wishcraft energy she tried to manipulate. It left Nonnie's mind extremely addled. Her behavior since then has been odd, to say the least, as you well know."

"It's all Moloch's fault." Will bit down on his lip so hard that he could taste a hint of blood. "He killed Poppa, and Nonnie wouldn't be so mixed up if he hadn't. Now—"

"Now," Hollywood continued, "he's kidnapped Nonnie. We're certain he intends to use her to power the Tokens so that he'll be able to grant his own wish. No doubt, his encounter with Nonnie in Paris made him realize that she, as an Omni, is an incredible source of power—far greater than anything he's ever encountered."

"Why take Nonnie? Why not kidnap me to use as the power source? I'm younger, after all."

"Youth doesn't automatically equal greater power. Nonnie has had years of experience, much more time to hone her abilities, and that counts for a great deal. And since Tang saw several of your, ah, early foul-ups, he probably suggested to Moloch that Nonnie would be better suited for their needs."

Will stomped his foot on the floor. "How do we get her back?"

"Yeah, see, that's our problem," said Nixie. "We can't get a trace on her. She ain't making any wishes for us to hear, and she ain't using any power neither."

"That doesn't mean—" said Will.

"Oh, no, she's still alive and well," Hollywood said. "Moloch needs her healthy to enact his plans tomorrow. But he undoubtedly has her subdued and probably unconscious. There's little chance we'll be able to trace her until it's too late."

"How about the three Tokens? Can you find her by tracking those?"

Kalpatharu waved a branch at Will and then pointed to a computer monitor as three objects flashed onscreen. "We've been trying. The ring of Candrissa, the crown of Manasseh and the flame of Kronos must be used in tandem for their location to be pinpointed. Unfortunately, that was a failsafe device we implanted within them the last time we took them from Moloch so that no one would be able to locate them ever again. Now, it's working against us, and we have no way of reversing it."

Will studied the artifacts on the screen closely. The ring with its eye for a center stone was as hideous as he'd imagined. The crown was made of a rich mahogany-colored wood but without any additional adornments. The flame was just that—it looked like any ordinary campfire. "Why did you guys hide them in the first place? Why didn't you just destroy them so Moloch could never get hold of them again?"

There were a few nervous chuckles around the room. Hollywood said, "Destroying a Token of Tenet would be the equivalent of setting off about 10 of your people's nuclear bombs. The results, one might say, would be rather counter-productive."

"So what hope do we have of finding Moloch before he goes through with the ceremony to steal Nonnie's energy and grant himself his own wish?" asked Will.

"We've only got one chance," Hiroshi said. "We gots to hope the varmint uses his Genie abilities between now and tomorrow. Our security system is calibrated to pick up any use of Genie wishcraft. The computers can trace the energy signature back to its point of origin, and then we go in low and hit 'im like gangbusters!"

"Will the computer flash a red light when it happens?" Will asked.

"Yeah, kid, how'd ya know?"

Will pointed to the large monitor behind them, and they all whipped their heads around to see. "'Cause that computer's blinking like mad!"

Everyone rushed to the terminal. Hollywood pecked away at the keyboard, and in seconds a map of the earth covered the screen. There were at least 30 flashing red lights scattered across the chart.

"Why are there so many?" Will asked. "What does it mean?"

"It means the rumors about the Genies helping Moloch are true, blast them!" Hollywood pounded a fist against the computer causing it to blink out momentarily.

"Is one of them Moloch?"

"That's the point," Peske said. "We have no way of knowing. Moloch obviously coerced a host of Genies to use their powers all at the same time. He knew we'd be monitoring for Genie activity, and the others are providing him the perfect cover. We have to investigate each of these blips—we can't afford not to—but doing so will drastically thin our ranks and take time away from the real search. It's a diversion."

"But," Hollywood said, "we *must* investigate. We'll have to personally look into each of the occurrences. We've got to do it before midnight before it becomes the Day of the Divine and Moloch is able to manipulate the wishcraft energies to his own evil ends."

Nixie stepped forward. "Give me the location of one of those thingamabobs. I'll see what's what."

"We all will," said Kalpatharu. "If Moloch's behind one of these outbursts of Genie power, we will find him."

"Good," said Hollywood. "I'm afraid you lot are about the only SCENE employees up to the task, and we can't count on the Vanguard, those useless scoundrels. They won't move into action until there's been an actual incident. I'll assign everyone a location, and we'll all take a trans-dimensional walkie-talkie to stay in communication. If anyone spots Moloch, we radio the others for help."

Hollywood pointed to the map and called out names until everyone had an assignment. Everyone but Will.

"Hey, what about me?" Will asked, waving his hand in the air. "I should be helping too—that's why you came to me in the first place, remember?"

Peske shook his head. "What help would you be? You've already used your Mizm today; you won't get another until midnight. If you were to confront Moloch now, you'd be putting yourself in grave danger ... which would put *your* world in grave danger ... which would put *our* world in grave danger. See a pattern developing?"

"He's right, Will," Hollywood said. "We can't have anything happening to you, and this area—the Trench—is the one place Moloch can't penetrate. The room's got mystical wishcraft barriers covering every inch—an Arcanian standing right outside wouldn't know if you made the biggest wish of your life; the barriers are so powerful they even block Telewishing. We really do need you to stay hidden until after midnight. Even if we find Moloch now, it would likely be the beginning of a long drawn-out battle, one that will require the power of an Omni to finish it. You're our ace, Will, and we must wait until precisely the right moment to put you into play. Besides, with all of us gone, someone must remain behind and monitor the computer systems. It's a terribly important job, and I need the absolute best covering it. What do you say?"

Will knew they were right. It wouldn't do at all to have come this far and then get slaughtered a couple of hours before midnight. He'd have to wait it out, like it or not. "Fine," he said.

Hollywood gave Will a quick rundown of the equipment, not that it was much different from his laptop at home. To ensure Will's safety while the SCENE employees were away, the wish agent sealed off the Trench from outside entry by causing the door he and Will had entered through to vanish. Then Will watched as Hollywood input the destination coordinates for those traveling to Earth to investigate the Genie power-bursts.

Once he was done, Reverie pulled a lever, and all of the chairs in the room came to life. They zipped around on their own, racing back and forth until they finally came together in a long line facing the south wall. Everyone took a seat and pulled out seatbelts from under the chairs. Hollywood took the final chair and twirled a finger in the air. The south wall slid into the ceiling, revealing a dark cavern spotted by twinkling stars.

"What is it?" Will stood at the edge of the cavern entrance and peered inside.

"We call it Space Mounting," Hollywood said. "This doorway is a dimensional aperture to the stars. It's powered with starlight and very similar to one of your roller coasters. We use it to achieve faster than light speeds so we can transport nearly instantaneously to your planet. It's fast but dizzying. Still, it's proven rather popular with children whose wishes we've granted over the years. One young man—Walt, I believe was his name— loved it so much that he wished for his very own amusement park with a ride just like it."

Will took a quick leap away from the entrance. He hated roller coasters and was now very glad they'd insisted he stay behind.

Hollywood pointed toward the dimensional gate, and the chairs slowly moved toward it in response. "We'll be back soon, so just stay put. No need to worry, my boy. Everything's under—"

The last word never made it out of Hollywood's mouth. He hit the opening and his chair rocketed down. The only thing Will could hear was a blood-curdling scream that sounded like Hollywood but about three octaves higher. Reverie was next, but leave it to her to nap. Her chair flew off in a completely different direction, sideways and then straight up. The rest all took off in turn, and Will waved goodbye to every last one. He was particularly delighted to witness Peske's pained wince and white-knuckle gripping of his chair.

When they were gone, Will was alone in a room of whirring computers. There was nothing left to do but sit and wait for the confrontation with Moloch. He wished with all his might for his grandmother's safe return.

★

For a while, Will toyed with the battle figurines on the center table, but when one shot his nose with a jellybean, he decided to entertain himself with something else. He examined the electronics equipment and discovered that one was rigged to grant the wisher any flavor of ice cream he or she desired. Strangely enough, Will wasn't that interested. Something nagged at his mind, something he knew he'd overlooked.

Will peered at the computer screen that displayed the images of the ring, the crown and the flame. He was drawn to the crown, as if its secrets could be told just by slipping it on one's head. It seemed so familiar; Will was certain he'd seen it, but where? He'd never seen a real crown before, not in person, only those cheap ones from fast food restaurants or the shoddy one in Mr. Peach's office.

Then Will heard it, a voice from the not-so-distant past. *Best way to go unnoticed is to hide in plain sight.* Those were Tang's words, and he'd used them to describe the way Genies hid among everyday things like lamps and bottles. Maybe it applied to Genies' possessions too.

Will didn't understand how—maybe it had something to do with him being an Omni—but as he traced a finger across the image on the screen, he knew in his heart that the crown of Manasseh was the very same crown he'd seen on Mr. Peach's desk!

A dozen questions raced through Will's mind. Hadn't his grandfather given Mr. Peach the crown? But Hollywood had told Will that Poppa had died in Paris trying to get it. Had Poppa and Nonnie used a Genie trick to hide it from Moloch before he came after them? If so, why had Poppa left it in the care of Mr. Peach, of all people? Did Mr. Peach know that his worthless tin crown was an artifact of immense and deadly power?

As much as those questions needed answering, they could wait until the crown was recovered. Will glanced at his watch—it was 11:00 p.m. There was still time to grab the crown before midnight—before Moloch could find it—and hide it away at the SCENE. The Genie's plans would be dashed, and two worlds would be spared.

Will raced around the room in search of a walkie-talkie like the one Hollywood and the others took. He needed to radio them right away and get them over to the Peach Preserves offices. But there was no radio, and no one had shown Will any other way to make contact. He couldn't make a wish and get through to Hollywood—the Trench was wish-proof. From what HW said earlier, there wasn't anyone else at the SCENE he could rely on to assist him with the mission, not that he even had an exit door to leave the Trench and return to the main office building to seek help. Out of options, Will plopped down into one of the few remaining chairs in the room. As he sat, a frightening idea developed.

He felt the seatbelt beneath the chair and looked at the south wall. His heart raced and his stomach did back-flips, but Space Mounting was the only way. Will ran to a computer and punched a few keys, mimicking what he'd seen Hollywood do earlier, only he entered an entirely different set of coordinates: the offices of Peach Preserves. If he couldn't contact anyone else to do the job, he'd just retrieve the crown on his own.

As his chair rolled toward the opening, he couldn't believe what he was doing. Roller coasters were at the top of his list of phobias, along with planes, speaking in front of crowds, darkness, closed spaces, strangers, dentists, blood, insects and albino squirrels.

Nearing the entrance to the Space Mounting, Will gulped down as much air as his lungs could hold. He tested his safety belt over and over again. As he gave it one last pull, one of the arms to the chair fell off. Suddenly Will wasn't so sure he was doing the right thing. He started to yank the seatbelt loose, but then he looked down—the floor was gone! He was in space!

"Well this isn't so bad," Will said as the chair strolled along at a leisurely pace. "Maybe this old chair likes to take its time."

As if on cue, the chair suddenly dropped from midair and raced downward at speeds faster than light, leaving Will to hang onto its one remaining arm for dear life.

Even though he wasn't sure his stomach would ever catch up, Will was on solid ground again. He found himself in an elevator car, though still seated in the old beat-up chair. As Will unbuckled his safety belt, he examined the elevator; he was at Peach Preserves, alright—he didn't know any other place that wallpapered their elevators with pictures of sarcophaguses and ancient Egyptian burial chambers. Will checked his watch— midnight was just under an hour away. There was still time.

Will hit the button for the third floor, and the car immediately went into motion. When the doors opened, darkness engulfed Will. A few exit signs gave off faint orange glows, but otherwise, there was little light ... except at the far end of the hallway. One of the offices was lit up—Mr. Peach's, to be exact.

The halls were perfectly silent, and Will couldn't make out any noise coming from the office, either. Still, he crept without making a sound. As he approached the open door to Mr. Peach's office, he was glad he'd moved so quietly because someone was within! Had it not been for the person's shadow, Will would've never known.

What if it's Moloch? Will thought. *I can't face him right now. I won't be able to make a wish to contact Hollywood, either, not without tipping off the Genie since he'll have Telewishing like all of the other Arcanians.* Will checked his watch again—forty-nine minutes to midnight. There was no way he'd get a new power in time to stop the thief from absconding with the crown of Manasseh.

Maybe it's not Moloch. Maybe it's just a janitor. Doesn't matter—I've got to find out. I'll just stay hidden until I know it's safe for me to act.

Will slowly poked his head around the corner. The intruder was slumped over, reaching into the desk drawer where Mr. Peach had stowed the crown during Will's visit on career day. When the intruder stood upright again, Will couldn't help but gasp. The thief had found the crown, but it wasn't Moloch as Will had suspected.

It was Tang!

DAY 7.3

Tang's hair flashed from turquoise to manila to hot pink. The smug grin covering his face confirmed what his colorful locks had already hinted—Tang was thrilled to have recovered the crown of Manasseh. As he shined the coronet with his forearm, a puff of mist exuded from the fake jewels and surrounded the crown. When the haze dissipated a few moments later, the crown had changed—it looked exactly like the picture Hollywood had shown Will back at the SCENE.

Will's heart sank as he spied on his one-time friend. He'd held out hope there had been some kind of misunderstanding—that Tang wasn't an evil Genie bent on helping Moloch destroy the world. Now there could be no doubt.

Will's only solace was that Moloch wasn't present. He knew Tang had enormous power, but at least Will was bigger. If he took him by surprise, Will might be able to overpower him and strip the crown away before Tang knew what hit him.

Before he could talk himself out of it, Will plunged into the office, barreling toward Tang at incredible speed. The half-Genie turned around just in time to catch Will pounce. Tang tried to get out of the way, but Will was surprisingly quick. They both tumbled to the ground, and the crown flew out of Tang's hands and skidded across the floor.

"Will!" Tang shouted. "What are you doing?!"

"I'd ask you the same thing, but I already know. We all know, Tang." Will rolled over and pinned him to the floor. He grabbed the half-Genie's skinny arms with one of his oversized hands and locked them in place so he couldn't so much as wiggle an elbow.

"You'd better let go of me, Will. I've got to get the crown!"

"Your days of stealing artifacts are through. I'm taking the crown, and you're not getting anywhere near it. If you think I'm going to let you and Moloch take over the world and hurt Nonnie, you're crazy!"

Tang's hair settled on a single color—lime green—which meant he was concentrating on something. He opened his mouth and calmly said, "You're making a serious mistake, Will. Just listen—"

"Shut up, you traitor!" Will slapped his free hand over Tang's mouth to prevent him from singing out a wish enchantment.

Unfortunately, Will had forgotten the most basic element to Tang and all Genies' genetic makeup—they were shape-shifters. Tang's arms suddenly felt different in Will's grasp. They were scaly and slippery, and then a few seconds later, they were gone! There was a tail where his hands had been—Tang had transformed into a boa constrictor! He easily wriggled out of Will's grasp and quickly slithered toward the crown.

Will grabbed Tang by the belly, stopping the half-Genie just short of his prize. Tang hissed and turned back on Will, coiling around his neck and head. Will pounded on Tang to get free, but the snakeskin seemed impervious to every blow. Will became weak and collapsed to the floor. He inched back and slammed against the wall, catching Tang between it and himself.

The force was enough to jar Tang loose, but there was still fight left in him. He bore his fangs, although he didn't move in for a bite. His eyes jumped from the crown and back to Will, but he wasn't staring Will down; he wasn't trying to intimidate him.

Tang had the look of fear in his eyes.

Suddenly, there was a noise just outside the door. Someone approached. The person broke through the outer veil of darkness and into the office. It was Lincoln Peach.

"Mr. Peach!" Will cried out. "Thank goodness you're here! This snake is after your crown. I know it doesn't look like the crown you had before, but you have to trust me on this. It's very dangerous!"

Mr. Peach calmly sidestepped a hissing Tang and picked up the crown. "Believe me, William, I know all about this crown and the danger it holds. I know that, in the wrong hands, it could help lead to the end of the world. It's fortunate I came along when I did. Very fortunate, indeed ..."

Without warning, a wave of energy burst from Mr. Peach. His skin melted away like candle wax, but he grew a foot in stature. His skeleton slowly regained its flesh, but it looked chiseled and hard like dull red brick. Two of his fingers vanished, leaving behind only the other two and a thumb. Razor-like thorns sprouted from the sides of his arms. His misshapen spine lifted out of his skin so that it ran down his back and formed a tail that whipped in every direction. When the process was complete, Mr. Peach was the most terrifying creature Will had ever seen.

"Allow me to properly introduce myself ... my *real* self. My name is Moloch, but you may call me 'Master.'"

With a wave of his hand Mr. Peach, now Moloch, forced Tang back into his human form. Dark circlets appeared out of the ceiling and covered the half-Genie's body. They tightened so that it was impossible for Tang to move.

Will expected the same but received no such restraints. The chilling laughter of Moloch, however, was enough to keep him frozen in fear. "T-Tang?" Will said.

As Tang struggled inside his mystical prison, he said, "I tried to tell you before, but you wouldn't listen. Moloch kidnapped me as HW and Peske were taking me back to Mythos. He's been holding me prisoner all this time. I overheard him talking to some other Genies about how he had the crown in this office. So when I managed to escape being locked up downstairs in the basement, I snuck up here, hoping to get the crown and take it back to the SCENE. I'd have wished for help, but he's made the whole building wish-proof!"

Will's heart rose and sank at the same time. If Tang was telling the truth, he hadn't betrayed the SCENE at all.

"I ... I don't understand," Will said. "We all saw the video footage of you stealing the ring of Candrissa."

Moloch laughed uproariously. "Apparently you haven't heard: Genies are masters of deceit." He took a step toward Will, but as soon as his foot touched the ground, he wasn't Moloch anymore. He looked exactly like Tang. "Unfortunately, your half-breed friend isn't nearly as adept at deception as I am. I learned he was trying to find me—"

Tang's special project, Will thought. *The one he'd never tell me about. He was trying to find Moloch! That's why when I snuck up on him he said Moloch's name—he must've been afraid that the Genie had tracked him down.*

"I almost had you too!" Tang shouted.

"Yes ... almost. Luckily for me, you didn't share your findings with that buffoon Hollywood. I imagine you thought locating me on your own would really impress that boss of yours and show everyone you really were that rare trustworthy Genie. But holding your tongue proved your undoing, half-wit. When I snatched you away from them, they believed you'd abandoned them and turned to my side. They are duplicitous idiots, aren't they?!"

"I'd never work for you! I'd never betray my friends!"

"Which is why impersonating you to 'steal' the ring of Candrissa from my own warehouse was so delicious. Not only did it make Mr. Peach seem innocent, but your one-time friends now believed you to be a traitorous scum." Moloch took a step back and returned to his demonic form.

"Tang," Will said, "I'm sorry I ever doubted you. After all we went through together, I should've known you'd never betray me. I mean, you were there for me every day, helping me learn how to use—"

"The bathroom," Tang said, out of nowhere. "Right, I know. You had a problem wetting the bed at night, but it's nothing to be ashamed of. Happens to the best of us. But you certainly don't need to give that another thought. No need to mention it again, either ... not like Moloch wants to hear about it."

Will's jaw dropped. He'd been plagued with many a problem these last several days, but wetting the bed was certainly not one of them! Why had Tang said that? Why had he cut him off before he could mention his ... and then it hit Will. Tang had stopped him before he could say "Mizms." He was covering it up! He didn't want it known that Will was an Omni. Moloch must've thought Will was just a normal meddling kid!

"Oh, right!" Will finally said. He took his time, choosing his words carefully. "I ... I just can't believe that Mr. Peach and Moloch were the same person the whole time. Tang, how come you didn't know it was him when you met him at my house that night you helped me fix dinner?"

Tang shook his head. "I had no clue; he's tricky."

"Hah! But I knew exactly what Tang was, if not who," Moloch smirked. "I also knew you were in the Cricket household for a sickeningly noble purpose. In fact, you were there for the same reason as I—you were there for the Omni."

Will gulped. Maybe Moloch really did know he was a super-powered agent for the SCENE. Well, if this was the end, he wasn't going to cower in the corner. He was going to give the

Genie a piece of his mind. Waving a finger in the air, Will said, "So the secret's out, huh, you oversized briquette?"

Moloch's face lit up, as though Will's display of backbone delighted him to no end. "It was hardly a secret. I've known of the Omni's identity for years."

"Years? But I've only known for a few days."

"Not surprising. You humans are terribly dull-witted. Except for that Omni ... I never could pull anything over on her."

Her? Will thought. *That means he came to our house for—*

"Nonnie. That old bat realized who I was right from the beginning, despite her madness. But her addled state of mind played right into my hands."

"You," Will whispered. "You manipulated my mom and dad into sending her to that nursing home."

"Of course. I had to get her away from the prying eyes of your household. After all, I couldn't be sure how many other Arcanian spies were lingering about. Once she was in that nursing home, it was a simple matter to use the fire to distract everyone long enough for me to abscond with her."

"I guess you weren't really a student in my Poppa's archaeology class?"

"I used that story to ingratiate myself with your mother, to bring her into my company so that I might keep close ties to your grand ma ma. I needed a connection if I was to convince her to abandon Nonnie to an old folks' home. But understand, I did know your grandfather ... I knew him very well. In fact, we spent the very last moments of his life together."

Will's pulse raced and his vision blurred. He folded his fingers into a fist.

"Don't do it, Will," Tang said. "Stay calm."

"Listen to your friend, William. I'd hate to see you follow in your Poppa's footsteps. I despise getting my hands bloodied."

"Why ... why did you kill him?" Will growled.

"Because he had something of mine, something that didn't belong to him." Moloch lifted the crown of Manasseh and placed it on his head. "It was mine to begin with. Your Nonnie and Poppa, under the auspices of those misguided fools at the SCENE, went to Paris to recover it. Fortunately, I beat them to it. But those two insisted on putting up a fight. So I popped Poppa like a balloon, and watched as Nonnie turned into a ninny. After that, I changed the outward appearance of the crown to be able to hide it out in the open. Then I set about searching for the remaining two artifacts, having to rely on humans to do my work for me since any use of my wishcraft abilities would have alerted that buffoon Hollywood to my whereabouts."

"That's why you started Peach Preserves," said Will. "The Ancient Prophets collection is really the Tokens of Tenet."

"Give the boy a gold star! I created the identity of Lincoln Peach, antiquities dealer, so that I could search for my treasures undetected. Thanks to archaeologists like Dr. Donnatelli, I now have the ring of Candrissa and the flame of Kronos, as well."

"The flame?" Will gasped. "You have that too?"

"My dear boy, you've held it in your very hands!"

Will thought about it for a second. "No ... not the opal Charlie and I fixed."

Moloch burst into laughter. "The very same! Had you not fixed it, I would have never gotten this far! Humanity's downfall will be as much on your shoulders as mine."

"Don't listen to him, Will!" Tang hopped over to his friend and gave him as much of a nudge as he could manage.

"But—but I've seen a picture of the flame. It's a real fire, not an opal."

"The flame of Kronos resides *inside* the gem. Don't worry, you'll see it soon."

Will glanced at the clock on the desk. He still had a half hour before midnight. He had to stall; he had to keep Moloch talking. "You really are a monster. I don't understand how my mom could work for you all this time and never realize what a creep you are."

"Don't be too hard on your mother, William. Few mortals can see past the veil of the Genie. She has no idea that when I enticed her away from her previous job I was doing so to gain access to Nonnie. Speaking of whom ..."

From a pouch around his waist, Moloch pulled out something small. It had the stem of a flower, but instead of petals were what appeared to be bone fragments. "It's a dandelioness flower. Just as the lioness is more dangerous than the lion, so too is this flower more deadly than the dandelion." Moloch sucked in an enormous breath. He closed his eyes, as if making a wish, and blew out breath so stagnant that Will could see the fumes. As soon as his gulp of air hit the bone petals, the office vibrated like an earthquake had hit. Will couldn't keep his balance. He toppled over as the room went pitch black. He expected to fall onto the stained concrete, but when he hit the floor, he landed in something wet and slimy.

The tiny bone fragments tinkled to the ground, and suddenly torchlight filled the room. Tang was still beside him, and Moloch was there too, but they were no longer in the office. The walls were curved and made of glass the color of tangelos. A thin film of swamp water covered the floor, and torches lined the wall.

There were cages and two tunnels on either side of the dank room.

None of it frightened Will as much as what lay in the center of the room. Hanging by a pair of oozing ebony coils over a pit of green flame was Nonnie.

Will couldn't see Nonnie breathing. "Is—is she ... dead?"

"If only!" Moloch said. "Her entrails would be filled with maggots, but I need her alive for the moment. She will serve as my source of power, to fuel the three Tokens of Tenet and allow me the unique opportunity to grant myself a single wish, which I will use to become a god! That can only take place after the stroke of midnight, when the wishcraft energies are wild and unbound. So she lives ... for now."

"Hollywood will find a way to stop you!" Tang exclaimed.

"Oh? How, pray tell, will he do that? Even now we're in the catacombs of Peach Preserves, and a whiteout spell keeps us shielded from prying eyes. Even if they knew where to look, my Genie accomplices are currently engaging the various SCENE do-gooders around the globe. They'd never get here in time. The last known Omni in the entire universe is in my possession anyway. And clearly her offspring didn't inherit the Mizm genes." Moloch sized up Will and gave a chuckle.

Tang snarled and said, "You ugly wretch! You're gonna get yours!"

"You first." The evil Genie's tail lashed out at Tang and sent him flying backwards into one of the open cells.

"Tang!" Will screamed and ran toward him.

Moloch whipped his tail at Will and pinned him against the wall. "Relax boy, unless you want to be next."

Will shook his head as he watched his friend writhe in pain. Moloch blinked his eyes, and the dark circlets binding Tang melted off and slithered across the ground. As they approached the edge of the cell, they reformed as bars, locking Tang inside.

"Tang, quick! Turn into a mouse and scamper out of there!"

Moloch picked up Will with his tail and brought him around to his face, close enough that his spittle dotted Will's nose. "Those bars are made of firestorm ebony, boy. It's the same substance from which your Nonnie hangs. It comes from a realm where nightmares—not dreams—are granted, and it renders all Omnis and Arcanians powerless ... all except full-blooded Genies."

"'Cause Genies belong to the nightmares," said the scratchy uneven voice of Will's grandmother.

"Nonnie!" Will shouted. A burst of joy warmed his insides. "You're awake!"

"What are you doing with my grandson, Moldy-loch? He doesn't have anything to do with this," said Nonnie.

"Oh, but he does, Sylvia," Moloch said. "You see, the boy inadvertently repaired the flame of Kronos for me only two days ago. And just now I caught him trespassing in my office. I can only imagine the damage that might have been done if he were an Omni like you, old bird. But look at him, he's useless. There isn't an ounce of power emanating from him."

"All the more reason to let him go! He doesn't belong here." Nonnie bucked in the direction of Moloch, but the ebony bonds kept her in check.

"He stays. For his part in my ascension, I'm allowing him to witness the end of the world as you simple creatures know it. Once the ceremony is complete, I'll give him the honor of being last to die—right after you and the half-wit Tangible." Moloch licked the air with his spiked tongue and a sundial appeared. "Well, look at the time. My, how it flies when you're having fun.

Midnight is almost upon us. I think we should get started, don't you? After all these years, I've grown a little impatient."

Will held the tiniest bit of hope. Moloch hadn't been able to sense his status as an Omni because he'd already used his power for the day. That was about to change. As soon as the clock signaled a new day, a brand new Mizm would be his.

Moloch chanted some words that Will didn't understand, and two stone columns rose out of the slime covering the floor. Resting atop the pillars were the ring of Candrissa and the flame of Kronos.

With the crown of Manasseh already on his head, Moloch placed the ring on his finger. Will tried not to look, but gave in to temptation when he noticed Candrissa's eye blink. As he stared back, the eye seemed more sad than evil.

"Behold! The flame! That laughable sun-god Kronos was a fool to have ever opposed me. I trapped the fire of his spirit inside this opal centuries ago. It yearns to be released again, to set aflame all that stands in its way. Now, I shall grant its wish."

Moloch wrapped his hand around the flame, and Will heard the sizzle of heat against Moloch's flesh. The Genie laughed and bore down harder on the gem. There was a cracking noise and suddenly the gem burst under the pressure of Moloch's iron grip. The pieces of opal fell to the ground, leaving behind a true flame resting in Moloch's hand. The fire quickly engulfed his entire fist but didn't spread any further. Even though Will could see and smell Moloch's burning flesh, he knew the flame of Kronos was now at the Genie's command.

Moloch let out a throaty sigh. "It's been too long since this power was mine to wield. Finally! After wasting two years masquerading as a pathetic mortal, I'm able to reclaim what's rightfully mine! This time, no one can stop me."

Nonnie chomped down on her dentures and gave her best imitation of a lion's roar. "If you weren't such a wimp, you'd let me loose, and I'd show you a thing or two."

Moloch feigned a smile. "You know, I need you alive for this, but you don't have to be conscious." From the Genie's fingertips sprung tapered paper the color of mold. It flung toward Nonnie and wrapped around her waist. She gasped and convulsed at its touch.

"What is that?" Will shrieked.

"Wishue!" Tang replied.

"Gesundheit."

"No, Will," Tang said. "That stuff is called 'wishue.' It's super absorbent wish tissue. It drains a person's wishcraft energy and zaps all their physical strength too!"

As Moloch continued to draw the Omni energy out of Nonnie, a loud bong shook the foundation, causing Moloch to drop Will into the swampy mire. Another bong followed, but it was drowned out by the Genie's mad laughter. "AHA! Midnight is here! The day of my ascension is upon us! Let the world tremble!"

Ten more bongs rang, and when the echo of the last one trailed off, the wishue that tied Nonnie to Moloch dissolved. Will rushed to his unconscious grandmother, avoiding the green pit of flame beneath her. She didn't appear physically harmed—her pink hair still held every last one of its curls. But when she slowly opened her eyes, Will saw a discernible difference. They were soft orange surrounded by a dead grey—like dying embers.

"Ugh ... I feel so cold, so empty," she said, shivering.

Fighting back a sob, Will said, "Nonnie, I'm so sorry. I should've taken better care of you. I was just so focused on getting my wish granted."

"I know. I knew about all of it. I am an Omni, after all ..."

She's known all along, Will thought. *It all makes sense now—her stranger than normal behavior, how she gave Tang the third degree, the way she knew things that no one else could've known.*

Nonnie continued, "... but my mind just isn't as clear as it used to be. I couldn't help you like I wanted. Make no mistake, this isn't your fault. Moloch's the one who choreographed this whole dance, but you've got to step on his toes."

Will craned around his head. Moloch paced the room in maniacal glee. Sparks of purple energy crackled around him, and the spikes on his arms pulsated up and down.

"How, Nonnie? How am I supposed to stop Moloch?" asked Will.

"Didn't you hear? It's midnight," she whispered.

Will patted down his chest, belly and waist, as if looking for something. "I don't know what my power is. It usually takes me forever to figure it out, and besides, it always seems like the Mizm is tied to a wish ... almost as if it knows an important wish is coming. I don't have a wish to grant."

"No wish to grant? Well, let me fix that for you, kiddo. I'll make one for the whole dang world." *I wish you'd put a stop to Moloch's plans ... and if you'd kick the stuffing out of him while you're at it, that'd be great too.*

Suddenly Moloch whipped around toward Nonnie and Will. "You!" he yelled, pointing at Will. "You're an Omni too?! But you're so ... fat." He pumped his arms in a fury and ran toward the two of them. His spiny-tail lashed out and smashed a few of the columns as he sprinted.

"He heard Nonnie's wish, Will!" Tang yelled from his cage. "He's got Telewishing too, remember? RUN!"

Too late. Even though Moloch was still several paces away, his tail jabbed at Will. It smacked him in the chest and sent Will sailing through the air. He collided against a wall, knocking the wind from him.

Moloch ran his flaming hand through the pit of fire beneath Nonnie. He caught a handful of the green blaze and tossed it at Will. The shock of hitting the wall had slowed Will's reflexes, but he scrambled out of the way just in time. When the fire collided with the glass wall of the dungeon, it oozed through, leaving a trail of inhuman blood in its wake.

This was serious. This wasn't Diego or some school bully.

Moloch leapt through the air and landed a few feet from Will. "I should've known you were an Omni—talk about a wolf in pig's clothing! That elegant dinner, the way you fixed the flame of Kronos—it was so much more than a pathetic boy such as yourself should have been able to do. I'd wondered when I dined with your family if Nonnie might have spawned another of her kind. You, your mother and sister were so ordinary. You, especially, seemed far too insignificant to be someone who fights for wishes. Still, if one of you had to be an Omni, I'm glad it's you. The others might've had a fighting chance, but you—ha! I should be able to finish you off with my eyes closed. Speaking of eyes ..."

Holding out his hand with the ring, Moloch flicked Candrissa's eye open. "The disintegration beam, if you will, Candrissa."

A sickly yellow beam of energy shot out from the ring. Will tried to jump out of the way, but the beam cut a bagel-size hole through his shirt and then to his flesh.

But nothing else happened. If anything, it kind of tickled.

All right! Will thought. *I don't know how I got it two days in a row, but I'm invulnerable again. Just what I needed!*

"What?! It's not possible!" Moloch turned the ring toward himself and stared down the eye. "No, it wasn't you that failed me, Candrissa. It was my own underestimation of the boy Omni that caused me to falter. I won't make the same mistake twice."

"Too bad for you, Moloch!" Will said, dusting himself off and waving a confident finger at the Genie. "I'm invulnerable to harm, so you can't do anything to me. You might as well give up now because I'm ... hey, what's that?" Suddenly Will felt a tingling sensation run through his body. It was the same feeling he'd gotten every time during the last seven days when he'd fulfilled a wish and his Mizm vanished. "No ... I can't lose it yet," he whispered to himself. "I haven't granted the wish."

Moloch sneered and licked his lips. "What's wrong, boy? Experiencing a short-circuit?"

Will waved his hands about and slowly took a step back. "Who? Me? No, I'm still totally invulnerable. Yep, you don't want to mess with me, that's for sure."

"I think I'll risk it." He held up the ring again, but this time said, "Paralysis beam."

Will watched as a pumpkin orange ray eked out of the ring. He quickly dove to the right, hoping to dodge it in time. But as Will hit the floor and jumped back to his feet, he saw that the paralysis beam hadn't budged an inch. Will turned to shout to Nonnie and Tang, but they weren't moving either. *I didn't lose my power at all,* he thought. *It just changed. I forgot it's the Day of the Divine—anything can happen! I've got super-speed again! Now we're talking!*

Within the tiniest fraction of a second, Will zipped over to Nonnie. He had to free her first. She was his top priority. He wasn't going to let her down again. But ... how was he going to *get* her down? He knew better than to get near the ebony bonds that kept Nonnie powerless—they might immobilize him too. He couldn't just yank her down, not with those green flames licking at her feet. What was he supposed to do? Nonnie would know—she'd been an Omni forever, after all. But he couldn't ask for her advice while his body was moving so fast—she'd never be able to make out what he said. He had to slow down just long enough to ask for help, and then he'd get moving again.

Slipping out of super-speed mode, Will heard a blast behind him. The beam that Moloch had fired at Will only two seconds earlier hit the swamp water, creating a backsplash that sprayed the Genie's face. He screamed something in that strange foreign language again. He was spitting mad but distracted. Whatever was in the slime water had blinded him, at least for the moment.

"Quick, Nonnie," Will whispered. "We only have a few seconds. I've gotta get you down."

"Aw, no, Will, why'd you come for me? Your fast feet were maybe the best chance we had at stopping that Genie, but now it's gone."

"What?" Will felt his heart race, but then realized it was the tingle again. His power had vanished for a second time!

"Don't you see? You're cycling through all the Mizms you've had for the last seven days. The problem is you only get to use them once. After your invulnerability saved you, it was gone. When you stopped moving super-fast, it was gone too. You've gotta use the rest of 'em smarter! And you've got to do it before Moloch's able to grant his own wish."

Will's brow furrowed. "Nonnie, I don't understand. Why hasn't he made his wish yet?"

"I shouldn't have to explain this to you, Will. You know there are rules you have to follow if you want a wish to be granted. Even a near-omnipotent Genie has to obey them, otherwise, the wish won't work. Now, you already know this, but he won't make the wish as long as—"

Suddenly Nonnie's eyelids closed, and her head slumped. She wasn't dead—she was snoring. Will turned around, and there was Moloch, wiping his eyes and saying, "Sleep ray."

Tang yelled out, "Will! Nonnie was trying to tell you that—"

Moloch fired another shot from Candrissa's eye, and now Tang collapsed on the floor of his cage. Will could hear him snoring too, but that didn't put his mind at ease. Will was alone, defenseless and cornered, trapped between Moloch and Nonnie's fire pit.

"You're trying my patience, boy." Moloch stepped cautiously toward Will—he had no idea what power the boy might have, and his concern showed in every calculated move he made. "I've waited an eternity for this day, and you will not interfere. You've lasted longer than I would have thought, but now fate's pendulum swings my way."

Will looked back to Nonnie and the flames that blocked his passage around and suddenly had an idea. *Sorry, Nonnie,* he thought to himself, *but you're tough, and I know you can handle it.* Will took a running leap at Nonnie, grabbed hold of her, and the two of them swung away from Moloch. The ebony bindings kept Will's grandmother from slipping, and Will's weight provided just enough push to send him over and past the green flame. He turned loose of Nonnie and fell to the ground.

Moloch moved toward the pit, but Nonnie was still in motion from Will's swing. Just as the Genie raised his fiery hand toward Will, Nonnie's foot swooped up and cracked him in the jaw. His aim went wild, and he missed Will by a mile.

"Way to go, Nonnie!" Will yelled as he scrambled backwards. He quickly searched the dungeon for a place to hide, for an escape. One of the two cavernous exits was just behind him—though its opening was so dark, it nearly blended into the black walls that surrounded it. He couldn't be certain what lay through the tunnel, but maybe if he traveled far enough into it, he'd be able to find help or get a message to Hollywood.

Moloch was nearly recovered. Will had no time to be frightened or second-guess his decision. He grabbed a torch from the dungeon wall and darted into the tunnel. Even with the fire in hand, he was still engulfed by the darkness. He could easily hear Moloch yell, "You miserable cretin! When I catch you, there shall be no end to the pain I will force upon you!"

What's it gonna take to stop this guy? Will thought. *I wish I knew what Nonnie was talking about earlier. How am I supposed to keep Moloch from making his wish?*

He was only a few yards in, but already a distant light at the cavern's end gave him a surge of hope. A few steps more and Moloch could again be heard yelling, "Ebon flow!" All of a sudden, the shadows around the wall started to take shape. But they weren't shadows at all—it was the same substance that bound Nonnie and Tang; it was firestorm ebony.

The darkness peeled away from the wall and ceiling, taking on the forms of a panther, a raven, a wolf, a bear, a mamba snake and a giant widow spider. They formed a barricade, preventing Will from going further down the tunnel. Even worse, the creatures hissed, growled and snarled as they moved closer to him.

Without even thinking, Will shouted, "Ebon yield!" but it wasn't his voice that came out of his mouth—it was Moloch's. The creatures came to an immediate halt but still blocked the passageway.

Will glanced at the torch in his hand, and a brilliant idea came to mind. "Ebony flambé," he said, licking his lips.

He carefully extended the torch so that the tip of its flame brushed the raven's wing. The bird-like shadow immediately burst into flames. Sparks shot from it in every direction, igniting the rest of the dark creatures too. In no time at all, there was a wall of fire that burned as high as the ceiling.

"Oh boy," Will said. "I think I just figured out why they're called *firestorm* ebony. Maybe the flames will die—"

Before Will could finish his thought, the raven exploded, knocking him back several feet. There was a chain reaction and the other ebonies exploded too. The entire tunnel shook, but Will managed to get back to his feet. The walls near the explosion started to collapse, and there was no way Will was going that direction now. In fact, he was going to be lucky to make it out at all!

A crack suddenly appeared along the ceiling, and giant chunks of stone fell all around Will. Dodging left and right, Will tried to make his way back to the main room, but he was too slow. Straight ahead, an enormous boulder broke from the ceiling. Will dove through the air and stretched with all his might to squeeze beneath it. He shut his eyes tight in anticipation of being crushed under a half ton of dirt and concrete. But when seconds passed, and he'd felt no pain, Will opened his eyes to find that he was still in the air. He was flying again!

More debris continued to fall, but Will zigged and zagged around it. He could see the opening to the main room. His reflexes were sharper in flight—Will had missed that feeling, and his heart leapt to have it back. He dodged the last of the falling rock and zoomed out of the tunnel. He'd hoped to fly across the dungeon to the passageway on the opposite side, but Moloch stood directly in front of it. He ran a hand across the crown of Manasseh, and suddenly Will heard a voice inside his head. It was like Telewishing, except that with this voice, every word felt like tiny needles being shoved into Will's brain.

You're a very bad boy, William. The voice was the Genie's. *Firestorm ebony is hard to come by.* Moloch slapped his other hand on the crown, as well, and dropped to his knees. A pulse rang out from the crown—but there was no way to dodge it, not even if Will had the entire sky for flying. It was some sort of mind wave, and it hit Will's brain without mercy.

Everything went haywire in Will's head. For a single moment, he went blind, while his sense of smell registered only the aroma of his mom's sugar cookies. His sense of touch was magnified a million-fold, and Will could literally feel the microbes in the air around him.

Like a badly-damaged World War I Sopwith Camel fighter plane spinning out of control, Will plummeted from the air. He couldn't see or balance himself to control his descent. He crashed to the ground and hard. Fortunately, the impact jarred his mind back to its proper state; unfortunately, the first thing his brain registered was intense pain.

Will tried pushing himself up, but his left arm throbbed. Hesitantly, fearfully, Will examined the source of his pain. What he saw almost made him pass out—there was a gash the size of a banana running down his arm. Blood poured out. Will felt his body getting cold. The room spun around him. *This can't be the end,* he thought to himself. *If only there was some way to ... fix it.*

A plan formed in his mind. It was beyond him as to how he knew it would work, but he didn't question it. He forced himself to forget the pain and nausea for the moment, long enough to get to his feet. Will ripped off the left sleeve of his shirt, wrapped it around his hand and dunked it into the slime water covering the ground. Looking back, he could see Moloch approach, but slowly, cockily, as if he believed victory was his.

Will ran to his grandmother, just a few yards away. His left arm felt like dead weight. He heard Moloch's pace pick up as Will stopped beside the trench of green flame. He flopped down on his belly and crawled to the pit's edge. Wincing, he lowered his wrapped hand into the flames. He pulled it out a split second later, and, just as he thought, the material around his hand had caught fire. But the flame wasn't green anymore; it was indigo, and it didn't scald him at all.

He ran the flame up and down the wound on his left arm. Instantly, the cut healed. Somehow, the swampy sludge and the green flame interacted on a chemical level, forming an entirely different sort of fire: a healing flame.

Unfortunately, Will's Mr. Fix-it power faded before the real problem could be solved. A gust of wind rushed at Will from behind, snuffing out most of his indigo flame. He didn't have to turn around to know that Moloch stood right behind him.

"William, if you insist on continuing to live, I'm going to be forced to saw off your ears. Now be a good boy and die!"

Still holding a spark of indigo flame in his hand, Will tossed it directly at Moloch's face. The healing properties it held for Will did the opposite for the Genie—Moloch howled and batted at the fire to put it out.

The distraction was enough for Will to get back to his feet and dash toward the other cavern exit. He didn't have super speed anymore, but he was pretty sure Lamone Pledge's track coach would've recruited him on the spot. He was a few yards away, then feet, then inches.

"Not another move, William!"

Will turned to find that Moloch had plucked the unconscious Tang from his cell and was holding him up by his tiny neck.

"Don't even think of heading down that tunnel, boy! If you do, your friend Tangible will pay the price! As you well know, I can't harm your Nonnie just yet, but I have no such qualms about bringing this half-wit's life to an end!"

Will dashed behind a series of large boulders near the cavern. He needed to think. He couldn't save anyone without escaping the dungeon, but he couldn't be responsible for anything awful happening to his best friend.

"Show yourself now or he dies! Five seconds, William! Five! Four! Three! Two!"

"Okay, okay." Will stepped out from behind the mass of rocks. "Just don't hurt Tang, please."

"Come here, boy," Moloch ordered.

Will did as he was told, sloshing through the sludge.

"You did your best, William. Unfortunately for humanity, your best was nowhere near enough. Now, it's time for me to take my place as a god." Moloch held up the ring of Candrissa and said, "Sleep."

Will's eyelids grew heavy. His tummy went full, and his body felt warm and cozy. He couldn't resist. The last thing he would remember was the slime running through his hair as he collapsed backwards into the water.

"Finally," Moloch said with a heavy breath. "That little meddler almost cost me everything. Now the world is mine." He threw his hands to the heavens and yelled at the top of his lungs, "I wish to be ruler and master of all humanity!!!"

The Tokens of Tenet sent up bursts of energy, but unlike a fireworks display, the explosions were murky like sea water and sucked the light from the room.

When the energy died away, the light flickered back to normal. Moloch cackled. "At last! My time has finally come!" He took a deep breath and looked at his hands and body. "I ... I thought I would feel ... different. Why do I feel the same?"

"Good question." From the same rock he'd appeared just moments earlier, Will stepped forward.

"No," Moloch gasped. He turned to the Will lying unconscious on the floor. "I-I-I put you to sleep." Right before his eyes, the slumbering Will vanished from existence.

Will shook his head and smiled cunningly. "Actually, that was my pal Ditto. I'm surprised he agreed to go along with my plan, honestly, but I'm ... he's a little braver since I saw him last. Ditto pretended to be me while I sat behind the rock and listened. It's an old trick I learned from my Nonnie. Sometimes you have to pretend to be asleep to hear the good stuff."

"But that means—"

"That I heard your wish? How could I not with you yelling like that?"

Moloch clutched his throat, as if he had trouble breathing. "But-but-but—"

"I finally figured out what Nonnie was trying to tell me—the reason you wanted us unconscious when you made your wish. No one was supposed to hear you make it, especially not some human kid. You messed up the one stipulation that every six-year old blowing out birthday candles knows: if you tell your wish to anyone other than your wish-granter, it won't come true."

"No!!! You meddling brat! You've ruined centuries of planning!" Moloch's tail lashed out at Will, but the Genie doubled over in pain before he could connect. He dropped to the ground and howled. "NO! The artifacts turn against me! They seek to enslave me!"

Will took a step back and shielded his eyes. The flame of Kronos burned brighter than ever and traveled up Moloch's arm. The ring of Candrissa gave Will a wink and then turned on its former master, projecting an unknown beam of energy right between his eyes. The crown of Manasseh spun around the Genie's head, faster and faster until it projected a field of energy around his entire body.

Without warning, there was an explosion. Will braced himself, but the shielding from the crown contained the blast. When it lowered, dozens of sickly but harmless blue-black moths fluttered up from where the Genie had stood. But there was no Moloch. The Tokens of Tenet were gone, as well. There was no indication that the Genie or the artifacts had ever been there at all.

Will should've been happy, but as he looked at his Nonnie still hanging from the ceiling, all he could do was cry.

Suddenly, the swamp water at his feet dried up. The pit of green fire vanished, leaving behind solid floor. The cells turned into storage lockers. The ebony that held Nonnie gently lowered her to the ground and then vanished. The curved glass walls of the room twinkled and glowed, as if someone had just rubbed them clean. Will found himself in an ordinary, average, run-of-the-mill basement.

Soft moans came from both Nonnie and Tang. Will wiped his eyes and ran to them. "You're okay!" he yelled and giggled, wrapping his arms around his grandmother.

"You did it!" she said, getting a look around with her brown eyes. As she sat, she raised a foot to her ear, gave a listen and said, "My Omni power's back too! Oh, I don't think I've ever been more proud of anyone in my life." Nonnie planted a whopping kiss on Will's forehead and squeezed him with all her considerable might.

"Unbelievable," Tang said. "You beat the baddest baddie of them all, and you did it without any help."

Will dropped his head and shook it. "If I'd faced Moloch a week ago, I wouldn't have lasted more than two seconds. I couldn't have done this without you, Tang ... without either of you."

"Well, I should hope I had a hand in it too," said a familiar voice. A warm glow shone from an open doorway that was once a tunnel exit. Hollywood stepped into the room, and the whole basement filled with a calming light.

"Hollywood, you're here!" Will shouted, smiling.

"There are no words to express how deeply proud of you I am. This room still echoes with accounts of your deeds. I'm your biggest fan, and even I'm surprised! You took everything you learned and used it to overcome impossible odds, to vanquish the worst of foes," he said as his gaze drifted to Tang.

"He's innocent." Will jumped to his feet and moved in front of his best friend. "Moloch framed him and held him prisoner."

"Then there's even more reason to rejoice today!" said Hollywood. He held out a hand for his young partner to shake, but instead, Tang hugged him for all he was worth.

"I missed you, HW," said Tang.

"How'd you know we were here?" Will asked.

"Obviously Moloch used a whiteout spell to block us from locating him. But when you defeated him, Will, and the Tokens took their revenge, all of his magics died away. The mainframe computer back at the SCENE alerted me immediately, and I came flying—literally. The others will be here soon, as well. For now, allow me to thank you on their behalf.

"My people have no concepts such as fate or predetermined destinies. We have only one thing, and we cling to it with all our might. That thing is hope. It carries us through times like the Frost Epidemic, when it's hard to remember there's still good left in the world. In a way, hope is decidedly like a wish. They both act as a shield against the harshness of reality. But hope is more powerful because it's kept alive, not by wishing, but by its pursuit. It's both a shield and a sword. It can change everything. You, a single human boy, were that agent of change in a fight that no amount of wishing could solve."

THANKSGIVING DAY

The Crickets had never had a better reason to celebrate Thanksgiving than they did this year. It had been several days since Will had returned home at 2 a.m. with Nonnie at his side. Hollywood had accompanied them, posing as an officer of the law, explaining that Mr. Peach had been taken away on a number of charges, not the least of which were kidnapping and insurance fraud. As Hollywood explained it, Nonnie had deduced Mr. Peach's plot to steal his own artifact, frame an innocent boy of the misdeed and collect the insurance money on it. According to Hollywood's story, she confronted Mr. Peach, and he didn't take well to it. He kidnapped her and held her hostage in the basement of Peach Preserves. Thanks to a call from her persistent and insistent grandson, the cops investigated, found Nonnie and took Mr. Peach away for what would certainly be an extraordinarily long prison stay.

"Sometimes you just know these things," Will told everyone when asked how he'd figured out Nonnie's location. No one questioned him further. They were just thrilled to have Nonnie safely home again.

Hollywood gave Will's father an exclusive interview for the newspaper, though he had to fudge a few of the details. To keep the people of Corinth and its real police officers in the dark, the wish agent reported that Mr. Peach had been turned over to the FBI, who had taken him away to be judged by a much higher court. Will imagined that Peske would be furious at the legal ramifications behind the cover-up, and especially with Hollywood for talking to the press; but Will knew there wasn't a better reporter for the story than his father.

Not everyone's job fared as well.

"It's official," Will's mother said as she finished placing the silverware on the dining room table. "As of Monday, I'm no longer employed by Peach Preserves. Actually, according to the lawyer who called—a Mr. Peske, I believe—as of Monday, Peach Preserves will be shut down permanently."

"I'm really sorry, Mom," Kaitlyn said as she dropped ice cubes into their dinner glasses.

"Yeah, me too, honey," said Will's father.

Will looked at Nonnie, who stuck out her tongue and gagged in jest.

"Well I'm not sorry at all." Will's mom crossed her arms defiantly and stomped her foot. "Why would I want to work at a place associated with that awful Mr. Peach? Why would I want to work for any company that keeps me away from my family so much? No, if anything, I'm thankful for the chance to get a clean start. I'll find something new soon, something a little less demanding of my time. Until then, I intend to enjoy every single moment I get with the best family in the world!"

"You're going down the street to stay with the Simpsons?" Nonnie asked, scratching her pink hair.

Will's mother laughed (she'd been doing a lot more of that the last few days), "I'm staying right here. With my incredible husband, my beautiful kids and my mother, who happens to be the best judge of character."

"Oh, those guys!" Nonnie said. "Yeah, I like them, they're good people."

The doorbell rang, and Kaitlyn ran to answer it. She returned with Jensen, who looked rather dashing in his suit and tie.

"Thanks for inviting me to Thanksgiving dinner, Mrs. Cricket," said Jensen as he fumbled for Kaitlyn's hand to hold. She beamed.

"Thank you for being here, Jensen," said Will's mother. "Kaitlyn insisted you come."

Kaitlyn giggled. "I ... I just wanted all the people I'm thankful for to be together today. Even you, Will." She glanced at Nonnie and then back at her brother. "Okay, especially you, Will."

"Since we're all being so thankful," Will's father said, "let me tell you what I'm thankful for. Two things. First, I'm grateful my editor is sending me more work after my—if I may be so bold—brilliant article about Mr. Peach's unscrupulous activities. Secondly, I'm thankful I didn't have to cook Thanksgiving dinner this year."

"We all are!" said Will and the rest of his family in loud unison.

The family's laughter was interrupted by Nonnie banging one of her galoshes against the table. "You'll all be grateful for my contribution this year—I brought the eggs for hiding and seeking!" She held up a basket of brightly colored eggs and proudly showed them off to everyone.

"They look beautiful," said Will's mother, taking the basket from her mom. "I think an Easter egg hunt after dinner would be a wonderful idea."

When the doorbell rang again, Will insisted on getting it. He was expecting a friend of his own, but instead, he found three. Hollywood, Peske and Tang stood on his doorstep, all with eager grins—even Peske.

Tang was dressed in a top hat and a long black cape, and he had a cane to boot. "I never know how to dress for these things," he said.

"Norv and I can't stay," said Hollywood. "We just came to drop off Tangible ... and to discuss a bit of business with you."

Will peeked inside the house to make sure no one watched. He shut the door and joined them outside on the porch.

Peske whipped out something Will hadn't seen in weeks: his signed wishing contract.

"Terribly sorry we haven't been able to discuss this with you until now," Hollywood said. "I'm sure you can imagine all of the business we had to attend to after Moloch was banished by the Tokens. There was the situation with the police and the question as to what to do with that company he ran. And of course every talk show in Mythos requested a few moments of my time. The spotlight can be so demanding."

"Ever try turning it off?" Peske said.

"And disappoint my legions of fans? Are you mad, man? Do you want a full-scale riot on your hands? We just averted one crisis, Norv, let's not go looking for another."

"The point Hollywood was trying to make before he somehow managed to start talking about himself again is that we're here to discuss the fulfillment of your wish contract," said Peske.

"Right, right, right." Hollywood snatched the document from Peske's hands and quickly glanced over it. "As I'm sure you recall, Will, you agreed to assist us with seven wish-grantings in exchange for a wish of your own. In addition, you went above and beyond the stipulations of your contract and aided us in bringing to justice the most notorious Genie of all time, though we're still not exactly sure where he vanished to."

"So, in other words," Tang said, "we're here about granting your own wish."

Will gulped. He felt a little dizzy. After all this time, he was finally going to get what he'd always wanted: a new life.

So why did his hands shake so much? He'd had days since rescuing Nonnie to think about his wish for a new life and family. There'd been some substantial changes in the Cricket household over the last two weeks: Kaitlyn was kinder, his dad's job was more stable, his mom was making more time for them, and Nonnie ... well, her crazy behavior finally made sense. For most of his life, he'd wanted to shuck his body and his family and start over from scratch. But those people inside did love him—it just took crossing a few hurdles for Will to see it.

"I ..." Will said, "I don't think I want the wish. I've changed my mind."

"Sorry, Will," Hollywood said, "the contract is binding."

"What?! But my family loves me. And I love them. I can't go through with this. I made that wish without realizing all the problems my family had. We worked together and got past them, like a real family should. You can't hold me to that old contract. I ... I signed it without, um, full disclosure of the facts or something like that."

"Sounds as though there's a budding lawyer underneath all that wishful thinking," Peske smirked. "But it doesn't matter. Your argument won't hold up. I do believe I warned you when we first met to be careful what you wish for, as it just might come true."

"No! You've got to listen to me!"

"Will, let me finish," Hollywood said. "We *would* be obligated to fulfill your wish, if not for one thing. Tell me again, what did you wish for?"

"To be a different person, a better person."

Hollywood said, "Will, it seems your wish has already been granted."

"What?"

"The Will Cricket who stands before us today is already a different person than the one we first met. It seems that someone else granted your wish before we could."

Will was stumped. "I don't understand. I think I'd know if another Arcanian had popped up to grant my wish. Who're you talking about?"

"He doesn't get it," Tang said.

"I suspected he wouldn't," said Peske.

"Will, my boy," Hollywood said. "The person who granted your wish was *you*."

"What?" Will said. "You're not making sense."

"Coming to work for us, you granted other people's wishes, but you did more than that. You faced your fears. You became daring and courageous. You found a way to use your talents. You fought battles that needed to be fought—with and without the benefit of your powers. You faced that bully at school because it was the right thing to do. You stood up and defeated the greatest evil either of our worlds has ever known, and not because you had to in order to receive your wish. You did it for your grandmother, for your family and for billions of people you don't even know. Tell me, is that the same Will Cricket we met at 11:11 p.m. on that fateful night just weeks ago?"

Will thought back to the day he'd met Hollywood, Tang and Peske. Then he thought back to the day before that and the one before that. Never during that time would Will have imagined he'd experience even half the things he'd done since signing his wish contract.

He undoubtedly was a different person now.

"You see, Will, mortals make millions of wishes every day. There are a select few who do more than keep that wish in their heart—they pursue it; they fight for it. Like you, they earn it all on their own."

Will put his hands on his pooch of a stomach and grimaced. "There are still a few things I'd change about myself, though. Maybe you could let me make a new wish."

Hollywood bent down and put a hand on Will's shoulder. "You don't need our help, my boy. Even if we were to grant your change, you'd never genuinely appreciate it. There's only one way to get the most of life: Live the wish."

There was more laughter at the dinner table than Will ever remembered. Tang's outfit got a round of applause, and he even shared his top hat with Jensen. Nonnie juggled the dinner rolls, and Will's mom didn't get upset—in fact, she joined in! Kaitlyn played hostess, constantly filling everyone's drinks, especially Jensen's. Will's mom and dad held each other's hands far longer than they held their forks.

At the end of the meal, Will's mom ducked into the kitchen and returned with something for Will. Every Thanksgiving, she made a special effort to put this one thing aside just for her son, knowing how much it meant to him. She took the seat next to him and laid it in his hands. "Here's the wishbone, Will. It's all yours."

Will ran his thumb up and down the bone. He knew precisely the right spot to position his fingers so that when he and another person gave it a tug, he'd be guaranteed to get the bigger piece and, therefore, the wish. Now that he was on a first-name basis with so many wish-granters, Will was almost certain that he could use this wishbone to convince one of them to grant him a wish—he had saved their world, after all.

Gently, Will lowered the wishbone to his plate. "I think I'll pass this year, Mom. I've got everything I could wish for."

EPILOGUE

From her bedroom window on the opposite side of Summerhill Road, Chloe Fourleaf leered at the Cricket house. She'd witnessed all manner of oddities across the street over the last few weeks. More importantly, both in their neighborhood and at school, she'd noticed a dramatic change in Will Cricket.

The night sky was unusually black. There were no shooting stars; in fact, not a single star specked the heavens. Chloe made a wish anyway.

At that precise moment, a bolt of blue shot across the sky. Chloe gasped in disbelief. Then a peculiar thing happened. Another bolt joined the first. They crisscrossed the atmosphere together until finally they changed directions and left their playground in the heavens. The bolts were coming closer and closer to Earth! They were headed right for Chloe!

She stumbled back from the window. Her entire room became drained of all light—even the soft glow of her nightlight vanished.

Chloe's heart beat so fast, she feared it might burst. As the bolts came within a few feet of her window, she dove out of the way, under her bed. She wrapped her sheet around her head, leaving a small slit to see through. Chloe lay perfectly still for a long time. Finally, the absolute darkness faded, and the light from her alarm clock blinked her back into composure. She took the sheet off her head, thinking she'd imagined it all. That's when two pairs of feet appeared beside her bed.

Chloe yelped and pushed herself further back under the bed, but to no avail. A moment later her bed frame was wrenched from the floor and soared to the ceiling. A man dressed entirely in black and a teenage girl stood over her, pointing and chuckling. As she laughed, the mysterious girl's skin tone changed from elephant gray to the orange and black stripes of a tiger.

"Pardon our intrusion," the man said, "but we're here about that little wish you just made."

"I can't believe it," Chloe said, her heart skipping a beat. "You're wish-granters?"

The man and the girl gave each other a sly look. "Delicious. You've done your homework. This is going to be easier than we thought," said the man in black. "The name's Quantum. As far as wish-granters go, I'm the absolute best. This is my ever-faithful sidekick—"

"Partner!" the girl interrupted.

Quantum rolled his eyes. "This is my ever-annoying *sidekick* Animalia."

Chloe eyed the two for a long moment. Nodding toward Animalia, she said, "You kind of look like a boy I've seen hanging out with my neighbor."

Animalia's nostrils flared. "Could we stay on track already? You don't see us making stupid comments while you're trying to work."

Quantum flicked his partner on the nose. "Forgive her, my dear Chloe. She's a bitter little sea monkey. But you—you are about to get your wish granted. We work for the WORD Group, and it's our business to see that wishes like yours come true."

"WORD?" Chloe asked.

"Word," said Animalia, flashing the peace sign. "It stands for Wishes of Revenge and Destruction."

Chloe clutched her hands together. "Then I'm not going to get in trouble for wishing such bad things?"

"Trouble?" Quantum laughed. "There's unquestionably going to be trouble, but not for you, my dear. We're here to make a deal. You help us grant seven *selfish* wishes over the course of the next seven days, and we'll grant your wish."

"I'll do it. Anything for my wish to come true."

Quantum plunged his hand inside his black knit turtleneck, inside of his very body. When he pulled it out, he held a wishbone. "The contract is all in order. For the record, just state your wish aloud. No worries, it will still come true."

Chloe glared out the window toward the Crickets' home. "I wish for revenge."

"Against who, my dear?"

"Will ... Will Cricket."

*If you enjoyed reading **Wishing Will**, please consider leaving a review on Amazon.com and/or GoodReads.*

For other books by Daniel Harvell, visit DanielHarvell.com or Amazon.com.

Made in the USA
San Bernardino, CA
28 July 2014